THE RESURRECTION OF...
DUTCH COURAGE

First Published in Great Britain 2023 by Mirador Publishing

Copyright © 2023 by Lazza Ogden

All rights reserved. No part of this publication may be reproduced or transmitted, in any form or by any means, without permission of the publishers or author. Excepting brief quotes used in reviews.

First edition: 2023

Any reference to real names and places are purely fictional and are constructs of the author. Any offence the references produce is unintentional and in no way reflects the reality of any locations or people involved.

A copy of this work is available through the British Library.

ISBN: 978-1-915953-22-3

Hey Peter Test Tube Cock of the South!

Here's

THE RESURRECTION OF...
DUTCH COURAGE

BY ME

LAZZA OGDEN

ENJOY! xxx

ALSO, BY THE AUTHOR

THE CURSE OF DUTCH COURAGE

INTRODUCTION

ACCORDING TO STATISTICS MOST OF us will meet eighty thousand people during our lifetime.

This very day I happened upon two of that number that I would have happily done time for.

Person One: Was a guy I know called Jeff who drove his car into the supermarket petrol forecourt, used the pay at the pump lane, and then after filling up his vehicle, locked it and went to settle up with the employees in the kiosk. What a complete bastard! This always seems to happen when there is a large queue of cars waiting to buy gas and annoyingly I'm sat in one of those waiting cars. These creatures annoy me as much as human beings who don't wear belts with their trousers when they clearly need to. These are people who are content to let the bottom of their sagging trousers bunch up and sweep the floor as they walk.

Person Two: Was one such non trouser belt wearing member of the human race that I encountered at the optometrist store 'Spexsave' last week, and he went by the name of Harvinder. Harvinder was my allocated optometrist who was going to put my mince pies through their paces. Nothing wrong with my eyes I can assure you dear reader, as I can pick out a fit bird at a thousand yards. "Mr McCarthy would you also like to take a free hearing test whilst you are with us today?" Harv asked whilst pulling up his trousers with his left hand for about the third time during our brief encounter. 'Why not?' I thought to myself, and I was sure I heard the word 'free.' mentioned 'It'll be good to get the all-clear today on both eyes and ears.'

For the ears I was placed in a soundproof booth and given headphones to wear with the instruction from Harv to press down on the red button that sat in front of me every time I heard a beeping sound in my cans. The procedure reminded me of recording my extreme metal band 'Erectile Dysfunction's' last album. Headphones, blast beats, beeps, and white noise. (That wasn't the title by the way.)

After five minutes and only about seven beeps where I pushed down on the red button and broke a bloody black varnished nail, the test was over. I extricated myself from the soundproof booth and the waiting Harvinder told me that the results would be ready after the imminent eye examination, which I was certain I would pass with flying colours. Well, I'm sure that was what he had said to me as I followed him to another area of the store for test number two.

Fast forward twenty minutes and I'm picking out some glasses to wear after failing the eye test. I was then informed that the results of my free hearing test showed that I was also going partially deaf. What a fucking depressing day this was turning out to be!

Why was my hearing shot to bits? Probably the same reason that I am fat, balding, and very single. I had been in an extreme heavy metal band for the last eighteen years of my life.

At least I'm still here. I may have a bad back, high blood pressure and at times have to walk with the aid of a a stick. True, I can't see well or hear so good these days and have more tablets than 'Curries' but my religion is still rock and roll. Born a rocker, die a rocker.

As I said, some of you reading may know and remember me as the bassist and singer for death metal grind core band 'Erectile Dysfunction' who in near on two decades together had a back catalogue of just five albums, two deaths and a former drummer awaiting a liver transplant.

Our stunning recorded aural arsenal included the epic "Blistering Wind" album. This record found us back in the 'World Rock Book of Hit Records' for having the most tracks on a vinyl recording (113 in 32 minutes) to go alongside our other record of also having recorded the shortest album ever released. (We thought this was amazingly funny until we realised it cost the same to put out as a full-length vinyl LP. We self-released our stuff at this point, so of course had to charge the same amount of money for a truly short collection of songs as we did a long collection. End result: Very few people actually bought it) and we became bankrupt.

I was also in a band once called Dutch Courage, an indie rock outfit from the late nineties, who literally sunk without a trace. Does this statement have any specific meaning? Well, we did lose all our gear and sadly the singers life when the ferry ('The Aquaholic') taking us home to Blighty after a truly disastrous but monumental European Tour went down in the English Channel back in 1999. My name is Martin 'Mac' McCarthy, pleased to meet you and this is my short story.

It was a cold day in February 2019, and my mobile phone was going off. I could hear the ringtone which was blaring out the classic heavy metal tune 'Paranoid' by Sabbath, but I couldn't find my fucking mobile phone anywhere? Why did this always happen to me. When I didn't want my phone it constantly fell out of my pocket and bits broke off it on impact when I forgot it was even on my person, and when I did require it IE Too answer the damn thing, I could never bloody find it despite the loud noise it emitted. (Full volume was always on, I'm going deaf remember?)

After shifting around discarded Pizza boxes and a few easy chair pillows I located the thing lodged down the side of my settee. Obviously, who-ever had rang had long since given up trying to speak to me and had gone onto doing something else whilst I had turned my flat upside down trying to find the bastard. I brought the phone up close for inspection and looked at it, the screen was more cracked than either Fred or Rose West (I'm all for equality). That was something else that I needed to get around to replace.

It was probably Elena who called. She was an ex-girlfriend of mine and the current guitarist in my band. Other than my drug dealer, she was about the only person who rang me these days. Even the 0800 scammers didn't bother me anymore. They obviously knew I had less than fuck all to rob.

Ah Elena. Sweet big breasted Elena. We had met somewhere in Europe

(Possibly Poland as she was from there) and it was lust at first sight. I soon manoeuvred it so there was a place in our band for her which was done by leaving behind the original guitarist at a service station on a motorway near Krakow. It had been fun for the next three records and then came the difficult fifth album. We bickered, we fought, we also took more drugs than the local pharmacy stocked. The end result, we bickered, we fought, we continued to take more drugs and then split up as a couple. She soon moved out of my flat but at least the band kept going. This was the only thing in my life at present keeping me on an even keel and keeping me sane.

I gathered up my phone and flicked through to check my call history; it was indeed Elena who had rang. She had probably seen sense about our latest break up I deluded myself into thinking. She will want to kiss and make up I thought. I rang her back….."Hey baby-kins, err…. I mean hi Elena, sorry I missed your call. What's up babe, erm, I mean fellow band member guitarist?"

Five minutes later, I disconnected the final call I would ever get from that cow bag. I had just been sacked from my own band. Apparently I was bad for band harmony (As if any of them pricks could sing any better), a bad vibe merchant to be around, not good for anyone's health with my constant need for alcohol and drugs and being high constantly on alcohol and drugs. What bollocks! I'll show them ungrateful bastards I thought as I chopped out a big fat line of Charlie and poured the first of several of the days big Cognacs. It was 10am after all.

I took a huge glug of the oak brown liquor that I had been swirling round in a cracked glass tumbler and switched on the television; The first thing I saw when the TV burst into life was an advert that was promoting death and a company called 'Hot Cremation' It seemed that I had tuned into Channel 4A. A Home Counties accent boomed out of my TV with the usual spiel. "Have your funeral your way" This appeared to be their tagline. The ad was as cheap as it was nasty.

Picture the scene: A woman was sat behind a desk at the Hot Cremation offices. The phone rings and she picks up the receiver and answers with the words "Hot Cremation" as the camera pans in to reveal not only great teeth but a huge happy smile emanating from her lips. 'Why is she so chuffed?' I thought to myself. The phone rings at a funeral directors, 99.9% of the time it's not going to be good news you hear from the person calling is it? What kind of ghoul did this place employ? Ring, ring, hello, oh good, there's another gone. WHAAHAHA! (Evil laugh), Ker-ching! Que: Beaming smile.

The next advert was a little more my scene and a bit more light-hearted than arranging funerals at 10am. 'I bet this one is about donating money' I thought to myself, as daytime TV ads only seem to advertise funerals and charities. Why? I don't know. The only people who watch it are the unemployed and students who have no spare change. Anyway, I was right. A deep Scottish voice filled my flat from the TV speakers. "Can you spare just three pounds a month? Drunks in Britain today are having a hard time functioning. At 'Guide Dogs for the Drunk' we can train a dog from a month old to look after their inebriated owners" (Any older than that and they probably try to kill themselves I ruminated.)

I was intrigued. My eyes reverted to the screen to watch the advert playout.

The scene: A drunkard was coming out of a pub to find a collection of assorted guide dogs tied to a nearby lamppost. He unties one and walks away with it. The Scottish voice resumes to advise the viewer how to make donations as the drunk is led to a nearby kebab emporium by his four-legged guide.

As the sauced human goes through his pockets collecting up change to pay whilst staring blankly at the takeaway menu in the restaurant, the dog barks four times. This signals an order for 'Number Four' on the menu. 'Chicken Kebab and Chips' which the guys in the takeaway then prepare. The scene then cuts to the drunkards journey home and the piss head has made a huge mistake by sitting down on a wall with his head in his hands and has unfortunately then passed out. The Scottish narrator returned. "Despite barking for assistance our guide has to use the last resort to stir his owner from premature slumber." The scene then cuts to see the dog cocking his/her leg to urinate on the sleeping drunks head which in turn wakes him.

I go to write down the number on my notepad, but frustratingly can't find a pen. I wasn't going to pledge money but maybe ask about some assistance from them in the near future.

After the adverts, it was back to part two or maybe three of some mid-morning gossip show crap that was on. The programme was called 'On the Telly with Our Kelly' It was the usual boring mid-morning banal drivel, but it made for some background noise whilst I skinned up. It was fast becoming a busy day.

After listening to some actor bore on about the soap series she had just left, this segment was then followed by some mundane gardening tips from 'Green Fingered Jake Peters.' It was after this that I nearly choked on my spliff. The smoke all went down the wrong way and I half coughed my lungs up along with some horrible looking black tar. Was I hallucinating? Just what the fuck was my old Dutch Courage band mate and one-time best friend John Leonard doing on the box?

I scrambled around to find the remote. I had only just had it, but where was it now? I moved the Pizza boxes again, chucked the cushions across the room, but it wasn't on the settee. I got up to manually adjust the volume on the TV and eventually after losing the colour to the picture, adjusting something called contrast and having the words being spoken by the host and guest flash in huge white sub-titled words across the screen, I finally managed to pump up the volume.

Kelly was speaking in her dulcet Liverpudlian tones "So John la, 2019 marks the twenty-year anniversary of you surviving the infamous 'Aquaholic' Bella Liners ferry sinking and I believe you have authored a book that is coming out next week that tells the story of your dramatic escape from it to tie in with the anniversary la?."

My old band sparring partner John Leonard looked at ease appearing on television as he would have been at a slaughterhouse butchering lamb. "Yes, that's right Kelly, my book 'The Curse of Dutch Courage' is out next Monday." I laughed so hard snot shot out of my nose and landed on the arm of the chair as John Leonard squirmed in his seat. Ants in his pants that boy. Kelly continued to take the lead in the interview. "Oh yeah, in the book title, 'Dutch Courage' was, I believe, the rock band you were in at the time of the disaster? (Leonard nods) Your book is so dramatic la. I've read it twice like in five days, and I can't believe the amazing action-packed escape you had. Not only that but you describe in great detail the dangerous situations you put yourself in to aid other passengers who you heroically helped to save. The books got it all kidder. Helicopters, daring escapes and the part how you summoned a pod of nearby swimming dolphins to help aid kids who couldn't swim get away is nothing short of miraculous. It was amazing to read how you got them dolphins to transport those kids to nearby rescue boats, boats that couldn't get too close to the stricken ferry due to the drawdown. That's a whirlpool to me and you at home kid. They are caused in the ocean by big sinking vessels. So, you managed to command the dolphins by imitating a distressed aquatic mammal, what an incredible skill. Then there's the bit about the NATO submarine that was luckily on manoeuvres nearby. I believe it was the subs captain who saw you through the periscope waving a pair of trousers, your trousers I think, that you had the foresight to set alight and wave around to create a beacon like effect whilst you stood on the flooded top deck of the ailing ferry. Unbelievable. You even managed to put out an SOS using semaphore smoke signals from those burning jeans. Finally, the bit about the World War Two mine that you pushed away from a rescue ship with a multi-coloured telescopic duster that you found on deck had me on the edge of my seat. Am I also right in thinking that you were also the last person to leave the nautical disaster for safety. What a guy you indeed are John, and so brave. So, what we want to know is can you, for all the viewers out there, recreate that dolphin call for us here today" Leonard winked at the camera. "Yes Kelly, it is indeed a miracle that I am here today to tell the tale" Leonard offered in the way of reply. "Err...I hope we and those watching aren't too close to any aquariums as I've been told by a couple of marine biologists that my imitation is a powerful call? Are we ready? Ok, Here we go, 'click-click-clack-clack-click-click-click-clack.' How was that? Kelly looks on in awe. "That was spellbinding John la. Anything else you would like to add?" John strokes his chin before speaking. "Yes please. Can I just add that If there are any survivors from the ferry watching then please get in touch with me via this show. I would love to hear from you. I must also mention that there is also a documentary commemorating the disasters anniversary being shown on this channel later this week."

What was going on here? Submarines, dolphins, World War Two mines, this guy had obviously had more drugs over the years than me, as I too was on that ferry and John Leonard was knocked out almost immediately after being one of the first who got straight into a lifeboat. No women and children first with that fucker.

This was worse treachery than playing folk music for the last double decade and that was what John Leonard had been doing as well. First he had betrayed his rock and roll roots and now this nonsense. I decided there and then to visit him, but not until I had consumed the rest of the Cognac and drugs I had lined up for the day ahead.

FOUR DAYS LATER

IT'S MONDAY MORNING AND TV celeb and survivor of the 'Aquaholic' ferry disaster and former Dutch Courage band member John Leonard was sat in the waiting area of the North Park Health Clinic on Butthole Lane in his hometown of Hungerton, England. He now takes up the story.

A young nurse who had the name tag of Mona appeared and called my name.

"Mr Leonard, will you follow me please." She was Scottish. Nice.

I gathered my limbs and peeled myself off of the green Formica chair, got to my feet and followed as instructed.

We walked along a shapely corridor as my eyes darted down to look at her equally shapely backside as it wiggled from side to side inside her crisp blue uniform. Since my wife had left me two years ago I just couldn't help myself these days and tended to ogle everything female wise in sight. I was embarrassed to admit it, but I was getting aroused just at the sight of a good female arse.

Mona entered a sterile looking and smelling room, beckoned me inside and then closed the door. She turned to face me and spoke slowly. "Ok, Mr Leonard. My name is Mona. I believe you're here today to have a boil drained, one that is situated on your rear end by your anus is that right?" Mona continued to speak without waiting for any answer from me. "If you could get undressed for me please." "Damn!" I thought as I made a downward bending of my head like a nodding dog. Why do nurses who do this kind of work always look so fit and have to be so young. My half lob erection from staring at her arse hadn't yet fully dampened down and dissipated. "Err, yeah sure." I responded as I stood behind the blue covered screen, removed some clothing, and then stood before her half naked. She turned to face me, looked me up and down, smiled and then spoke.

"No, Mr Leonard, you need to keep the top half of your clothes on. It's the bottom half you need to remove so I can see and dress your injury."

I immediately regretted my schoolboy error and put some clothes back on, took some off and then assumed the position. I guess that's why lying on a couch with your bum in the air is called ass-uming the position I amusedly thought to myself.

This had been the first woman I had got naked with for over a year now. Not that she was joining me in the removing of the threads stakes.

Mona pushed her dark black hair around her well-crafted ears and placed a mask over her mouth and nose (Good decision I thought) "Ok relax please Mr Leonard." Would now be the good time for me to say 'Just call me John' I reasoned?. Then darker thoughts entered my mind like 'Was it clean down there?' 'Did it smell?. It had been hours since I had showered?' before I could think of any other complaints I might have the nurse spoke to me again. "Oh yes that is nasty. It looks quite infected as well. Why on earth haven't you done something about it sooner? It looks a right state and very sore."

This nurse had the right name I thought to myself. Mona. I guess I could take asking her out for a drink off the table. She continued to address me "Now then Mr Leonard. We usually like to take a picture of the affected area before proceedings. So, do you mind if I take a photograph?"

"Yes of course. You're not going to put it on Social Media are you?" I deadpanned, but this gag went down like a lead balloon. She bed panned me back. "No. Of course not Mr Leonard. More than my jobs worth I can assure you Sir. It's just for our records." Nurse Mona then moved in and got as close to my pus spouting bum boil as she dare. She was so close that I could feel the air exhaling out of her nose on the base of my spine, then I heard the clicking sound of her camera phone.

The nurse moved away from the couch where I was still lying with my arse in the air. She wiped a cloth over the screen of her phone and then returned to me with a syringe the size of a ladle.

On seeing that the colour drained out of my face and then from the rest of my body. At a distance, I probably looked see through to invisible at this very moment. "Right, Mr Leonard. I'm afraid this is going to hurt a fair bit. But it needs to be done. The wound is badly infected, so you need to keep taking the antibiotics that you have been prescribed until they are completely finished with. I find in these situations talking about something else helps. It will hopefully take your mind off things whilst I perform the draining procedure?"

My brain at once told me to talk about my book which had been released that very week.

"I, I, oooowww, have a book I've written come out. It's a truuuuuue story. Do you like music or disaster films?" "Oh, you're an author. Lovely. Yep. I love both to be honest with you Mr Leonard. What's it called this book?"

"It's called, 'Theeeeeeeee…..The Curse of Dutch Courage'" I replied as I gritted my teeth.

"Oh right. I will check that out for sure. I love reading. Sounds interesting. I'll probably buy one. Nearly done now. Let me put some dressing on your under buttock for you." Just recalling her saying that last line put me off salad for life.

That was it there. I had it! One up on famous multimillion selling Canadian horror writer Steven King. I bet he never sold a book whilst having a boil drained on his arse.

THREE DAYS PREVIOUS

THREE DAYS EARLIER AND MARTIN McCarthy is just waking up and realising he is lying on the floor of his front room flat. The first thing he notices is that the television was still on. He knows he saw or heard something on it yesterday and had planned to do something today with that information but right now whatever it was had escaped his recollection and been filed in that part of the mind called 'The Black Hole.' This was the area where all those drunk unremembered memories are kept on the dark side of the brain with the reminders to pay bills.

But first things first. He needed to remove the sick encrusted t-shirt he was wearing. He must have puked all over himself after finishing off the Cognac bottle the night before.

Mac could taste his own alcoholic breath; and it made him gag like hair of the dog never could. It was breath that could currently toast bread at twenty paces or even peel the paint from the walls of his Bristol flat, but the council wouldn't be happy with that as they had only just redecorated for him.

He peeled himself off the floor and could feel a second damp sensation from within his slept in clothes. Ah, he had pissed himself during the night. Some things in McCarthy Land just never changed.

RE-ENTER: MR JOHN LEONARD

AFTER THE KELLY TELEVISION INTERVIEW JOHN Leonard had thanked all the staff he could and left the London studio of Channel 4A to head for breakfast at a nearby 'McDonough's' restaurant. Leonard didn't really care what the government ministers and nutritionists said about their food, he would have still eaten the burgers they sold it if the specialists had confirmed that it was made entirely from human meat.

With food consumed John's next stop was his favourite capital city pub 'Ye Olde Roode Boozer' (Pronounced 'Rude') which was situated in a sleazy part of South London just three stops from the TV studio on the Victoria Line.

I made my way through the tube station. It was already a hive of activity. I passed many transport staff telling holiday makers or day visitors that they needed 'That line' or 'This line' I knew what kind of line I needed, and it wasn't the bloody Circle one. I had of course promised myself, my manager, and my ex-wife that there wouldn't be any more drugs. I had lied so well that I nearly believed it myself. I reminded myself of some graffiti I had recently seen on a toilet wall that said 'I'm pissed again despite all the promises' That was me down to a tee.

Being on the TV was stressful and I needed to wind down with a cheeky toot and a couple of pints minimum. It didn't matter that I had dressed down for my day in the spotlight and looked like a bohemian tramp, I was still besieged by beggars as I made my way out of the tube station. Great Britain.

Ha! Nothing great about it anymore. I ignored all the requests for money, but one guy decided to follow me on my onward journey, and I had to admire his persistence.

"Excuse me Mister. You got some change? A couple of pound for a Coffee please." I stopped immediately in my tracks and turned around and surveyed the scruffy mass of humanity that had shuffled along the street after me. This guy was covered in what looked like shit and straw. His accent sounded Eastern European. I stared hard and the dosser held out his grubby hand in anticipation of some coin. I can remember times when the beggars only asked for ten pence and now it was a couple of quid for a coffee. That said it even cost two pounds to put air in your tyres nowadays at a supermarket petrol station, but that really is inflation for you.

This guy was aiming high though. Two quid. For that price he could possibly afford a brew at 'Buckingham Palace' but let's face it, no coffee was ever going to hit this annoying humans lips. Why lie? He just wanted to get high. If I gave him any dough he would just blow it on booze. Like I would. He asked again and stepped closer once again holding out his hand in anticipation of the payoff. But in this instance he was wrong and outfoxed. I quickly produced my credit card and addressed him. "Sure. Do you take Card?"

Much had changed since our last written engagement together dear reader which was some twenty years in the past. The internet and the mobile phone were now the greatest source of entertainment and hard cash was slowly being phased out of use all over the planet. Pubs had sadly closed by the thousand in the UK, Brexit was now a thing, the words 'woke,' and 'snowflake' had new meanings and bizarrely Leicester were now a powerhouse of English football, and ridiculously supermarkets had self-service check outs. Who could have foreseen any of that in 1999? It was mind blowing.

The heaving mass of inhumanity looked at me gone out. I launched into one.

"Look mate, if you are going to ask for money at least have the fucking decency to carry a card machine. Yeah? No one carries cash these days. Up your game son. Do you have such a device about your person?"

I already knew the answer to this question and turned quickly and went on my merry way, eager to get in my favourite London pub and to add alcohol and narcotics to my own blood stream. Two quid my arse.

I waltzed into the pub and could hear that the old striptease music was playing. What good timing. I took a gander at the stage and noticed a 'Jack the Ripper' (Stripper) was down to just her black underwear and left leg stocking. The décor in the place was more dust than spit but I liked it that way. I bet myself a Pound to a Penny that there was no cleaners on the payroll for this gaff, none that used hoovers at least.

I took a seat right by the stage and checked out my surroundings. There was only one other punter in the place, and he was a balding old man nursing a half pint of some dingy looking ale. Waste of time going out if you're only gonna order halves but then again looking at him second time around he was clearly here just for the birds. In fact, I noticed he had bought his own box of tissues which were sat next to him.

A bored looking petit young blonde girl came and took my order of a pint of Bitter. This was the life I thought. It was only 10am and I had a beer coming and beaver winking at me from the stage. It was at this point that my mobile phone rudely interrupted my crude train of thought. The name that flashed up and illuminated on my beat-up blower was that of one word: 'GOOCH.' It was my agent checking up on me I was sure of it. How times had changed. I answered. "Hello"

"Goodness gracious John boy where are you? The jukebox is way too loud wherever you are Buddhist. I can hardly hear what you are thinking."

Carlton Gooch, the owner of the 'Planetoid Agency' (Showbiz supplier of Stars), one time 'Dutch Courage' band manager and sometime kleptomaniac was the man doing his level best to get me work despite the fact that I was sure I had fired him at some point in our past working relationship.

The Gooch had hit it big in the noughties with most of his signings to the agency actually doing good business. I mean who would have put money on a pair of posh boy, Oxbridge University graduates forming a techno double act called 'Treble 17' then going on to have the biggest chart hit of the year with "Stand Up If You Love the Arts" This tune wasn't massive just in the UK but also in most of Europe and North America as well.

Gooch had gone from being a guy who shovelled shit to having the Midas touch that everyone wanted to know. No one thought that a band with four drummers would work. How do you transport four kits to gigs? But again, Gooch saw the potential and 'Conundrums' were a bona-fide hit machine for twelve months. Add in guitar darlings of the day 'The One Bounce Four' whose "Human Spin Cycle" album was a mega million seller. But his big, super smash was his vision for taking dead beats and making them bona fide stars. For example, no-one could have dreamt auditioning high-class hookers who could sing, and he turned four women into the singing sensation of the late inbetweener years that became 'The Vice Girls' Even now as I think about them their song "Want to Be" immediately enters my mind. It was as infectious as Malaria, but everyone all over the world knows those opening bars and lyrics backwards.

"If you want us to all be your lover, you've got to slip us a grand, then we will make you come by vagina, mouth or hand" A true disco classic that was number one for weeks absolutely everywhere.

Unfortunately, 'Vice World' wasn't the best name for the movie he produced which went on to lose him a lot of dollar and may have drawn the wrong clientele to cinemas but for ten minutes the 'Vice Girls' were the biggest band on the planet.

Carlton Gooch had also branched out from music and taken on a couple of sports personalities at 'Planetoid' There was the Irish boxer 'Pyro' Jacky Sparks, who within twelve months of signing with The Gooch had somehow gone from third on the card at Kilburn Town Hall to light heavyweight NOBB (Nation of Boxers Belt) Champion of the World. This feat was mainly thanks to what commentators called 'The Invisible Punch' As no-one saw it coming and the recipient of it 'Brown Suga' Joe Suggs most definitely didn't. Gooch was also lucky that French Air Traffic Control had gone on strike for a week prior to the fight and Suggs knowing about this took three weeks to get here from America on a boat. I'm certain people smugglers would have got him here quicker in a dinghy.

There was nothing that The Gooch hadn't done. He had even won a national pun competition that was held and broadcast on radio from a convent in St Albans. His winning line was about how many times he had laughed at the other entrants in this competition? He simply said…..Nun.

Carlton also now employed a huge Scottish bloke as a security guard / minder / odd-job man called 'Bullock' whose main duties were to shadow him and stop his boss from trying to steal useless objects that A) He didn't need & B) He didn't need the scandal of being caught.

The Gooch had also signed the first openly gay dart player in history. Clarke 'Good Arrows' Lestrange had caused a bit of a stir on a mainly manly male dominated sport by having "It's Raining Men" by the Weather Girls as his walk on music as he skipped to the oche.

He started to lose his grip on reality and money though when he agreed to manage disgraced female Tory MP Bunty Cooper, who was of course famous for 'Onion Gate' If you aren't old enough to remember, then 'Onion Gate' was the story of where Bunty had sliced and diced her abusive onion magnet husband Hooper Cooper to death at their Dorset mansion. 'Onion Argy Bargy' was how the Gooch sold it to the tabloids.

Such was the outrage at Bunty's long sentence that Gooch managed to get permission from the authorities for Bunty to become the first prison inmate to have then been allowed her own podcast show called 'SuperDuperBuntyCooper' which aired every Thursday night from HMP Pentonville. He also now managed me. A deadbeat who had nothing on the horizon but one acoustic pub gig.

I had unexpectedly received a call a year back from The Gooch on New Year's Eve of 2018. He had somehow heard about my woes, no work, loss of wife and kid to divorce and the death of my pet Goldfish 'Swim Shady' to fin rot. I was not in a good place. Neither was he as he called me from some business he was doing in Wolverhampton.

The Gooch probably still felt guilt that he hadn't been aboard the 'Dutch Courage' ferry disaster of 1999. The band had played at a festival in Bilbao, Spain that had turned into a bit of a riot and then we had to drive all the way back to Rotterdam, Netherlands for a gig with some rave star and more importantly, to get our travel connection home from the Hook of Holland port. The Gooch had in his infinite wisdom decided that a sixteen-hour drive would have creased his strides so booked himself out of Spain on a flight to London whilst the rest of us went home the long and hard way round.

The sunken ferry had claimed the lives of two of our travelling party and 137 other unfortunate souls. Band vocalist Chris 'Bosco' Boscombe (Body never found) and merch guy Baz Oakes AKA Mr Orange had perished when the worst storm Europe had seen for eighty years had whipped the ocean into such a frenzy that it claimed the 'Aquaholic' ferry for its own. The meteorologists had later named the storm 'Toby.'

I left the bored looking stripper to now perform to the one single gent left in the bar as I looked for an area of peace and quiet to receive the rest of the phone call from my agent.

"Can you hear me now?" I asked him. "Yes of course poppet" He quickly replied.

"So, did you see the show?" I asked.

"No of course not Johnny John, John. It was on far too early for me. Late night last night at the Hippodrome Buddhist. I was just ringing to make sure you appeared, appeared sober, didn't swear on air, and plugged the ring ,ting ,ting, ting, belly-boo tele documentary about the ferry disaster that's being broadcast this week? I assume all was honky dory as I haven't woken up to find my Clockspace social media account gone into spizzing overdrive."

"Give me some credit Gooch." I yelled back. "Yes it all went like clockwork. Yes I was sober and when I could get a word in with 'our Kell' I advertised our wares as you instructed."

"Good, good, John Buddhist, but it could have been bad." Gooch replied before adding "Amazingly, on the back of my recent hard work of raising the anniversary and profile of the disaster, I have some more work to put your way my tip top Botanist. Bizarrely yours truly has been approached by Kai Tipping, you know him right, left, right, he's a top banana music promoter. Top man in his field. He's more than a little interested in going 'Dutch' and having you crew, the one and only 'Dutch Courage' play a set at a BIG festival in the UK. Not only that but hey presto there's also a possible mini tour of the US of A being bandied about. You as the special guests to another reformed Americana act may be in the offing. How does that sound c'est quoi ca?"

Hearing those two words ('Dutch Courage') stunned me like a Pyro Jacky Sparks punch to the solar plexus. I hadn't thought about my old band for near on nineteen years after the farewell gig we did at Rockets Bar, Newbury, where Bosco's wife stood in for our deceased singer on vocals. "Hello, Hello, for God's sake….These bloody cell phones are more trouble than they're worth. Hello. Earth to John Leonard, Buddhist, talk to me Johnny."

I gulped my pint down in one and then heaved half of it back up back into the glass and then swallowed it again and kept it down once and for all. I composed myself. "I'm still here Gooch." I could suddenly picture him running a hand through his hair whilst dressed in a white satin robe having only just stumbled out of bed in his huge ten bed house in Hampstead with his greasy balls swinging wild and free. Why on earth was I thinking of him like that? I had to shake that image quickly and sear it from my mind.

"Speak man, speak you crazy toothless Haddock. What do you think? Can you get the rest of the boys onside? Can you put the band back together? I mean it'll looks a good earner; I meant to say there will probably be a good few crumbs in it for you. Can you find the others? I mean that tight bastard drummer Chester is already in America if you do get to go there, so that's at least one less air fare to budget for, and Mac, do you know where he is these days?"

Again, I went into a daze. I began to taste salt in my mouth and the Toastie Eggy Bacon Sausage McDonough's meal I had eaten earlier began to stoke my internal boiler so much that I had begun to suddenly piss sweat. It got so bad that I could have wrung out my t-shirt there and then. Had anyone actually been in the foyer of the 'Ye Olde Roode Boozer' I may have given the impression that I had just walked to the pub after having a quick fully clothed dip in the nearby Thames river.

I thought about my old partner in the band and one-time best mate. Martin 'Mac' McCarthy (The Bass Player). We had gradually grown apart following the charity gig we performed in 2000. I thought some more. The band drummer Chester Rataski had returned to the country of his birth and left the UK to reside once again in New York some years back. For a while we communicated regularly but then, it became like one of those Holiday relationships you have. You meet someone in the sun, have a laugh for a fortnight, ring them a couple of times when you get home and then slowly but surely all lines of communication stop as you assimilate yourself back into your humdrum life. Then I thought about singer Chris 'Bosco' Boscombe (Deceased.) and became melancholy. So, we had no vocalist or drummer. Not much of a band I thought to myself and then vocalised it.

"But Gooch we don't have a singer or drummer and seriously, who on earth would be interested in us? I mean we were hardly 'Top of the Pops' material first time around."

The Gooch launched quicker than a cruise missile. "I've got you covered John. I have a guy, a lovely happy chappy called Brandon Slam who I think will be just the ticket. Great vocalist, nice blokey bloke, and short ...errr....of work at the moment, hello, yes. Drummers are ten a penny cocker. That and Channel 4A think that there could be a follow up documentary in it after the ferry anniversary programme. Mucho Pesetas Monsieur! You are coming on trend my friend. Hashtag John Leonard Survivor and all that"

I was cornered. I didn't really have a pot to piss in thanks to the CSA (Child Support Agency) and worse DAAA (Drug, and alcohol addiction.)

I desperately needed a paying gig and hadn't had one of those now for months, well actually, years. "I guess it's time to put the band back together." I said to Gooch as I cut the call, then burst back into the bar to see what looked like a cute looking Asian girl on stage artfully dancing whilst half naked.

This chick had full sex doll type cherry lips and was struggling to remove her red panties that had got snagged in her suspender belt. Things were looking up and so was I. "Need a hand?" I shouted stage wards.

Leonard sat back down in his chair and the girl on stage tottered around on high heels picking up her clothes following the completion of her slot.

Instead of leaving the stage the 'act' came and took the seat next to me in the big empty room. I tried to act cool and non-plussed as my penis went poker stiff in under two seconds flat, which at my age was a big deal. Quick as a flash she put her bra on and then a lacy t-shirt.

"That's typical that." I said aloud. "A hot scantily dressed girl comes my way and immediately starts putting on more clothing."

She giggled and held out a hand and then quickly retracted it when she saw my face.

"Hey! You look like a guy who was on the TV earlier today. It is you isn't it? The boat sinking guy. Oh, man I'm Erika, Erika Puck."

She had a strong accent and a keen eye. American I think. The accent and the eye.

"Erika from America?" I asked.

"Oh man, yeah, is it that obvious." She responded with a giggle as she sadly continued to put on more clothing. "I'm John Leonard. Don't hurry with those clothes on my account." I said as I wiped sweat from my brow and this time it was I who extended my hand. Talking of extensions…. "Do I make you nervous?" She purred. I just nodded at her.

"As it appears you are scared stiff." Her eyes dropped down to my crotch and more importantly my 'stick shift' which was now straining the gusset of my dirty jeans. She continued to talk. "No need to be scared of me John. I'm just a big pussy really."

From the moment she said that I just stared at her and didn't see a woman before me but a throbbing vulva. Never had a truer word been spoken. Thankfully, I snapped out of my reverie and continued to yap excitedly.

"Well yes Erika……Muck, did you say?" I tried to recall her surname once again and untangle the words from the sentence she spoke as it was difficult making out what she had said with her heavy East Coast American accent.

"Puck" she replied sharply. I got that, so I thought.

"Ruck?" I responded having guessing incorrectly again like a dimwit on a quiz show.

"Puck" She shouted loudly just as the background music playing in the venue dropped in decibels. "I'd love to!!" I said licking my lips, but I had sadly misheard for the last time as she strode away. She did, however, turn to wink at me, well it maybe was a wink, I hoped it was as I wasn't wearing my glasses, though it could have just been her removing something minutely small that had just flown into her face.

TWO WEEKS LATER

Two weeks later John Leonard was sat at home staring at a scrap book of 'Dutch Courage Press Clippings' as was written in Sharpie on the front of a dishevelled looking book.

"Hmmm not looked at this for ages" I said softly to myself. In truth, the contents had mostly been pictures I had taken at gigs or flyers from shows we were bottom of the bill at. On turning a page, I let out a stifled laugh as I started to read what was written.

Ha… The only bit of press we ever had was from the now defunct music paper 'Give Voice to Music' (GVM) It was written by some aptly named prick called John Thomas who wrote (and I quote) "The indie four piece 'Dutch Courage' come across like a wannabe Madchester band, and it doesn't quite work with their well-rounded vowels that they pronounce as they sing. The crowd at 'The Ear Worm' in Duffield had them down as a hit/miss live band. As some of the people in attendance threw pints at them and some hit and…."

Ha! The reactionary left-wing music press I thought to myself. Where is it now? Disappeared up its own Jacksie. It failed to move with the times. I mean they banged on about this and that and being inclusive of all, yet 99% of the people who worked in this field it had to be said, exclusive world, were white males.

I wondered where John Thomas was now?. He had probably hoped to be writing about the arts now for 'The Preserver' newspaper but reality was more that he was rotting in his bed with his own farts, unemployed. He who laughs last and all that as I farted myself, whilst sat home alone at just after mid-day on a working weekday.

    I turned another page in the scrap book and it was from a time after the band had split up. It was a headline from the daily Hungerton paper 'The Tombstone' Mac was out of control in his life at this point and was arrested for throwing a monkey wrench or something equivalent at a guy he had chased through the streets. This bloke he was chasing had taken refuge in a shop that sold stationary and children's toys and was full of mums and kids. The headline read 'Local Band Bassist Throws Spanner in the Works' It was all over something as trivial as the victim refusing to pay for the next game of pool at a nearby pub. Macs boozing was out of control and this incident caused him to up sticks (Shame he wasn't the drummer) and move out of Hungerton after he had of course completed his community service.

    All of a sudden there was a loud knock at my door. I closed my scrap book and dropped it to the floor and rose out of my chair. As I did, the detritus of the morning, toast crumbs, fag ash, and hair that would rather embed itself in my dirty navy jumper than stay in my head, also fell to the floor.

    Who the fuck was it? If truth be told I had been thinking about having a wank. So, this unwanted intrusion was not required and immediately put me in a bad mood. I half thought about ignoring the knock, but the knock came again but more pronounced this time. It occurred to me it must be someone who really wanted to see me. I racked my brain. I didn't owe Owen my dealer any coin did I? Nah, who on earth would it be at eleven-forty in the morning. I surmised it must be the Gas / Electric Meter reader. I mean I was half surprised I was up myself. The knock then turned into a full-on number of BANGS as I reached to open the door to my living room, and I could now hear muffled shouting from outside.

    When I opened the door I was momentarily lost for words. There before me were two people joined arm in arm. The male was this bald metal type, sporting a long grey beard which made him look like Papa Smurf. He was cradling a walking cane with his right arm and on his left was a creature that looked like it had crawled out of the 'Vantablack Lagoon.' It was a woman I again surmised. She smiled I think. Her mouth when open resembled an empty chess board. White with black spaces as there was that many teeth missing. The male spoke but I let the word 'John' float off into the ether as my brain tried to work out what or who was in front of me.

I looked again. They were definitely two separate people and not one complete hideous human centipede. It wasn't the postman with an apprentice as the female only had one arm I noticed. A combination not good for posting letters.

The male said my name again and finally my brain sent recognition to my vocal box. "Fucking hell….Macca. Is that really you?" It was. My old 'Dutch Courage' band cohort Martin McCarthy. "You gonna let us in then? I'm busting for a piss. Old age innit! Edmund Bad Bladder the band use to call me, after that comedy show on the Beeb. Remember the theme song "Bad Bladder, Bad Bladder" We had to have to stop every thirty miles on tour just to empty the bottles I'd already filled." Mac said as he barged past me dragging his one-armed girlfriend behind him.

I closed the door a little too hard and the picture frame holding a colour photo of 'Spud' my deceased Guinea Pig fell over sending up a puff of dust from the cabinet it resided on.

Mac was pointed to the direction of the toilet 'Just follow your nose' I shouted as the one-armed girl took a sit down on the settee and I took the chair opposite. Before we got down to the pleasantries we heard the toilet flush and then the internal heating pipes began to rumble constantly like an empty stomach.

Mac re-entered the room. He was slow coming down the stairs but quick to piss. I stood and we embraced. His hands were wet. I hoped he had actually washed them. "Long time no see buddy. How you doing? , are you going to introduce me to your wife / girlfriend then Mac?" Mac stood back and smiled at me.

"What her? You got the wrong end of the stick mate. She's for you John. A sort of sorry that I've been a such shit mate over the years." I looked over at her and the woman flashed me a half-hearted gap-toothed smile.

Something didn't add up, but the penny soon dropped. I had recently been on television and in some of the daily newspapers like 'The Pun' and 'Daily Non-Binary' so people I hadn't seen for years were possibly going to come out of the quite rotten woodwork.

"Oi bitch. Stand up and get over here and meet my friend John." Mac commanded.

The black Lagoon girl stood and slipped her woollen coat off quite easily, quickly dropping it from her one arm to the floor in one fluid movement. Mac spoke again. "This is Wendy, known simply around our way as 'Bandit.' She'll do whatever you want mate. I mean if I get involved it might be hard work for her as she's only got one arm but call it a late Christmas present, you can just go first on her if you like?"

Mac then retrieved a bottle of Vodka from Wendy's handbag. He unscrewed the top and took a long swig as if it was tonic water. "Decent turps that for Polish stuff" he said as he wiped his mouth and burped. He then took a wrap of white powder out of his dirty blue jean pocket and smiled at me "Here's to the Septic Siblings being back" and he opened the bag and threw the choppy white contents down his throat as if that was kids Sherbet. Wow, and I thought I had problems where pharmaceuticals were concerned!

I politely declined the invitation of sex and going first on Wendy the one-armed prostitute and also the offer of a male dominated three-some. So, I went back to maudlin about my life and resumed looking at the 'Dutch Courage' scrap book whilst I waited for Mac to get his money's worth out of the amputee hooker. We decided that as he had already paid-up front that someone should at least do the business. It would be poor form to let the money go to waste. The sounds emanating from my bedroom were more akin to a stock car race than any love making. Still needs must and all that I guess.

The grunts sounded pig like, the groans more like someone had just received their gas bill than any sexual stimulation. It was at this point that I dropped my scrap book back down to the floor and went and joined in. That night plums came up constantly on the one-armed bandit. Her speciality was the 'Jack off pot' which involved a lit spliff, a candle and a willing participant. I will leave that to your sordid imagination.

I had been through many experiences with this man (Martin McCarthy) but lying beside him and a one-armed prostitute smoking a post coital threesome cigarette was a new one for the diary.

"So, what brings you round these parts?" I asked casually in-between bouts of coughing. Wendy answered, and I had to politely tell her that she was the hired help and to go and make a cuppa or something as I was actually talking to Martin.

"You weren't asking me to make a cuppa when I had your dick in my mouth" she shot back at me instantly.

"Tell you what I will put the kettle on" I lamely replied. I got up off the bed and bent down to pick up my underwear. On doing so Wendy screamed and all I could hear was Martin shout, "What the fuck is that?" as they had copped sight of my anal swelling that was due to be drained again.

THE RESURRECTION

IT TRANSPIRED THAT MY OLD band sparring partner was similar to me in one respect. We both had absolutely nothing. He reckoned that we should get 'Dutch Courage' back together and get some purpose in life. Who knows where it could lead? He would say. I'll tell you where it led......Huddersfield, Yorkshire, United Kingdom to start with and then onto the good ol' United States of America. But first we had to find some missing pieces IE A drummer and a singer to replace the originals who were residing in New York State and presumed dead, lost at sea, respectively.

Getting the singer was piss easy. Brandon Slam, 34, (Press name and age) was put forward (With little choice from us) by our manager Carlton Gooch during a band meet in his office.

"You need to meet Slammers dear boy. He too has been on TV. It was about two years ago now, but he has star sparkle dust all over him. You must have seen him" The Gooch told us enthusiastically whilst prancing around his office gradually getting louder and more excited by the second. "He is the perfect fit for your band. Bless my blue skin barnacles. Put your trust in me my fine finks."

"What TV show was he in?" Mac (Seated left) asked of our erstwhile manager whilst trying to deal with what seemed to be an irritating itch on his back, it was one of those awkward one's that is just out of reach. "UK's Got Very Talented People" Gooch quickly snapped back. "He made the last eight of the competition before being voted off by that slime Simeon Howell" (Who was also the show creator, writer, director, producer, you get the picture)

"He must be a decent singer if he got to the last eight" I vocalised.

"No, you misunderstand." Gooch retorted before continuing " He appeared on there as a magician. But the bottom has most definitely fallen out of the magic world since Howell described it on dismissing him from the show, as, and I quote, 'An old, archaic form of entertainment which should have died in the seventies with flares, spam fritters and paedophile glam rock singers' I can't even get him panto in Cleethorpes for French sake. He will sing for his supper bwana, and he is cheap."

"So, you want us to take on a guy who can pull a rabbit out of his hat as the singer in an indie rock band." I gasped whilst Mac opened the office door to rub his back on to deal with the nagging itch.

"He has rock star quality my finks. He is also desperado, and I could get him at the drop of his magic hat. He is box office material but is currently in an office….working as a cleaner….Which I'm not making ten percent from Daddio. THIS IS A WASTE OF HIS TALENT…. Shall I arrange the meet?" Gooch dropped down to his chair and began to gargle with some mint mouthwash straight out of the bottle.

John Leonard knew he had to strike whilst the iron was hot and nodded his acceptance. With the vocal situation seemingly in hand, it was now time to broaden the search for a drummer.

We couldn't really be bothered to look for a drummer. Surely with The Gooch once having a band like 'Conundrums' on his books it shouldn't be too difficult to source a skin basher. It wasn't.

A rehearsal with former magician Brandon Slam and ex 'Conundrums' drummer Enoch Izzet was confirmed by Gooch's Serbian PA Dorinka Stupor for four days' time. We were to meet at 'Hairy Helmets' a well-known music rehearsal studio in South London which was owned by members of the heavy metal band 'The Micro Aggressions' This was to lead into an evening's social where it was agreed upon that we would share some food and hopefully bond over a couple of drinks and a Ruby Murray. I was looking forward to it. Things had come together quickly and with little fuss.

Before that though, I had to get back to my flat in Hungerton to pack up a few things for my temporary relocation to London which was a necessary evil to take full advantage of this current media interest in me and my life.

John Leonard was strolling toward his street of residency, he headed to Glen Close so he could take the jetty short cut through to his hovel and was heading towards his flat when he was accosted by one of the few people locally who actually bothered to talk to him.

Mr Robins was trundling along slowly in his mobility scooter walking his dog Hector when he collared me. "Hello young John. You doing ok. I hear you have only gone and wrote a whatsaname.?"

"A book? Yes Mr Robins. You heard correctly." I answered.

"Yeah, yeah a book." Mr Robins replied before continuing to talk whilst tugging harder on my arm with each passing phrase.

"You know what you ought to do next young John? You need to write another. Then another, then another, and another, and another, and another, then another, and another, and another and another, then another, and another and another. That's what that horror writer Steven King did and look at him now, his books are everywhere. Even on that there Inthenet"

They say old people are slow. This of course is bullshit if you have ever been to bingo? Here you will see the older generation marking the cards with their dobbers / dabbers (Delete as you see fit) at great pace. Some of them have six bingo cards to play with and I struggled to keep the pace with just three.

The conversation with Mr Robins then took an about turn as the tugging of my arm continued.

"Did you know that if you had fifty thousand six hundred and twenty-five whatsanames.... err.... bingo cards then you are guaranteed to win the whatsaname. You just can't lose."

I thought about that for a moment and wondered how much that amount of cards would cost as opposed to how much reward they would reveal in getting a bingo- the jackpot. I was beginning to tire of this conversation when Mr Robins finally said something that made my ears and another part of my anatomy prick up.

"Anyway John. I haven't forgotten that whatsaname I lent you last month in the whatsaname, but it looks like you have."

This wasn't what made my ears prick up. I had also forgotten about the fiver I borrowed off him in the local pub. Old people as sharp as a tack when they want to be.

The sound wave that entered my outer ear and travelled through the narrow passageway known as the ear canal which in turn leads to the eardrum was this.

"Oh, and there's some dodgy looking woman stood outside your flat. She's got one of them tight whatsanames on son. Looks like a dog in a catsuit if you ask me. That's it a whatsaname! Not like my Edith. She was a proper lady. I miss her you know young John."

My eardrum was now vibrating from the incoming soundwaves and sending some of these vibrations to three tiny bones in my body. The bones vibrating were the malleus, incus, and of course penis.

I unhooked my arm from Mr Robins grip as Hector started to defecate on the pavement.

"No worries sunshine. You make sure you bring that whatsaname round to me soon. Cauliflower is getting awfully expensive these days in the whatsaname."

And without looking around at what Hector the dog was doing, Mr Robins trundled off in his scooter at around 10MPH. If he had looked he would have seen his poor dog was halfway through having a shit. Poor guy had started and now had to try and run along to keep up with his master in the mobility scooter with half a turd hanging out of his arse. It was either that or be dragged along the pavement and strangled by Mr Robins dog lead.

My mind was working overtime. A couple of the neighbouring flats where I lived where empty. There were some residents though. There was an old couple called Alan and Agnes Foster-Childs who lived directly next door. They were that quiet I wasn't even sure they were still actually alive in there as the property they inhabited smelt of damp, death, and detritus.

I carried on my way and then my quick walk turned into a trot, the woman Mr Robins mentioned then came into view. It looked like her, but it couldn't be could it? I hadn't got my glasses on, but I thought I could just about detect jet black hair, rose coloured lips and lumps all in the right places, but from this distance it could have been the bloke who reads the gas meter.

As I got closer I tried to act cool. It was her. Erika, the stripper from the pub in London wearing nothing but a skin tone coloured catsuit and thigh high leather boots.

How had she got my address? I didn't really care. At this point I just wanted to shag the arse off her. She saw me approach six inches before the rest of my body did.

"Hey man. I didn't think you would ever show. I've been here ages. It's freezing, just look at my nipples they are stood to attention like those ham burger guards at the Queens house. I'm here to show you how much of a pussy I am."

She was drinking from an opened bottle of Gin and suggestively licked the tip and then moved the top of the bottle into her mouth. She then offered it to me. I grabbed the bottle in my left hand and took a huge gulp. I grabbed her arse with my right hand. This unfortunately left no hands to get my key out of my pocket to open the door. I now had a dilemma. As an alcoholic its always difficult to put a bottle down but then I didn't really want to let go of her arse either just in case she disappeared in a puff a smoke.

That was a ridiculous notion as I was to find, as Erika Puck would be exceedingly difficult to shake off in the coming weeks and months of my life.

In the meantime, I let go of her rear, pulled out my keys and dropped them to the floor twice. Not cool.

Finally, we gained access to the property and started kissing passionately. I gently nudged her towards the bedroom, where the curtains were still drawn and had been since last March. We continued to kiss and grope each other as I managed to dislodge both shoes that I was wearing.

On entering the bedroom Erika shoved me hard towards the far wall and I knocked over a lamp with my flailing arm. I staggered backwards and ended up stood on a discarded pizza with my left foot and in a Chinese takeaway carton with my right.

The American knew what she wanted, and it was some prime British pork. She pushed me down on the bed and began to grind herself on top of me.

"I fall in love so easily you hunk, take me, I'm yours." Erika shouted and demanded.

This was the point when I realised that I had left the Gin bottle on the floor outside of the flat on the pavement and struggled to properly concentrate. Ridiculous really Sex v Alcohol. There should only be one winner when you were my age and opportunities like this only came round once in a blue room. (One arm prostitutes aside)

Forty-five minutes later and it was all over or so I thought, but Erika wanted Extra-Time and maybe penalties if I could rise to the challenge. She had just started to give me a blow job when my mobile started to ring, and ring, and ring.

Erika removed my glistening lower body gristle from her mouth.

"Fucking answer, it, asshole. It's putting me off." I did as I was told as she resumed suction. The name on the mobile flashed up as 'GOOCH' but it turned out to again be his secretary Dorinka Stupor on the line. She was straight to the point as per usual.

"John. John. Can you come quick?" She asked in her strong Eastern European accent.

Wow! How did she know what I was doing? Had I somehow accidentally answered and put the video mode on? I wasn't much good with these new modern technological things.

"What's up?" I asked as I took a sneaky look down towards my erect member and immediately felt like a proper rock-star, porn-star, star-turn, and king type all rolled into one.

"Is Gooch. He need to urgent chat with you today. It is big deal."

I agreed that I would be back in London as soon as humanly possible but first I had a third innings with Erika to attend to. She was insatiable.

During the third shag Erika disembarked from 'Rumplefourskin' (My pet name for my penis) and burst into tears. I didn't think it had been that bad. The first outing was a little quick granted, and I had withdrawn before climax and covered her in my seed but then I found a bit of form and stamina and as far as I could tell it had gone well during round two. She seemed to make all the right noises in all the right places. I tried to placate her. "Baby what's wrong." She fixed me with a hazed stare and if looks could kill they would have done."

"GET THE FUCK AWAY FROM ME MOTHERFUCKER!"

"If it's about the thing on my arse" I interjected.

"FUCK OFF!!" She yelled so hard in my face that it was my turn to be covered by her bodily fluid.

Erika wiped the tears away from her face and started to manically stare around the room. She then proceeded to get up out of the bed and skipped over to my dressing table where she picked up some small manicure scissors. I then watched in horror as she begun to stick the sharp point made by the blades repeatedly into her arm until they had drawn blood. What the fuck! "What are you doing?" I cried but transfixed, made no effort to stop her. "It's just another small prick in me today, it's just another small prick in me" she repeated in a zen state mantra. Erika then dug the scissors deeper into her wrist and dragged them downwards towards her wrist, scraping off skin and drawing more blood.

After cutting herself a couple of times Erika then threw the small scissors at one of the walls and then hurriedly went around the room gathering up her clothes from the floor. By doing this she had unwittingly re-created the scene that was reminiscent of the day I met her at the strip bar. A day I was beginning to regret now deeply. Then without another word she moved towards me and gave me the bird an inch away from my nose as blood dripped down her arms, going everywhere. Damn! I wasn't sure how I was going to get the blood out of the mattress. She then backed away from me before slamming the first of three doors during her exit from the house. BANG! CRASH! THUD!

Door Number One: The bedroom one.

Door Number Two: The picture of Jimbo 'Bad Moon Rising' Morrison was violently and deliberately knocked off the hallway table to the floor.

Door Number Three: The front one to the flat.

I jumped in a succession of times and then finally out of the bed. She couldn't have left could she? What on earth was that all about? What had I done?

John opened the door to the bedroom, saw Jim Morrison lying on the floor surrounded by shards of glass and decided he needed to put some shoes on before attempting to walk in the hallway. It was now clear that Erika had left as there was a small blood trail to the front door. She had also most likely left naked. There was no way she could have got that cat suit back on that quick as it had taken Leonard over eight minutes to peel her out of it prior to love making earlier.

As John turned back to his bedroom he stumbled around looking for the light switch and stood again on both the discarded Pizza box and Chinese takeaway carton. These would have to do for now as feet covers as he needed to sweep up the glass, but first things first he needed to see if that bottle of Gin were still outside his flat. He needed a glug badly to calm his shredded nerves after that display in his bedroom.

Leonard opened the door just as the neighbours, the Foster-Childs were passing by with their shopping outside his door. Mrs Foster-Childs saw naked John, screamed and as she did, so did John but for different reasons. That Gin bottle outside had gone.

This whole scenario had started when The Gooch had phoned via proxy. Whatever he had wanted had better be top fucking drawer thought John.

Three hours later after a train and tube ride, John Leonard was back in London in the offices of 'Asteroid' ready for his supposed urgent meeting with his friend and manager The Gooch.

Dorinka Stupor the PA knocked the door of Carlton's office and opened it just enough ensuring that she kept John Leonard from being able to look inside. She quickly closed the door again. "He not ready yet. He is masturbating with window cleaner." She said as a matter of fact as if wanting to know how many sugars I might want in my tea. Dorinka continued to talk. "He won't be long now. He probably on the, how you say, vehicular stokes." She meant vinegar strokes, but I let that go despite the fact that the revelation put me off my unopened bag of vinegared chips that I immediately threw straight into a nearby waste bin. The image of Gooch pulling on his plonker that popped into my mind had suddenly made me not very hungry at all and downright sick. But what was this window cleaning business?

Five minutes later and I'm sat in a leather chair at Gooch's table. A table that only had a lap-top present on it and some fierce marks where it was obvious that it had recently been wiped. Vigorously. These streaks were clearly visible as the last of the days sunlight poured through the open blinds of his office window which was when I noticed the rather busty female window cleaner with an opened shirt outside one of them stood on her ladder soaping the glass.

Ah, The Gooch. He was stood in the corner of the office spinning a large globe of planet earth that was situated on what I suspect was a drinks cabinet with his left hand whilst running the right mitt through his recently transplanted hair. He'd come a long way from running operations from the cellar at his Dad's bar in Newbury.

I decided to wait no longer and spoke. "That's probably why it all fell out. You wanna stop putting your hand through your hair mate. That and masturbating."

Carlton Gooch turned to face me. I hadn't noticed his attire of blue silk Paisley Kimono. His attire was out there at the best of times, but this was something else.

He fixed me a stare but no drink. That was a massive disappointment.

"Thank you Samantha, same time next week?" he shouted at his windows before he turned to face me.

"Buddhist. It's all happening groover. It's going down. Now is your time to strike. It's within your grasp. Hashtag in the bag brother. You have been sprinkled with stardoms pixie dust, you…."

I decided to cut him off from his flow as I watched the impressive figure of Samantha descend from her ladder.

"Gooch, Goochie, Gooch, Gooch. Why the fuck did you need my presence here and now so urgently? I was….busy."

Ever the exhibitionist Gooch walked around the office and then began to do a pirouette and he jumped up high in the air to reveal a pair of baggy white undergarments under the kimono.

"En point John. En point Buddhist. Take a seat" I already had.

The Gooch turned and banged both fists on the table and leaned his head as far forward towards me as his body would allow it to. It reminded me of one of those huge sea turtles that I had recently seen whilst tripping around the local zoo which is something I highly recommend. "Johnny boy. This is your time." Gooch picked up some papers from a drawer and continued to speak. "See these dear Botanist. These are all for you. I've got more offers than Hungerton High Street during sales week, yes I know most shops there are basically all charity shops now anyway, but you get the picture. You are A one banana. A One bwana. You're more desired than the number one on the FBIs most wanted list." All I could manage in response was a "Huh?"

Gooch carried on his diatribe whilst waving vast amounts of A four paper around. "These are offers for your services both musically and personally. Everyone loves a hard luck story. You have struck a chord with promoters, the tv producers, night club owners… somehow dear boy." Carlton picked up a sheet of paper and continued to speak not to me, but at me.

"See this. It's an offer to appear on the TV show 'Celebrity Mating Agency' with some other minor Z listers. The celeb version usually has one disgraced minor celeb like a footballer or soap star appearing alongside scum who really should never work again from that summer show all the youngsters watch. You know, that show called 'Meat Market,' you know the gig where they go to a Villa in 'Marbs' or Greece, talk shit and try and pull each other for eight weeks. It's all scripted though. Anyway, get this brother, Anna Phylaxis, the Greek model who was caught shagging that married, expense swindling Labour MP Weir Harman in a London taxi is definitely onboard. Could be a good Bunsen me old China."

John Leonard just sat stock still in his chair looking non-plussed shaking his head.

The Gooch picked up another sheet of A four paper. "No….Ok. I'm not sure where to start JL. These are actually all for you. From radio, TV, even offers for Dutch Courage to play live again."

The offer of music suddenly piqued by interest. "Gooch. That's what I desire. I just want to make music man. I also want to clean up my act and get my wife and kids back. I don't think going on some sex show or whatever the hell it is, is going to help in that quest. What would I be? The old man comedy element??"

The Gooch sat down hard into his leather chair and had to immediately re-arrange his underwear under his Kimono. In all the years I had known him Carlton Gooch had an uncanny knack of sitting down hard on his knackers.

"Quid pro quo Buddhist. Quid pro quo. You scratch my back. The big bucks is in television. This is your chance to shine out son. I can put together some music stuff for sure, for sure, for sure bwana. We have offers. It's coming up for the Bedding Festival. I can get you on there, NOW, piece of bliss brother. Just say. They are more than interested. It looks a good line up. Already confirmed are 'Swipe Left,' 'Concession Popcorn' 'Gaye Bykers on Acid,' 'Suburban Toys' 'Disco Naps,' 'Transmogrification,' 'Bumfuzzle,' comedian 'Chris Cromulent' 'Expensive Looking Teeth,' you can stop me when you've heard of one bwana, oh and funky rap posse 'Bin Dipper's are headlining. It's a two hander. A good ruddy deal is on the Aunty Mable with one leg in Yorkshire and one in Berkshire. Do you dig Por favor?"

Wow the 'Bedding Festival' I thought to myself, a real pinch me moment. This was one of the United Kingdom's biggest alternative festivals. It had started as a bit of a left-wing festival to raise funds for the homelessness in the country, where you could get in free if you turned up and donated a brand-new duvet, but It had now got so big that the promoters had spread it out for bands to appear simultaneously in two counties and even extended it to four days in duration. This of course was because of demand and for the cause and had absolutely nothing to do whatsoever with the financial greed of the promoter.

"Ok, I'm all ears." I replied to Gooch.

"No, no Captain. That is definitely your cohort Mac. He really is all ears. What the fudge happened to him? He looks rougher than sin these days. Is that what the world of cadaver metal or whatever it's called does to you…FRENCH! Glad I don't listen to that metallic rock garbage."

We both chuckled at the Gooch's reference to my band colleagues rather large lugholes.

"Look Carlton. I'm pleased, no ecstatic about this. It's what I want, trust me. I will do some television, but no reality type crap. Anyway, why did you need me to come in to see you so urgently?"

The Gooch beamed a wide smile and the white light that bounced off his gold tooth nearly blinded me. He fixed his stare on me as his left hand opened another draw in his table. I looked down to see what looked like a vintage porn mag looking back at me.

"Is that one of Chester's old mags?" I asked (Referencing our old drummers penchant for porn). Without looking or hesitation Gooch closed the table draw and opened the one on his right and in one swift, but camp movement produced another document and slapped it on the desk in front of me.

"It's upside down." I told him. He quickly swizzled the paper around, so it was legible to me. I looked down and saw that it was a contract and suddenly after reading two lines my heart began to race. I looked deep into Carlton Gooch's blue eyes. "A, American Tour!!" I stammered.

"Yes, yes, yes my liege. I want your inky drip on it before they change their mind. We are talking LA baby, and I'm not meaning a show in the London Area."

I speed read through the contract thinking it all looked too good to be true. Little Dutch Courage had been invited to be special guests to some American rock band called 'Frog Splash' All I knew about them was the name. It was something I recalled I had recorded in my memory after reading something or other about them from twenty years plus ago in the British music press. I may be doltish but I'm sure it wasn't April the first. This had to be a put on. It amazingly wasn't.

"How come you only need my signature though. What about Mac and any others we conscript into the band?" I asked.

Carlton Gooch rose from his chair and swept his hand through his hair again. A few strands of it came away in his fingers. He turned to face me and clapped his hands. "Hear me now. You are Dutch Courage John Leonard. You deserve this. Mac fudged off to the world of denim and leather at the drop of a bikers hat when the chipolatas were down last time. Heavy metal. I mean that term was never really in our lexicon was it old fruit? He sold out bwana. He is also a liability. I'm not sure he can be trusted. America. The land of milk and syrup. Lady Lib and all that Jazz, see what I did there?. The country where no-one had any idea why a dollar is called a buck. Think about it. Have you thought about it? Now sign the fudging contract. I will deal with any other associates of the good ship Dutch Courage."

I stalled. That wasn't a good adage. "But what do we do with the others?" Gooch was as pragmatic as usual.

"FUCK THEM. You are the talent JL. Sign the damn blinking contract. We'll put the others all on a retainer, minus my fifteen percent commission for finding them work. I will only take, say just fourteen from you for providing your new drummer and singer. Tell McCarthy that the offer going forward to resurrect Dutch Courage is for a straight wage all round. Simple sausage. Just like him."

By the time Gooch had got to the word 'Simple' the ink was already dry on the contract.

Wow!. The Gooch had finally proved his worth. We had gigs to play in 'The Fall' (Whatever the fuck that is?) in the US with newly reformed flamboyant heavy rockers 'Frog Splash' (Fronted by two ex-wrestlers on vocals) We were too be billed as 'Special Guests' on the 'Prepare to Die a Thousand Deaths' Tour which was to run for the grand total of seven dates across both the East and West coast of America.

Before that though, Gooch had lined Dutch Courage up with a stint on the biggest gig that the United Kingdom had to offer on the fest circuit, two dates at the prestigious 'Bedding Festival' He also revealed a one-off single deal with renown indie label 'Smooth Sale Bikini' Records. (SSB Rex)

I had to admit that I was quite excited about the prospect of the festival, as despite my love of music I had never actually been and camped at one so now I had my chance to witness this no doubt wonderful experience.

Our band were booked to play the Yorkshire leg of the festival on the Friday and then the Berkshire version of it on the Sunday, which I'm sure would be like a home coming for us of sorts. I needed to source some camping equipment for the opening Thursday in Huddersfield.

Thanks to my TV profile and book release The Gooch had also procured me a slot on entertaining BCB TV music / comedy quiz show "Too Much Pressure" where I was to appear as a guest to one of the regular team captains. This also intoxicated me.

My brief going forward was simple. Consolidate a line up for Dutch Courage. Write some new radio friendly tunes, do some warmup gigs and festivals, and most importantly keep off the drink and heavy drugs, especially prior to any television appearances and especially whilst in America. It all sounded so simple. But like most things in life, it wasn't by a bloody long chalk.

DUTCH COURAGE LINE UP MARK TWO: CONSOLIDATION

I THOUGHT I WOULD BE the first to arrive at 'Hairy Helmets' rehearsal facility in Lewisham, South London, but I found a short bald guy who had a disturbing facial twitch already in my rented space playing about on a in house keyboard. This rad dude was decked out from head to toe in denim. He was going to get decked alright if he didn't move out pronto. It appeared that the geezer was also blind in one eye I noticed, so I decided to be a shade nicer in telling him to fuck off with my opening gambit of "Aye, aye mate. This room is booked for today. So can you piss off out of it….PLEASE!" I shouted as I dumped my guitar and pedal gear onto the sticky, mucky carpet less floor. The bald twitcher looked my way but didn't appear to be in any hurry to shift. He then spoke and here I found that the bloke also had a horrific stutter.

"Are you, J, John. J, J, John Len, Len, Leonard? I, I, I, I'm E, E, Enoch, Iz, Iz, Izzet. Your, you, you, your n, n, new blind dr, dr, drummer. I'm, I'm called that because there is only one 'I' in Izzet" (He said smiling as he pointed to the dark socket on his face that no doubt once housed the missing eye) He then burst out laughing before adding "I, I, I'm ho, ho, ho, hopefully your new, new dr, dr, dr, drummer." It was no ho-ho-ho laughing matter. The guy continued trying to converse with me "Ca, ca, ca, Carlton G, G, Gooch asked me to come and au, aud, audit, aud….p, p, p, play for you." I got the feeling the way he announced his surname to me was going to be some sort of repetitive catchphrase joke from him. He was also about as cool as molten lava.

Enoch Izzet ventured towards me and outstretched his hand. I shook it but first impressions and all that were not great. He even stuttered his wobbly handshake, but it could have been because he was cold as it was bloody Baltic in the practice room.

Martin 'Mac' McCarthy was next to arrive, and he did not arrive alone. He was accompanied by a six-foot-tall guy wearing an impressive black top hat with an even more impressive handlebar moustache. He had an incredibly crooked nose, probably from playing rugby I guessed, and from what I could hear a posh accent that could cut glass. At least he was better dressed than Enoch, but then again so were unemployed farmyard scarecrows. This hip cat I was soon to discover was Mister Brandon Slam, our potential new vocalist.

A short while later and I was actually rooted to the spot in amazement. Izzet, one eye in Izzet and all that, played way better than Chester Rataski our previous tight-fisted, big balled American drummer, now residing back in the Big Apple ever did. Enoch Izzet had a quick wristed jazz style about him and seem to effortlessly hit the drums and cymbals. Slam also did the songs Bosco (RIP), use to sing justice. He possessed a decent set of pipes. The lad.

"Wow, you play good Enoch. Why on earth did 'Conundrums' get rid of you? I mean they are still going right?" I asked Enoch. Carver locked his good eye on Leonard. "They said it, it, it, wah, was, be, be, because I couldn't spell the word Emu. So, so, they k, k, kicked me out." And just like that he then went onto play a jazz fill and drum solo. He surely couldn't have been serious, could he?

We dusted off some of the old tunes that Gooch had recorded from our one and only Compact Disc release for both our new members to learn from. The tune "Fruit of the Poisonous Tree" went well. It was always one of my personal favourites (About the Unabomber in the US) and I really dug the lyrics and still remembered them without the need of a crib sheet.

"He stuck it to the authorities, posting bombs to many cities, He shudda just bombed the bass, instead of innocent people all over the place. Bombs, bombs, not what it's about, should have done an 'E' he should have chilled out."

We then did "Chalk It Up" and "Bubbles" which we surprisingly got down easy. This was turning out to be a fairly simple process until we attempted the number "Bagman" This tune yet again foxed the new players as it once did the old, but we eventually got it sorted after several aborted attempts. We also took on agreeing to learn some sort of new cover version to cement the new working relationship between us.

The one thing we all had it common was a love of the eighties smash hit song "West End Girls" So, I produced some lyrics replicating my recent experience of having visited the local Hungerton East End Working Men's Club for bingo. So "East End Club" was written in haste, and I began to sing the tune in the style of 'West End Girls' karaoke whilst strumming the tune to the original on my guitar to my new playmates.

"West End Club" (John Leonard)
Trying to get served, you might as well be dead.
There's a fiver in your hand, kids need to be fed.
Going mad, becoming unstable
Wanna get some drinks back to the table.
In a club, in East End Street
Call the doorman, there's kids running around.
TV on can't hear a sound.
In this dive bar, in East End Town
Chorus
It's a East End Club, in a drab dull world.
Bingo boys and disco girls.
The East End Club

Lots of rooms, lots of tellies
Blokes stood about with beer bellies.
Kids who don't know the word no
Fish wives playing bingo.
Lots of laughs, Council estate wit
A sign at the door asking you not to spit.
Repeat Chorus
Got a pint of Lager and a pint of Stones.

Not sure how you're gonna get home.
Cabaret singer on stage singing.
The last orders bell starts ringing.
In every club, all over the nation
Scenes of drunks and degradation
East End Club (Have you ever been?)
East End Club
You don't know what you've been missing.
Watch where you stand when you're pissing.
At the East End Club.

When I had finished I hadn't expected applause. But I hadn't expected the slack jawed gawping that greeted me by the others. Izzet had even managed to hide himself within the bass drum of his kit. A neat trick in itself. "Ok, ok, I get the picture" I shouted, and we worked on the more lyric friendly original "Nothing Good is Easy" instead until a decent cover to do could be agreed on.

After seven hours solid practice it was sounding quite good and we had eight tunes down, one half-baked new song and a couple of cover versions to add to our arsenal. No-one would expect us to knock out a raucous guitar frenzy version of the boy band 'Hunkatron' and their global smash hit single "Never Forget I'm Back for Good" (Which even hit the number one spot in Syria)

We had practiced hard and both Slam and Izzet appeared to be competent at their respective jobs. For once in the studio, it was the decibel count that was the highest not the players. I now needed to know what kind of people they were. I didn't want any nutters, political people, or drug addicts. It was time to get to know them both on a social level away from the instruments. We had a quick chat about where we should go for a drinky.

'Nocka' as he had now been christened AKA Enoch Izzet suggested we head to the local rock bar 'The Pig's Tazza' which he knew wasn't much of a walk away but Slam fancied food. He suggested Sushi so the guys agreed to go to 'Turning Japanese' which was a new restaurant in the High Street but only after I got my way in getting some liquid refreshment first.

'The Pigs Tazza' was a typical rock dive. There was absolutely zero welcome, it stunk of bleach, didn't serve food, the décor was hanging on for its life, one pull of the hanging wallpaper could well have brought down a supporting wall.

A song by punky metal combo 'Conniption Fit' called "Mental Anguish" was playing on the jukebox as we walked in. "Lads, take a seat I will get these in. Do we all like fruit Cider?" I asked.

"Just h, h, h, half please J, Jo…" I immediately cut Nocka off.

"Nocka. This is a fucking pub mate. They don't do halves. It is against my principal to order halves, soft drinks, water, or coffee. We are a fucking kick ass bastard rock band. You'll get a pint."

I hadn't even played any gigs yet and I was already getting into rock mode.

Ten minutes later we were seated with our drinks away from the smell of bleach by the toilets close to the vacant pool table. Macca was the first to speak. "So that was a good practice today. These lads nailed it. Slam was great and me and Nocka locked the rhythm section down pretty tight. Talking of tight…Are you getting the drinks in again? You must have some expenses off The Gooch?"

Re-seated and now with the second round of drinks I decided to tease our bassist.

"I think prior to the festival dates we need a warmup. We have had an offer to play with your old band 'Erectile Dysfunction.' I think that would be a good test."

Mac half coughed; half spat out his beer. "Whoa there Mr TV Star. We aint doing that under any circumstances you daft cunt. They replaced me with some foreigner remember."

It seemed that despite all his supposed left-wing leanings Mac was still a philistine when it came to certain matters of the heart. I gave him a broad cheeky smile.

"Oh, you bastard. You're just taking the piss aren't you? We aint got no warmup gig." He half laughed, half said.

No, we hadn't but I was determined to sort out something low key pretty soon. We weren't going to go into the biggest gig of our lives practice room cold.

I noticed that Nocka was lagging on the drinking booze front. "Come on Nocka. Sup up lad."

"I'm, I'm, I'm not one for dr, dr, drinking m, much J, J, John."

"Well, if you want to be in Dutch Courage I suggest you summon up some Dutch Courage and get that down you" protested Mac pointing at the full pint that Nocka was hoping would evaporate under the light beam he had placed the glass under.

As Nocka picked up his drink and slowly started to sip it down as the conversation turned to Slam who expressed his desire again to leave soon for food.

"If you can beat me at pool we'll leave immediately." Uttered Mac who bizarrely used his walking stick as his cue.

Six minutes later we were on the way to the restaurant. Mac and Nocka were struggling to walk far so we gave the Japanese place a miss and went to a closer sushi bar.

Inside 'Go-Go Boozy Sushi' we were seated on some table that had an elongated Scalextric racetrack that ran all around the other dining tables. This confused me to start with. 'Was that for kids to play on whilst the grown-ups ate?' I thought to myself. I put the thought out of my mind and posed a question to the others.

"So how did you pair think it went today?" I asked.

Slam was first to answer as Nocka started to look a little pale.

"Fucking A." Slam responded. A phrase that I utterly detested but decided to let it go on this occasion.

Nocka thankfully just raised a thumb.

Coloured bowls suddenly started to whizz by our table along the adjacent electric racetrack.

"What's the form here?" queried Mac, before asking all seated amongst us if 'They did chips?'

Slam took up the mantle. "Well Mac, the coloured bowls all represent a dish. I think chips might be a non-starter, but if you pick up the menu just beside you, it will give you an idea of what is contained within each coloured passing bowl."

Mac picked up a menu and started to read.

"How do we get the booze?" I asked Slam.

Before he had the chance to answer Nocka had removed an orange-coloured bowl. He took off the lid and the smell of the watery green contents hit him bang in the face which was enough to push him over the edge. Nocka barfed into the bowl. He then looked around to see if anyone had seen him puke before he replaced the lid back on top of the orange bowl and returned it to the conveyor belt as if nothing had happened. He then commenced skimming bits of sick left on the table onto the floor with his fingers. I watched the bowls onward journey aghast. It sailed by the next two tables which were both empty, passed another two tables which were occupied by people jabbering away and waving chopsticks around as they spoke. It then passed one further empty table before it was removed by a large behemoth of a man wearing brown coloured glasses. I looked closer at Mr Big who was dressed in matching brown coloured suit jacket and possessed crazy unkempt brown coloured hair which from this distance looked very much like a wig. This all-brown look made him look like the world's biggest turd. I watched with bated breath as he unscrewed the lid of the orange bowl, sniffed the contents, put the bowl down in front of him, picked up a spoon and then very quickly started to shovel up the spewy broth into his mouth. "Holy shit" I exclaimed rather loudly as I gave commentary on what was occurring.

Mac followed my eyeline. "I think that's what he will be doing tomorrow." He said doubled up laughing as the bloke continued to innocently spoon up Nocka's gip. I took up the mantle and started to chuckle myself. "Slam….Nocka….. I think you'll both fit in fine. Welcome to the world of Dutch Courage."

Who wouldn't want this gig. 'Dutch Courage' was on the up. It had taken the best part of two decades, but the band had a major UK festival to perform at, twice, and even though it was going to be short, a first prestigious American tour to look forward to too.

For the next two weeks intense rehearsals carried on, the band got tight, a set list was born, and it was to be a mixture of old songs, cover versions and a couple of newly written tunes.

A warmup gig was arranged in front of a small party of invited journalists and old fans we knew and was to be held at an Italian wine bar called 'Vino Zoff' which was situated on the Lewington Road in Fulham.

The gig was strictly invitational, and John was informed that an American female had tried countless times to get in even though her name wasn't on the Guest List.

Earlier in the night a huge bouncer who was working the door named Rio (Surname could have been Grande) had come into the bands dressing room to use the toilet and advised John that some woman had been relentless in trying to gain access to the gig. "Blimey my friend, she had said she was you, John Leonard's wife, then changed her story saying she was a member of the support band when I know there wasn't one. Then she insisted she worked for that gossip magazine 'Poke' and was here to review the show, but she had no credentials, and finally that she stated she was here on the councils behalf to check the venues health and safety certificate. Possessed even less credentials to prove that. She even came back later in a different outfit hoping I wouldn't remember her. She Mad man." On hearing all this from security Leonard checked his mobile phone. He saw he had several texts and missed calls from the half a night stand he had had recently, Erika Puck. She would have to wait, first there was a gig to perform, and well performed it was.

Leonard had been terribly busy recently, and he hadn't heard anything else from the American woman in the days since their one on one but suddenly out of the blue prior to the gig she had begun sending weird messages to him at odd hours of the day. The messages John was reading now had been sent early on in the night before the gig had started and kicked off nice enough. "Hey, am I on the Guest List tonight xxx?" then "Help. I can't fucking get in John x." To "Sort me the fuck out for getting in the gig. I'm outside NOW." And lastly "You Motherfucker. Rot in hell. No-one ignores me." John was about to text her back an apology when Carlton Gooch made his presence known in the small room that 'Dutch Courage' were using for a dressing room.

"That was hot, hot, hot boys. My sweat is sweating. The invites loved it. I loved it and I hope you've saved at least a fifth gear for the Bedding Festival this weekend. Am I right? I'm not wrong."

The gig had been a good one. No calamities and the new guys had nailed down their parts perfectly. It was onwards and upwards for Dutch Courage.

A few days later we were all back in Gooch's Office at Asteroid going over the finer details of our upcoming schedule.

It had been decided that despite his recent high media profile that John Leonard was going to camp at the Bedding Festival. This was on his 'To Do Before You Kick the Bucket, Bucket List' No-one could quite believe that he had never put up a tent and camped at a music festival.

"So, who is up for joining me?" I asked.

The silence was deafening. Mac who was still sporting the black luminous skeleton onesie that he wore at the warmup gig was the only one to speak up.

"Hotel for me John boy. I've played many festivals and trust me, it's ok if the weather plays ball, but if it at any point it takes that ball and pisses off home early, then I take bricks and mortar over polyester to protect me against the wind, rain, and freezing bastard cold every time."

Nocka and Slam both sided with Mac and decided to 'Hotel it' as well.

It was agreed that I would only camp at the first of the two Bedding Festival performances. Bring it the fuck on I thought to myself.

After failing to gain entrance to the warmup Dutch Courage gig, Erika Puck had returned home to her one-bedroom flat in Maida Vale. She didn't switch on the lights; in fact, it wouldn't have helped if she did as there was no lightbulbs in them.

Erika walked into the cramped kitchen and retrieved a box of matches. She then went into her bedroom and started to light a number of candles that were carefully positioned around the room. She then bent down in front of her altar. Here placed on a velvet blanket was a small effigy of John Leonard that she had carefully crafted. The head was beginning to go brown as it was just a peeled apple, which had the lid from a black biro stuck in it for a nose. The eyes comprised of two golden coloured drawing pins. The body and legs were made out of different sized pencils. A 2HB blue was stuck into the apple and that made the body. Two mini pencils had been broken in half and then superglued to the body to create the legs. The arms were made using an ice lolly stick which had an incredibly old childish joke about newspapers printed on the back of it.

On top of the peeled apple was some of Leonards actual hair sellotaped on that Erika had found the third time she had gone through his rubbish bags in his dustbin. She had been searching for the holy grail. Some pubes but hadn't struck gold. On the makeshift hands and feet were Leonards actual nail cuttings that had also been secured via the same painstaking method.

The apple was beginning to rot, so Erika lit some incense to rid the room of the smell and then got down on her hands and knees to worship to him. "You will be mine John Leonard. Roses are red, roses can be white, you will be with me forever, don't ever let us fight" She then lent forward and placed a big sloppy enthusiastic tongue kiss on the apple face.

Erika then got up off her knees and switched on her television. The video of John Leonard's recent television performance was already playing on loop from an old working video recorder that had been left by a previous tenant in the rented flat.

Erika opened her closet and removed a small black box she had stored there. When it was unlatched an angel sat on a cloud began to rise up as a musical waltz started to play.

Inside the box were more trophies from John Leonard's dustbin. A couple of used tissues, both which were stuck together, so she wasn't sure in what scenario they had been used. They were two colour pictures of Leonard that she had taken and had exposed at a local supermarket. There was also a few more nail clippings and a used plaster, but the star prize was a white sock that she had taken when she had fled his flat. Erika picked the sock up and put it under her nose and took an almighty breath in savouring the pungent onion scent that the sock gave off. The pheromones sent Puck into a wild frenzy, and she began to thrash about on her bed.

Who was Erika Puck? She was the troubled daughter of wealthy off-shore New York banker Buck Puck and his wife Shelly. Erika had picked up a drug habit during teenage life in New Jersey. Drugs were easy to get for a kid who had a huge allowance. The drug use started just after her best friend Meryl Flynn had been found choked to death on a pencil. It was a pencil that newspaper reporters became obsessed by as local police lost the evidence. Headlines guessed at the make of the pencil. '2B or not 2B' was one. 'Was Meryl Rubbed Out' was another. Erika was questioned by law enforcement over the incident as she had been seen quarrelling with the victim just hours before the tragic accident. No further action was ever taken, and Flynn's death was entered as accidental choking.

The Pucks thought they were doing the right thing by sending their daughter to London to straighten out after rehab, but it had proved to be an epic failure of a move. They had found her a nice flat in Chelsea and promised to pay the rent, but the rent only as long as she stayed straight. If Erika wanted more then she would have to earn it a phrase that had been the Puck mantra.

To start with it looked like they had made the correct decision as Erika got a job working in a clothes store on the Kings Road called 'Sputnik' and had slowly started to kick her drug habit the old-fashioned way by going cold turkey. Sadly, for her parents she didn't go full on vegetarian as good drugs may have been slightly harder to get in the United Kingdom, but the legal drinking age was a lot younger than the States and alcohol was available everywhere.

Puck soon started to spiral out of control when she hooked up with some punk rockers who knocked around the Camden area of North London. Parties were on every night and slowly but surely Erika developed an alcohol addiction and then got back on the hard drugs when she had spare cash.

The job at 'Sputnik' was the first to go. She just failed to turn up as the constant hangovers took their toll. Next she failed to report into her parents, so they threatened to stop paying her rent. In the end the threat became reality, and she was kicked out of an expensive flat in an affluent part of London.

After crashing on a friends sofa for a few weeks, Erika decided to put her assets to work. She was an attractive girl. Guys and sometimes girls were always hitting on her. She heard about a job opening as a stripper and as soon as she got the cash together she rented a room in a huge house that had been converted into flats.

Erika was going to make her own way and mark in the world. From that first meeting with John Leonard, she knew he was the 'one' But how could she show love? She had never really received it as a child. She was the runt of the litter. The last one born to aging parents who were too wrapped up in their careers to be bothered with her.

When she met Leonard she felt an energy. A connection, instant attraction. Ok, he was about twice her age, balding, and quite short sighted with bad dress sense but she loved his well-manicured hands and that accent. Wow! The way he pronounced the word 'Spoon' That alone could blow her underwear off. But when he penetrated her recently, she didn't feel it was right. It was too soon. She foolishly ran away. But now the gravity pull was stronger than ever, and she wanted him back as soon as humanly possible.

She had sent text messages to him, and they had gone unanswered. She had sent him flowers and they had been unacknowledged. She had sent a used tampon to him via 'Asteroid' but then felt that had maybe been too weird. She had even slept with a couple of guys for money as she had read on social media that Dutch Courage were going on tour, and she decided she had to go everywhere to see them.

Erika picked up one of the zoomed in pictures she had had developed of John Leonard and kissed it. "Soon my love, we will be together for ever" she whispered and then kissed the photograph again before lying back on the bed to watch Leonards recent television appearance play over and over on the archaic tv set.

THE BEDDING FESTIVAL 2019

PART ONE: THE JOHN LEONARD EXPERIENCE

DUTCH COURAGE WERE BOOKED FOR the Friday of the Yorkshire leg of the 'Bedding Festival' That meant that I had a whole day to myself as I pitched my tent on the Thursday at just after 8.30am in leafy Tramps Park in Huddersfield.

I had purchased a nice modern two berth tent which had set me back some eighty quid. If you were wondering and are a big fan of tents it was as blue in colour as the sky was on that there Thursday lunchtime.

It didn't matter how many times I read the instructions though I just couldn't fathom how to erect my tent. Out of the corner of my eye I noticed a couple of young girls point and laugh at the sad old man trying to sort his sleeping quarters out. I'm all for sexual equality and all that but neither of them lifted a false nailed finger to help. They just carried on drinking some sort of liquor they were sharing from a huge brown bottle and cackling every two minutes like fish wives. Jealousy was a bitch. I wanted to start boozing pronto myself.

Once again when I stood back to view my pitched tent it still didn't quite look like the picture on the bag it came in. I swore loudly again which got the attention of some guy sat outside one of the two red tents to my immediate left. He twisted his head and stared in my direction, then picked up a hat which was lying on the grass by his feet and perched it on his head. It was at this point that I noticed that the hat was in the shape of a large

Lobster in design and the lobsters three eyes also seemed to be looking in my direction.

The guy got to his feet, still staring right at me. He dusted his trousers down and walked over.

"E mate. Do you want some help with that?" He said as one of his hats Lobster claws began to point at my crooked tent whilst his own hands stayed fully thrust into his jean pockets.

The guy had an extraordinarily strong Northern accent. Could have been local Yorkshire dialect even but I wasn't sure. My forthcoming response made me sound very lame indeed.

"Oh Yes please mate. Any help would be hugely appreciated. I've never put this up before."

The guy turned around and shouted towards the identical red tent that was pitched opposite his.

"E, Mr Wiggles. I'm not going to be long duck. I'm just helping this here gent to put up his tent" The guy looked me in the eye and outstretched his hand. "Oh, that's poetry that isn't it. I'm Mark Michael J. Balderstone by the way from Derby. Incredibly pleased to meet you and your tents acquaintance. Have you given it a name? E, You should. Mine's called Terrance the tent."

So, if I had this straight I had just met Mark and his polyester shelter called Terrance Tent from Derby. Alarm bells should have been ringing immediately but I was out of my comfort zone.

After getting the pleasantries out of the way, Mark erected my tent in forty-five seconds flat. I couldn't believe it.

"There you go Joe. All done. Dead simple that."

"Thank you so much Mark." I let my incorrect name pronunciation / slip slide as I was just relieved to get my sleeping quarters habitable and pegged down.

Mark returned to his own red tent. In a moment of weakness, I shouted after him.

"Hey Mark, I'm just about to crack open a beer. Do you fancy one of mine? Just to say thank you for your help."

I pulled the ring pull off a can of fruit Cider and held it out to him.

"E thanks but no thanks for now cock. I forgot to bring any ciggies and got to go into town to fetch some, else Mr Wiggles will be annoyed if he can't smoke a tab soon Joe."

Again, the reference of Mr Wiggles went straight over my head. Mark continued to talk throwing words and spittle in my general direction.

"I have been in the festival, and they want eleven pounds for twenty tabs. I'm not paying that. E, It's bloody robbery that, like that Dick Turbine use to do on the York Road. Bugger that Joe."

He turned and started talking again in the direction of the other red tent that was adjacent to his. "Yes I'm going in a minute. Have patience will you. Are you coming or staying put here?"

I left him to his conversation with his friend who I assumed was in the other tent. I pulled open my deck chair, sat down and took a long pull on my first can of grog of the day just in time to see Mark wondering off alone with his Lobster hat jumping around atop of his head in time with his lolloping footsteps. He walked like he talked.

Four hours later and it was nearly time to make a move from the campsite to go into the gig early doors to hopefully see festival openers 'Kid Gloves' or at least noise monsters 'The Wonky Fences' who were second on. Worst case scenario arrive for third band the mighty Scottish anarchic punk band 'Subvision UK' I really didn't want to miss them. I was also excited for chirpy singalong duo 'Chav and Dave' who were playing. Chav and Dave were a duo who did a fine line in cheeky Chappy sing-along songs. The band consisted of one guy who lived on a council estate doing the singing and playing bass (Chav) and an upper crust gentleman called Dave from the house of lords on bass. I wondered how on earth they met. I looked through the whole line up for the day and also noticed that Leicestershire indie band 'Cool Rekz' were also playing. It was a fantastic bill, a bit like opening a letter to find it's a hundred-pound rebate from the gas board.

John Leonard had had a quiet morning observing everything around him. He saw all manner of crap flags of even crapper football teams like Forest, Coventry, and Scotland, along with strange, coloured windsocks and the like blowing around like crazy thanks to the strong breeze that was apparent. He also witnessed a random bloke who was just walking around the campsite with a tall stick that had a pink armadillo nailed on top of it with a vibrator attached to its cranium and a bold sign that read 'I'M ARMADILDO.'

A bit further down the campsite was a group of lads who had caught John out earlier on the return from one of his frequent trips to the toilets. As he walked along the grass John had spied a twenty-pound note on the deck and immediately bent down to pick it up. Despite the grab, the note had remained stuck fast to the floor and then howls of laughter emanated from the gaggle of lads who were constantly filming all those gullible fools on mobile phones who thought it was their lucky day finding twenty quid. On closer inspection it was a good photocopy of a 'score' nailed to a sod of grass. Three hours on and these youths were still laughing at the same joke as more mug punters took the bait.

John had also found himself staring at girls half his age who were dressed in virtually nothing when out of nowhere the familiar sound of John's camping neighbour Mark penetrated the air. "I'm back Mr Wiggles!"

I turned to see Mark was stood outside of his tent. "You get your fags?" I shouted as I raised my latest can of booze in salute to him. "Yeah Joe. E, I had to go into Huddersfield though to get them. But I got them for only eight sheets. Told you I wouldn't pay eleven that they were charging inside the festival. Bloody rip off that."

"So, what did you do walk into town? It's a bit of a way and a good stroll from here isn't it?" I asked innocently.

"E it is that. No, I got the bus like."

I was just about to disengage from the conversation when a thought occurred, so I asked one more question.

"Do you have a bus pass then Mark?."

Mark unzipped the red tent adjacent to his then threw the cigarettes inside and zipped it back up again.

I repeated my question as Mark approached me.

"Nah, I don't have a bus pass. Wiggles might have. I didn't think to ask him. How stupid."

"So how much was the bus?" I asked of Mark.

"Oh, I got a return ticket Joe. So, it made it cheaper like. It was four quid. E, a bargain that so I could get my ciggies."

Despite the alcohol that was already clouding my mind but not yet my judgement I knew that the eight pounds for cigarettes and four for the bus ride equalled more than the cost of eleven pounds that the festival was selling them for, and it would have saved him at least three hours of wasted time. I checked my watch. "But you've missed 'All Night Benders' and 'The Kipper Ties' whilst you've been out on stage two'" I said as I looked at the days musical itinerary on my 'Bedding' phone app once more.

"E, me not bothered about them. I only wanna see Adda-Hadda really. It's the only reason I'm here. I don't really like anyone else on the bill."

Mark was referring to the surprise inclusion of the notorious heavy rock outfit 'ADHD'(Known affectionately amongst their fans as 'Adda-Hadda') They were a band who courted controversy with their Satanic image, and songs like "Highway to Hades" and "Black is Blacker" It was a shocker them being added to a predominantly indie rock orientated music festival and raised many an eyebrow.

"Well make sure you check out the band 'Dutch Courage' who are playing tomorrow. I hear they are shit hot." I mentioned to Mark.

"Shit more like." Mark giggled back at me.

"Wiggles might go but I'm only here for Adda-Hadda" Mark reiterated.

"Let me get this straight. You've paid near on three hundred pounds to come to this festival just to watch one band?" I asked.

"E, that's right, plus a ticket for Mr Wiggles." Mark said as his Lobster hat pointed a claw towards the red tent adjacent to his red tent.

"It's ok, me ma and pa pay for it. They didn't want me to miss out."

It was at this point that not only did the penny dropped but the whole of Fort Knox's gold reserve. Mark was clearly as mad as a hatter, and I bet his parents would pay anything to get rid of him out of the house for a few days.

I stood up and folded away my chair. "Well, I'm going in Mark. Gonna check out a few new bands I think."

Mark had returned to his red tent and was on his knees trying to light a small portable barbecue. "I'm going to have sausages. We got to eat and be strong for

Adda-Hadda later haven't we Wiggles?" Yet again Mr Wiggles failed to answer. Mark continued. "Do you want some or do we save you some for later?."

It should have been a no brainer really but foolishly I agreed to return for a sausage or three after a trip to the bogs as I felt sorry for this simpleton who had though put up my tent when I couldn't. That and I didn't fancy paying seven quid a pint the app said the price of beer was inside the gig.

Whilst the conversation had been going on between John and Mark, the Dutch Courage member had failed to notice the woman who had been watching him intently from behind a face veil some distance away in between taking ample slugs of Gin. She noticed John walk away so decided to make her ascent to Mark and Wiggles tent where she could see him cooking something in a pan which was placed on top of a barbecue. The mystery woman approached Mark.

"Hmm... Sausages. They smell good man. Just cook them well on the one side they'll be ok. Here let me put this in. Just some special spice to add taste."

The woman took out a small bottle from her leather jacket which contained a mixture of untreated sewage water mixed with laxatives and hallucinogenic drugs and poured it over the sausages in the pan before Mark could even look up and answer.

"That's ok I guess" said Mark. "We like sausage don't we Wiggles. Do you like sausage?"

"Hmmm....Yes I do. Big long pink raw sausage." The mystery woman answered licking her lips and with that she turned on her heels and left Mark to his sizzling sausages with the phrase "Have a nice day now." ringing in his ears. "What a nice Australian woman Mr Wiggles." Mark shouted towards the adjacent red tent as the meat slowly began to burn on one side of the sausage as it cooked in the juice on the barbecue. "Block my texts, ha this'll unblock you fucker" Puck thought to herself.

Later that afternoon at the Bedding Festival, John Leonard had (Despite telling everyone he wouldn't be 'that man' as he really wanted to experience the fest through the eyes of the punter.), used his 'Access All Areas' credentials and became that man to get access to the backstage area.

He still hadn't realised that he was being followed through the crowds by

Erika from America who was dressed as a saucy nurse in latex gear. There was no way Leonard could ignore her dressed like this especially after she saves his life. She thought to herself.

Erika was just about to pounce on Leonard when she herself was accosted by a pair of festival going twats who were walking around the site on stilts dressed as clowns. During this untimely intrusion for Erika, Leonard had flashed his backstage pass and disappeared through an open door that was situated behind a row of blue polo shirt wearing security guards. 'Shit' she exclaimed. 'Too many guys there to blow to get beyond that bunch. Curse my rotten damn motherfucking luck' she thought to herself and decided to put Plan B into effect which involved tracking down the other members of the band instead who she knew were booked into a nearby hotel.

The reason for this backstage visit by John was that he was not overly chuffed with the fact that he felt the sudden desperate need for a dump and had no desire to hit 'Portaloo Sunset' which was the area of the green fields that the festival had turned into the toilets after catching a whiff of said area on passing.

John was a full-on toilet prude and didn't want anyone around when he had to go. He had been one of those people who wouldn't ever drop a log in the works toilet if someone else suddenly ventured in whilst he was ensconced in a cubicle in there. He would also clench up until the hand dryer went on before unleashing. Therefore, there was no way he was going to drop some mixture with the possibility of twenty thousand punters hearing his turd hit the water however unrealistic that possibility was.

John began to sweat profusely as he weaved around rushing roadies and other staffers going about their business and to his dismay the toilets backstage were in no better condition than the ones out front. He pulled open the door to his first pick of Portaloo and was greeted with the sight of shit splattered everywhere around it. "What the..." he muttered to himself as he caught his breath before doubling up from a rumbling pain that had become more pronounced in his stomach. He eyed his surroundings with a hand over his nose and mouth. Had someone been in and fixed a garden hose attachment to their ass hole, changed the setting to spray and then let rip? This was beyond the pale. How was it possible to get crap stuck on the ceiling? Thankfully, choice number two became immediately vacant, but it was still hardly tea at the Ritz, but those sausages he'd eaten back at the tent with Mark were obviously seriously undercooked and at this moment looking to come out well before the nights encores were finished.

Despite feeling so desperate to go, once seated John found that he had to strain hard to push anything out. He pushed and could only feel the tip of the bodily waste poke its head out his chuff. This beast wouldn't come out without a fight though. He huffed and puffed again until it finally started to move, and when it did start to come out into the world it then wouldn't stop. It came out as one huge, long faecal sausage.

Leonard started to clench and unclench his buttock muscles but found they couldn't break the turd off. It was too thick. It had now hit the water in the pan and was curling up but worryingly it was still coming out in one long fluid movement. There was smoke on the water.

John stood up to stop the shit looping round any further and immediately regretted his decision as he hit his head on the roof of the lavatory and slipped back down onto the toilet seat in shock. The bumping of the head and gnashing of the teeth was just what he needed though and had helped cut the massive shite's umbilical cord. Whilst unexpectedly knocking his head, John had ended up biting down hard on his tongue and the reflective action of his body tensing and pain had finally broken off the runaway brown rocket.

John stood again slowly, this time taking care of his surroundings by putting both hands directly on the back wall of the cubicle where someone had recently written 'Shit Muncher' with a black sharpie. He turned and looked down the pan. Looking back at him was something akin to a large brown Anaconda snake, the deadly type with large dark spots as it lay curled up on the plastic bowl.

'How on earth had three sausages turned into that?' thought John as he mopped his brow with tissue paper and continued to sweat bullets. Just as he thought he was over the worse he then vomited for good measure. Things couldn't get any more unpleasant he surmised until he realised there was no toilet paper, and this was the back-stage area for fucks sake!

Leonard removed his T-shirt which after being rolled up was now ready for its next function. It was handily damp as it was drenched in sweat. It was a yellow shirt of the band 'Fringe Benefits' It wouldn't be yellow for much longer as he rolled it up and got to work cleaning his sore arse hole.

Sweat was now pouring out of John. What was going on he thought to himself? He'd had several fruit ciders granted, but they hadn't really touched the sides, had they? He couldn't have beer-stroke? The sun had hardly been out all day. No, this, whatever it was, had to have been caused by Mark's slightly uncooked sausages he had foolishly eaten earlier. Did he have food poisoning? Whatever it was, it was causing his stomach to somersault more than a Chinese gymnast.

After John exited the toilet he noticed that the backstage area was suddenly a hive of activity, but no-one seemed to pay him any attention even though he was walking around topless, holding a t-shirt covered in shit.

He moved away from the toilet block and could now see a bar area where many hip people were sitting around cross legged talking and drinking on the makeshift flooring. Beyond them was a closed off area that said, 'ADHD Band Members Only' 'I'm sure I have that' John thought to himself referencing the disorder whilst he waited for the opportunity to quietly slip into this cordoned off area which was reserved for the rock band ADHD and crew. Thankfully for John, the bouncer, 'Chivers,' who had been stood outside guarding the area soon quietly moved away to take a phone call and Leonard took his chance.

Once entering the roped off area a still topless John Leonard headed straight for the huge fridge which had a massive pair of black stack heeled boots sat on top of it. He pulled open the door and was in luck as it was full of various bottled drinks.

This area seemed to be quiet and deserted or so he thought until he spotted a small bald guy sat on the floor sucking on what looked like a 'ADHD' emblazoned bong.

Some bald, short guy looked up and caught my eye. "Who the fuck are you? You aren't Chivers? How did you get in here?" he asked. By now the sweat was pouring out of me as I flopped down on an empty black settee holding a bottle of water. The bald guy stood up and reached for a nearby mannequins dummy head, which was situated on a dressing table behind him, flanked by a full-length mirror. He grabbed the wig that sat on it and placed it on his own head, checking himself out in the mirror. "You shouldn't be here." He said before looking at me closer and added "Christ, are you all right?"

The guy walking towards John Leonard was the recluse singer of the band 'ADHD' Scoot Adonis' (Stage name. Real name: Malcolm Boulton. Age: 66, Press Age: 43) A chap who John thought was most definitely not bald and had appeared a lot taller in all the photographs of him he had ever seen. 'Oh, them boots' thought Leonard to himself just before he passed out.

John Leonard awoke startled to witness the toilet in the back-stage area erupting. It was like the Mount Vesuvius of shit as hot crap shot out and slithered down the sides of the pan.

John looked to his left and there stood with his arms folded wasn't the stunted black clad follicle challenged singer of 'ADHD' Scoot Adonis but a guy with orange hair. On closer inspection the bloke was wearing an orange suit and sported an orange shirt with orange tie and rarer still he was wearing orange shoes. The orange man looked over at Leonard and spoke. "I never thought you were going to wake up." John recognised the voice but then became utterly confused. "Baz…Is that you, Mr Orange? But, but YOU'RE FUCKING DEAD! I went to the funeral. Mr Orange…What the fuck! Oh bollocks, am I Hovis too?" There stood before John Leonard was the ghostly spectre of one-time Dutch Courage fan, roadie, merch-seller, and hanger-on Barry 'Mr Orange' Oakes. "No. You aren't dead John." He replied.

Oakes was known by his nickname of Mr Orange (His best friend had the moniker Mr Vodka, they entered gigs on guest lists as Vodka and Orange) Baz Oakes had succumbed to the rampant seas that engulfed the ferry that had sunk when returning Dutch Courage to the United Kingdom from a disastrous European tour some two decades previous.

"Yes it's me John. I see twenty years on, and nothing's changed. You are still fucking things up for yourself and more importantly the band." John relaxed and assumed this was some sort of apparition or dream sequence that happened all the time in films and books. "What are you doing here Orange?" Mr Orange looked directly at the sweaty prone leader of Dutch Courage "Yes

I'm dead all right, but I chose you John. I will haunt you John Leonard. Only you can see me." John sat up immediately. "Only me, fucks sake... Why me? We were hardly the best of friends were we huh? Surely haunting your wife Holly would make more sense, I mean she is quite fit after all and you must want to see your child or even your old mate Garry Newman, AKA Mr Vodka." Orange appeared annoyed. "Well, that's gratitude for you." Replied the ghost who then continued to speak "Look you prick, it's the bands biggest gig tomorrow and you and Mac are intent on fucking it up. I'm here to try and guide you, to help you out and to stop that from happening." I started to reply "Mac, You've seen Mac what's he up…"

…. I suddenly felt a splash of water in my face and jolted awake. Before me was a guy not dressed all in orange but a bloke wearing a black lobsided wig, behind him there was a huge lump of a bloke with a badge that said, 'My Name is CHIVERS,' and the word 'SECURITY' was splattered across his chest. There was also someone else who was decked out in a green jumpsuit which had the word 'MEDIC' imprinted on it. Thankfully, it was the someone in green who was holding my left-hand checking for a pulse as unicorns danced around and a huge black bear was juggling chainsaws. "Is he alive?" Asked Wig guy. The medic nodded. "Good, now get him out of here NOW. I need to meditate and have some important me time before my show." Lopsided black wig man shouted. "I think it's a nasty case of food poisoning or a drug overdose" replied green jumpsuit. "Sorry again boss. Not sure how this arsehole got in here." SECURITY blurted out in apology.

Next I was on my feet being dragged towards the exit by the duo of Medic and Security, although I felt like I was walking on the moon as I looked down to see that my feet weren't actually touching the ground. Boy that medic was strong.

As the door to 'ADHD's' exclusive backstage area was opened with a kick by Security, the first thing I saw was an orange figure stood by a vacant table shaking his head and tutting at me in disgust.

John Leonard thought he had finished puking and shitting having been escorted out of the backstage area and left to his own devices. All of a sudden he was hit by another body spasm and involuntarily crapped himself. He stumbled on in the dark as the sound of a band playing in the distance and people having a better time than him filled the night air.

John slumped down to the floor and landed square on his arse, which in hindsight having just shit himself was an error. He had already lost his t-shirt to a toilet episode earlier and now he had soiled his jeans and underwear, of which he had now squashed the contents of against himself after falling hard to the floor.

Fellow festival goers gave John a wide berth oblivious to the fact that this guy would be appearing on the festivals main stage early the next afternoon.

"You ok pal?" A good Samaritan dressed as a Panda asked me. For a moment I didn't know if I was back in the festival or if this was another sort of ghostly vision. I chose it to be the latter option. "Fuck Off you cunt!" I yelled at the stunned bear. The guy removed his panda head to reveal a human cranium that was the shape of a potato with a fat chip for a nose. No wonder he was wearing a disguise. I would if I looked like that. The human Maris Piper shouted back at me "Huh charming, only trying to help. Jesus...You stink mate." "You should have dressed as King Edward not a bear" I childishly yelled but Panda head had moved on as other revellers passed by me. I suddenly regretted my choice of words. "I'm sorry mate. I thought you were my dead friend playing tricks on me" I shouted after him, but my words were lost in the noise generated by 'Concession Popcorn' who were blasting out a neat line in four-piece indie rock on the festival main stage to a massive adoring crowd.

I got to my feet. I just needed to sleep. I was so tired and dehydrated. Next stop for me was my tent which took the best part of another two hours to find. Festivals….Stick them up your arse!

THE BEDDING FESTIVAL 2019

PART TWO: ENTER MARTIN 'MAC' MCCARTHY AND BRANDON SLAM

EARLIER IN THE DAY MAC and Slam found themselves travelling to nearby Dewsbury as it was impossible to get a hotel in and around where the 'Bedding Festival' was being held in Huddersfield. They weren't really interested in seeing what the bands of the first day had to offer. Band drummer Nocka was travelling up separately on the day of the gig 24 hours later.

At first glance their booked accommodation 'The Hypnos Hotel' only seemed slightly better standard than John Leonards tent would be from outside viewing. Mac and Slam exited their parked rented car and made for the reception area. First impressions were how on earth had this place been deemed a three-star abode. "What the fuck does Hypnos mean Slam, any idea?" asked a confused Mac.

"Maybe something to do with hypnotism Macca? I'm not really sure to be honest with you mate." Replied Slam.

The answer to the hotel moniker question was sort of found at reception where a sign behind it read.

"We come to H pnos – The reek God o leep.'

It was pretty easy to fill in the blanks.

Mac and Slam were checked in by a woman with tight curly blonde hair, and bad dandruff. She bore the name tag 'Sharon' which was attached to a black waist coat that appeared to be at least two sizes too small for its occupant. Sharon also had the charm and warmth of Atilla the Hun. She directed the band members to a room on the fourth floor with a bored robotic voice. When it came to directions or instructions of any kind Mac found he was not good with them at the best of times. He had taken off his glasses at check in (As they didn't make him look Rock and Roll) and hoped that Slam had taken onboard the given direction to the room as he hadn't.

At the top of the first flight of stairs as Slam came to a crossroads he turned to Mac and asked, "Which way did she say at the top of the stairs right or left." It was like the blind leading the literally blind.

"I dunno Slam. I wasn't wearing my glasses so didn't really hear her." replied Mac.

Ten minutes later after more wrong turns than the incumbent Tory government, Slam and Mac were outside room 408, their rented abode for the night. It took them another five minutes of tapping the key card in every conceivable position until the familiar clicking sound came from the lock unlocking and the annoying red light barring entry being turned to a palatable green one.

"Hoo-fucking-ray" shouted Slam as he turned to high five Mac, but Mac had already pushed past him and entered the room.

"Sweet home of Babylon. I'm busting for a piss" Mac declared on entering the room. This declaration and run to the lavatory meant that Brandon Slam had the all-important (Or so he thought) choice of which identical bed to sleep in. There was a single one with white bedding to the left or there was another single one with cream bedding to the right. Slam went right and threw his meagre luggage onto the mattress which soiled it immediately. He then heard the toilet flush which made the water pipes in the room rattle which in turn made it sound like a train was passing beneath it.

Slam looked out of the window and started to shout at the still closed toilet door. "I don't think they've ever heard of double glazing in some of these towns up north. I could see none of the houses had it on the way here and neither does this hotel. The windowpanes are so thin I swear I've just heard a passing seagull fart outside. Come here and feel this draft."

The toilet door flew open at speed and hit the bedroom wall hard sending chipped paint and wood splinters flying across the room as Mac exited the bathroom wiping his nose with his left hand and holding his thick black rimmed glasses in his right hand. "I'm not coming over there if you've just farted. Feel your own draft." Yelled Mac as he put his glasses back on and immediately started vigorously rubbing his right leg hoping to remove the small wet piss stain he had created on his clothing.

"You got any valuables Macca?" asked Slam as he moved over to stand in front of the rooms visible in built safe.

Mac rummaged through his luggage and removed a large bag of nose candy from a side pocket. "Here stick this in there. Oh, hold on a minute." He then dribbled spit onto his fingers and stuck them into the bag of choppy white powder. "Quick toot for the road. Do you wish to partake? If so hurry up then we can get down to the bar. I'm right parched, as dry as a nun in the Sahara. Let's go get a good glug chief. Hit that turps hard. Yes?"

Slam had not only been told to by band manager Carlton Gooch, but he had also signed a binding contract with his 'Asteroid' agency which bound him to ensure that in his presence the 'Septic Siblings' Leonard / McCarthy wouldn't be able to get their grubby hands on any narcotics or hard alcohol that could potentially lead to them fucking up this nice little earner for The Gooch. "Nah, I'm not bothered by that stuff. But I'm more than happy to go and hit the bar my friend for a Lemonade." Slam took hold of the bag of drugs and placed it in the safe along with bizarrely enough, Macs glasses which he had now sensibly removed. "Can't afford to get them broken. Lost without them buggers these days. I've only got the one pair as well" Mac commented as he delicately patted the arms of them as they lay on the purple velvet flooring of the safe. Following the pat and removal of Macs hand Slam pushed the safe door shut and added his own random number code to lock it.

"Five, Seven, Nine, One. Ok Mac?" he said to the back of Mac's head as Mac made for the door. Slam double checked that the safe door was shut and by the time the last of the safes three clunks of the lock activating itself sounded, the room lights were off, and the singer and bass guitarist were well on their way down to the hotel bar.

The Dutch Courage duo had been boozing in the hotel bar which was named 'Bottle Grounds' for over four hours and were just shooting the breeze when (To Mac's eyes) a fit bit of totty presented herself at the bar. Mac was up in an instant. Then the rest of his body got up out of his chair and he waddled over to her. "Can I buy you a drink Miss?"

The woman turned around laughing. She was tall and elegant, wearing a sleek green and white swirled print dress. She had long brown hair that was tied neatly back in a ponytail. Mac caught himself being mesmerised by her ample large earrings that twinkled every time the light reflected off them. He couldn't stop looking at her large tits either. He had already checked out the other important parts of her, well had tried to, but found he had to squint really hard to ensure that it was indeed a woman he was ogling at first before walking over and making his interest known.

"Bottle of beer" she requested sounding like a ventriloquist dummy whilst seductively licking her thick synthetic filled lips. Mac suddenly felt like he had twenty-twenty vision despite being unable to see how rough this woman's complexion really was underneath the inch thick layer of make-up that she had applied to herself. Still, he was no oil painting.

A dark green bottle of booze was placed on the bar with a knowing smile by the barman. The woman who had now introduced herself as Kitty didn't even look or touch the bottle. She just wanted to talk.

Over in the corner of the bar, Brandon Slam had been joined by another woman who had just recently arrived at the hotel as the sun outside had gone down and the dark of night had come, she asked if the seat next to him was taken. "Please. It's yours." Advised Slam who got to his feet and ever the gentlemen pulled the seat out for the female to join him.

"What the fuck. This aint the fifties man." The female said with the hint of a seductive smile which showed off some neat pearly white teeth. Slams visitor may have had good teeth, but he himself hadn't noticed her pock marked mocha coloured skin which had been caused by heavy drug use. She displayed rosy, red lipstick and that was definitely an American accent he had picked up he thought to himself. Slam continued his charm offensive in between gulps of Lager from a two-pint glass.

"I detect you aren't from around here are you?"

The woman let out a hearty laugh. "Look if you want to take me to bed just get a bottle of Champagne sent up to your room. My name is Erika. I will see you up there. Give me your key."

Slam was lost for words. His hands moved down blur like to his trouser pocket faster than the speed of light. No sooner had the American sat down than she was stood up again. Slam marvelled at her curvaceous body through his beer goggles and suddenly started to perspire. He tried hard to think if it said anything about sex or heavily drinking beers in his Dutch Courage contract. If it did he was snookered as he was pissed as a fart and was definitely going to investigate this woman further.

Slam was used to conjuring up rabbits in a previous life as a magician, but this seemed to be his best trick yet. No sooner had she asked than Slam had produced the room key without seemingly to her, moving his hands or fingers. "Wow man! I'm impressed" said Erika. She leaned in closer to Slam and continued to speak in husky tones "I hope your fingers will work more magic like that later." Erika winked, then wiggled over to the bar, stopping every few paces to hitch down her skirt.

Erika ordered a bottle of Moet from the barman but asked for it to be put on the tab of room 408, showing him the key and then signed the chitty. She then turned to Slam, winked again, and gestured to him to give her five minutes with her hands before mouthing a much ruder signal to him which also required the use of her right hand and opening and closing her mouth as if it were sucking a stick of rock. The second gesture had blown Slams mind and his sweaty face began to crimson.

Back at the bar with pick up number one was Mac. He had now been in conversation with the woman named Kitty for almost an hour in which time he had gone through three pints of Premium Strength Lager and five shots of Limoncello Liquor, whilst her green bottled beer had remained untouched, with the liquid inside having gone lukewarm and the bottle probably taken root.

"How about a proper drink" Kitty purred. "Sure. W, w, whatever you want?" stuttered an inebriated Mac whilst involuntarily playing air guitar to the tune of the same Quo song that only he could hear. Kitty raised a long-manicured finger to the barman and suddenly a bottle of Champagne was uncorked and placed on the bar alongside a bill and a pen. Mac picked up the pen and signed the bill without looking or realising that he just agreed to pay two hundred pounds for a thirty-five quid bottle of cheap house plonk.

Upstairs in room 408 and Slam couldn't believe his luck. He was lying naked in bed with the American he had only met thirty minutes ago. He may now be a rock and roller, but this situation had surely called upon his time as a conjurer to be in this position within half an hour as he smiled and then laughed all happy with himself.

Slam had got into what was Macs bed with the white quilt. Slams mantra was that If he was going to be making a mess it was going to be on someone else's bedding.

Erika exited the toilet carrying her clothes wearing some skimpy, ketchup coloured lingerie. 'Saucy' Slams eyes had read. She cast her eyes towards the morsel in the single bed. "Pour me some Champers man. Cuz remember honey, if I get no Moet then you get no show…ay" Slam indicated with a nod of his head towards the fizzing glass of bubbles that was already atop of the table on what he hoped would be her side of the bed.

Erika dropped her carried clothes and confidently strode over and picked up her glass, looked the drunken Brandon Slam directly in the eyes and spoke using the huskiest and sexiest tone she had available. "So, Brandon, you are in that group Dutch Courage correct? And how well do you know John Leonard?" Slam answered quickly whilst licking his lips and poking his tongue out of his mouth constantly like a snake collecting information for its Jacobson's organ. His own organ was poker stiff under the covers. He grabbed his erection as he answered her. "Not very well really. Not very well at all. I've only been in the band a few weeks. Mac down in the bar knows him far better than me. That's not a deal breaker is it? Are you a fan, I am the singer of the band after all…?" The questions that followed would come quicker than Slam ever would in room 408. "Is John Leonard seeing anyone at the minute? Is he getting divorced? Is he good with children? Does he like children? Does he like Apple Pie?" All questions that Slam didn't really know the answers too. "As I said I hardly know the man to be honest with you" a confused and agitated Brandon Slam responded. "Look, I've been on telly as well you know. Would you like me to pull a rabbit out of my hat for you?"

Erika decided there and then that a rampant rabbit would be preferable than this boring drunk.

Brandon was also getting bored, but his reproductive organ was still rock hard. He got up out of the bed trying to conceal his ardour. "I'm going for a piss. You going to be ready for some Slam Slam action when I get back or what?" As the door to the bog closed, the Benzodiazepine sedative pill was already beginning to effervesce in Brandon Slams glass of Champagne.

Twenty minutes later Erika Puck was leaving room 408 and the Hypnos Hotel to return to her tent at the Bedding Festival site. Things really hadn't really gone to plan today with Scheme A or B.

Meanwhile back down in the hotel bar and Mac was still standing but beginning to slur his words badly. He didn't really like Champagne and hardly noticed that Kitty had not touched her glass of bubbly whilst he had virtually consumed the rest of the bottle.

"Sh, s, sh, shit, err, shill, I mean, shall I,I,I order us another bock, bot, bottle of spunk, err I mean punk, no p, p, plonk?"

Kitty moved in on her prey and grabbed him by the lapel of his shirt. "One hundred and fifty and you can take me upstairs and order me to do anything you like to me NOW." Mac started to reply, "I plan on doing everything to you …." It was at this precise moment that realisation hit Martin McCarthy square bang in the kisser. "What? You, you, want money to sleep with me. You're a p, p, pro, oh for f, f, fucks sake. I don't have one fifty. Can't we haggle. How about a score to fifty. Do you take card as well as cock? Not sure I've got any bread on me."

Kitty looked perplexed. "I've not fucking stood here in my finest listening to you bore the arse off me for fifty smackers you cheap piece of shit. You saying I'm not worth more Mister Rock Star or are all your stories about being Grammy nominated just lies?" Mac held up his hands in mock defence as Kitty became angrier and her faced turned devil red. "You've wasted my fucking time!" By now the other guests were looking over at the scene playing out at the hotel bar. The bar man tried to intervene "Kitty. Calm down. Are you on drugs again? I told you no drugs." Mac turned to look at the man behind the bar who's name tag read 'Leo' and it was the last thing he saw or remembered as the manky chipped white porcelain ornament Kitty had picked up from a shelf that had been standing next to some nearby pot plants came crashing down on the back of his head, sending him sprawling to the floor.

Leo rushed from behind the bar, grabbed Kitty around the waist and bundled her towards the door as she continued to kick and scream at the prone bass player. "Rock star, rock star my fat arse!" was the last anyone heard from her as she was ejected from the premises.

Leo the bar keep fetched help in the form of his mate Gavin who was also on the night shift. "We have to get this cretin up-to room 408 quick." He discreetly said. They picked Mac up off the floor and escorted him to the lift and up-to the fourth floor. They dragged him along the corridor as a couple approached. "Just had a few too many this one, It's all part of the service." Beamed Leo as the threesome passed the slack-jawed couple in the corridor.

Finally, they reached room 408. Gavin used his Master key to open up the room where they discovered another prone figure already in the rooms left side bed snoring loudly sound asleep.

"Chuck him on the spare bed and let's get out of here. Fucking Kitty went too far tonight" whispered Gavin. "Actually, not fucking Kitty done for this muppet." Laughed Leo as he switched the light off and closed the door.

THE NEXT DAY

THURSDAY BECAME FRIDAY AKA: GIG day for Dutch Courage. Nocka was just a couple of miles from the site of The Bedding Festival driving up in his white AMC Shotput 3000 car and was ready and raring to go for this show.

In the Hypnos Hotel things were deathly quiet in room 408 with the exception of two mobile phone alarms that had been going off solidly for over an hour. Brandon Slam was the first to begin to stir, he opened his sleep encrusted eyes, and took in his surroundings. He was in the right room he noticed but the wrong bed. He scratched his groin and that's when he realised he was naked under the duvet. As well as the alarm he could hear loud snoring coming from within the room and he sat up as straight as his body would allow at this assumed early hour of the day.

Slam glanced to his right and saw his room-mate Mac who was fully clothed but asleep in the wrong allocated bed. It appeared he had dried blood splattered across his forehead. 'God, I hope that's his.' Slam thought to himself as he exited the bed before bringing up a hand to hold onto the wall to steady himself and wonder what the hell had happened last night?. He sort of remembered the girl in the bar, Champagne in the room and then…. NOTHING.

Slam bent down to switch off his mobile alarm that had been going off for ages and that's when he noticed the time. "Oh shit. It's ten-thirty-five" He exclaimed. The reason for the panic was that the band were due at the festival by eleven to facilitate a soundcheck.

Slam approached a still sleeping Mac and begun to shake him vigorously. Mac opened one eye and saw the outline of a naked man towering over him. "What the fuck?!!?!"offered Mac. "Mac, Mac, calm down, it's Slam, come on shake a leg, shake anything, we're late, it's gone half ten." Mac just groaned and rolled off the bed to reveal a large wet outline where he had been lying and had routinely pissed himself during his slumber. "Christ Mac." Yelled Slam. "You got some sort of brain to bladder disconnect? You've made a right mess of that bed. Your urine stinks like boiled cabbage my friend."

"We need to get a shift on." Brandon Slam stated the obvious whilst putting yesterday's underpants back on. He moved quick for someone who not only had a hangover but had been drugged the previous night. He moved over to where the safe was situated in the room and posed Mac a good question. "What on earth happened to you last night? You look how I feel. It seemed like you were well in with that bird you were jabbering to at the bar." Mac to had a vision of the previous night and it wasn't good. "Oh her. Nah, nothing doing." He responded whilst removing his wet jeans and boxers before adding. "But I think some of that gear in the safe will sort me out for breakfast…. And I need my specs badly. My eyesight is getting worse." It was with that comment that the day ground to a halt as neither man could remember the code to the safe.

The arguing commenced. "You put it in you prick." Shouted Mac, "Yeah but I told you what it was." Retaliated Slam. "Just ring reception. Surely they can reset it?" reasoned Mac. "No. You tell them. What if they send someone up to open it and they see it has your big bag of Cocaine in it" "And my fucking glasses" countered Mac.

After consideration, the hapless duo decided to do a runner from the hotel. Gooch's firm had booked the room, so they could pay their drinks tab. They hadn't run up that much of a debt there had they?

Back at the festival and Nocka Izzet had parked up and was getting his festival credentials from the box office. He was all smiles and couldn't wait to hit the stage later.

John Leonard was woken by the sound of someone other than him being violently sick. He lent forward and unzipped his tent to see his camp neighbour Mark lying in a heap, dry heaving.

"You ok there Mark?" I shouted. "No Joe. I'm not having a good time. I even missed Adda-Hadda last night being sicky. E, I think it was the sausages. Wiggles said they were great, Adda-Hadda and the sausages, so I'm angry. Well, I would be if I had the strength."

Mark finally got to his feet and dusted himself down, flicking away bits of errant carrot from his jumper.

He turned unsteadily but then expertly packed away his pop-up tent in record quick time. He carried on communicating. "No point staying now. It's ruined. We're going Wiggles." And in a flash Mark took down the second red tent, the one which had been adjacent to his. He was a whizz with the camping gear, but no quality chef thought John.

John had been right in his assumption. Wiggles had been a figment of Mark's imagination all along. John looked down at his right hand, and what wasn't a figment of his imagination was that his 'Access All Areas' wristband was no longer there.

Later that day, at two-thirty-five Dutch Courage hit the stage slightly later than advertised at the 'Bedding Festival' They had pulled a reasonably sized curious crowd. Mac sadly, without his glasses on was a calamity on stage. He sent his microphone flying on more than one occasion, couldn't quite see what he was doing to play and hit more bum notes that the orchestra did on the sinking Titanic. Slam was also less energetic than the previous performances and had already missed more words than someone suffering from fluency disorder. The crowd, however, didn't seem to notice or mind the fluffs.

I looked down at the setlist. It was a mixture of old and new.

ELIXIR

FUNNY FARM

AWARD WINNING MARROW

MOUSTACHE SONG

TOP BANANA SUNDAY

FRUIT OF THE POISONOUS TREE

EXPENSIVE CLOAK ROOM
KITE
THE ALBANIAN EUROVISION SONG CONTEST ENTRY (*JL Vox)
ROCKIN' ALL OVER THE WORLD'S END
BUBBLES / CLIMAX

We were only on 'Funny Farm' Song number two, which was only three minutes in length, and it had started to feel like the World's longest ever song . We had to get our heads in the game and quick. I knew what was wrong with me down to the night of puking and shitting that I had endured but what was wrong with the others? Nocka was doing fine on the drum kit, but Slam and Mac were every bit as bad as I was. I should have guessed something was not right when they turned up just thirty minutes or so before we were due to go on stage. Flat tyre my glass eye!

A plastic bottle skimmed across the stage spilling some of its sticky content on route. I watched it bounce twice before it came to a halt by an Ug boot, which was attached to the bare right leg of our seemingly angry manager, Carlton Gooch. The Gooch had a face like a full-on thunderstorm and was bizarrely wearing a pink tartan kilt offset with a white double cuffed ruffled shirt. He was less than happy at what he was seeing from his charges.

I was going to be singing the last but two song on the set list the bizarrely titled 'Albanian Eurovision Song Contest Entry' so Slam could nip off and have a smoke. We had only practiced it a couple of times and it was a song I also had to play keyboards on. I had the words to the song running through my mind so much that they were stopping my brain from instructing my fingers what to do on the guitar fretboard. They started another recital.

'A far-off land,
In the Balkans
Small population,
A little nation
Didn't expect much,
Got a vote off the Dutch.
Cue utter mania.

In Albania
Hello Stockholm calling,
Viewing figures falling
Serbian man sings,
Dad dancing
A Russian Nun,
A Norton pun,
A lotta fun,
You ok hun?

Our most famous resident
Was heaven sent
Her name was Motha Theresa
She was like Ebeneezer.
A real cool geezer
And she was good.'

It was at this point that I noticed about eight thousand pairs of eyes of me and the cruel lone voice of someone from the crowd shouted "Do Sailing by Rod da Mod" as everyone watched and waited for me to start the next number.

I ambled up to the microphone, wiped away the white film that had encrusted itself around my lips and then spat out a huge lump of frothy phlegm before I spoke. "This song. This song is for anyone in love" and then began the guitar intro chords to "Top Banana Sunday."

Erika Puck was stood alone in the audience jumping up and down holding onto her shoulders and hugging herself shouting "Thank you John. Thank you for playing our song. I love you."

Dutch Courage managed to pull it round slightly and finished the set with the usual battering of instrument chaos that went with the tune "Bubbles" It was the only time Mac moved during the entire performance. I looked around as I rung the last notes out of my guitar before I kicked the mic stand directly in front of me over to ease the frustration / tension that had built up inside of me during our stage slot.

I unplugged my guitar post haste and left the stage to a smattering of applause and chanting by the home crowd. Wow the chanting was getting louder as we trooped off. We had done it I assumed. We had somehow pulled victory out of the jaws of defeat. As I got to the wings of the stage I could see the festival stage manager Ed Givens stood with his arms folded looking at me with daggers. As I approached him I spoke "They loved it in the end huh? Listen to them out there chanting Yorkshire, Yorkshire, which must be a good sign we went down well right?" A member of the next band 'The Dirty Bristow' weaved in front of me to place two guitars he was carrying in the aptly named guitar rack. Givens hadn't yet blinked. He then looked me directly in the eye and responded "Nope. They were shouting You're shit; You're shit." He unfolded his arms and barged straight past me.

SLOUGH - TWO DAYS LATER

I WAS DETERMINED THAT OUR performance and day as a whole at the second 'Bedding Festival' gig in Slough on the Sunday would go a lot smoother. This time we travelled together, and we all abstained from any booze or extra-curricular activities prior to our performance. We then played a lot better and got a warmer reception from the citizens of the south of England.

With the gig in the bag, I was just about to leave when I got word that an American girl had been trying everything she could do get backstage to talk to me. This news changed my projection of how I saw the day playing out. I decided to do the 'rockstar' thing of hanging around the backstage area with the hope it went better than it did in Huddersfield.

My first concern should have been that the bar was free for anyone possessing an 'Access All Areas' (AAA) pass. I checked my wrist. Yep, it was still there this time. The three magical letters of 'AAA' staring back at me in black offset by lemon. One for the road wouldn't hurt would it? It would give that American bird a chance to get bored and hopefully piss off home.

I saw Beve from 'Subvision UK' the Scottish punk band who had played just before us earlier in the day. "Great set" we both said to each other as we lied in that muso way as the honest truth was that neither of us had probably watched anyone play. He went back to talking to his posse as I ordered a pint of fruit cider.

After leaving the bar, I looked around for Mac but couldn't see him anywhere. "Looking for someone?" said a voice that sounded like it had a plum in it and an authority that said he owned the joint. (Maybe he did and was from the big top tent hire company) I turned to see where the sound waves had ruminated from and saw two young men talking to each other. The posh guy looking my way seemed familiar, but I couldn't place him. He was clothed in a cord jacket that was unbuttoned with nothing underneath to cover his shaved, tanned bare chest .He also sported a pair of three-quarter length tight white trousers, which left nothing to the imagination. His look was topped off with Prince of Wales check Espadrille shoes. A combo that to me, was a definite no-no for festival wear in the United Kingdom. Luckily, we hadn't had rain.

I approached the lad who had posed the question. By the time I was close enough he was holding his palm up in the high-five position. I sadly obliged him. "Miles A. Way" He said as our palms slapped one another. "John Leonard" I offered him by way of a return whilst wishing he were actually miles away. "Yes boy. From the Dutch Courage band. I saw you on the box a few weeks ago. Great to meet you. Gassed in fact." I immediately didn't like this cat, and when he said he was 'gassed' I again wished he had been.

The third person who had been talking to Miles then entered the conversation. "Hey, I'm Boomer Edison, guitarist of The Grunts. We were on first today" Was his opening gambit. "I saw you play earlier though John. It was like a rich badgers house. Great set." Laughed Boomer at his own joke. He was wearing the standard band t-shirt (His own for fucks sake) , white trainers and black jeans with home-made slashes in the legs. He had noticeably short cropped blonde hair and a number of earrings in both ears. But had he really seen us earlier?

As we continued small talk between the three of us a stream of people kept coming over to Miles to have a selfie took with him. Boomer noticed the confusion in my eyes. "You know him don't you John? He's the posh boy totty from the last season of 'Meat Market'" 'Ah 'Meat Market' I thought to myself. The crap dating television show where they bunged a dozen horny twenty somethings in a Marbella Villa, get them drunk and hoped the inmates would indulge in some sex that they couldn't then broadcast. It was a programme lower than whale shite as far I could see but was somehow as popular as fresh air.

Boomer continued to advise me about Miles as he was having another picture taken. "Yeah he's the bloke who picked some girl called Lana to be his girlfriend just because he said it was an anagram of anal." BY now another woman had sauntered over to grab a picture with the pretty boy. I could just about make out their conversation. "Oh really. My favourite county is Essex or Sussex. One hundred percent. Just a shame that there isn't a place called Sex and we could do away with having to pronounce the extra letters." I heard the laughter from the female as, yet another girl approached, and he started his patter with her…"You're at University? Really? I have a PHD. Yes a Pretty Huge Dick. One hundred percent."

Boomer and I eventually broke away from the pretty boy and continued drinking the 'AAA' wristband offered free booze. I still wasn't sure where the rest of my band had got to and none of them had answered my request for their whereabouts on the mobile phone 'Wotnot' Message Service Group Chat we had set up.

After a couple of hours of small talk and amusing anecdotes Boomer and I came to the same realisation that the beer we were drinking wasn't really doing much of a job.

Boomer went to the bar and came back to the table we had seconded with a tray of shots and a bottle of a large clear spirit with no label. I opened the bottle and took a slug. The liquid burnt my throat as it slipped down making me feel very much alive "Good call. VODKA FRENZY!" I yelled as I took another huge gulp from the label absent bottle.

We continued the chat as the late Summer sun went down, each trying to outdo the other with our drunken stories. Boomer apparently did 'Iron Man Triathlons' and I had just told him about the time I climbed Mount Everest when the words no hardened drinker ever wants to hear were shouted at us. "Last Orders! Sorry guys. We got to clear out the backstage bar. It's down to the headline act. We can't have anyone around when he goes on stage." Some faceless jobsworth informed us. "Serious, seriously, tha, that Sam Pyle. I remember him when he was just a kid at my school." Boomer said to the jobsworth. I felt duty bound to drunkenly join in the conversation. "Ha! Sam Pyle of shit more like. I remember him when he was a foetus."

I looked at the bottle of vodders which was nearly empty apart from some dregs and spittle at the bottom. Boomer then posed me a question. "What say we get out of here and get a proper drinkette." I suddenly had my sensible head on. "Would love to Booms, but I'm not sure where I'm stopping tonight. I need to get back to London and…" Edison cut me off. "C, come on man. I live in Bracknell. It's like about ten miles from here. You can stay at mine tonight friend. Come on let, let's make a proper night of it."

My sensible head was removed, and my piss head was back on, and I agreed to take the party to a nearby pub that was just down the road from the festival site.

We had about ninety minutes drinking time left by the time we arrived at the 'Three-Legged Mare' drinking establishment. The place was surprisingly not overly busy. Perhaps more people were staying to watch the headline act at the Bedding Festival than I initially thought would. I got the double vodkas in. It was quite easy to get served but a pain to now have to pay for them. Mind you it always is easy to get served when you are steaming drunk. Politeness goes out of the window, and they just serve you quick just to get rid of you from the bar. Anyway, it was time to teach this young pup a drinking lesson I laughed to myself.

Boomer returned from the toilet where I suspected he had gone to be sick. He had been doing a lot of swallowing and spitting during the last twenty minutes. I pushed the glass containing the double vodka towards him with my right hand and the splash of tonic that was left in the bottle we were sharing with my left. After this manoeuvre my right hand grabbed my goblet and I downed my double vodka and set off to the bar to refill our vessels.

I returned with the next round and Boomer finally got in the spirit of things and downed his drinks in rapid succession. His expression had now changed from 'I'm having a good time' to that of someone completely off their fucking head. Next thing he was off was his fucking chair as he fell to the floor. He clambered back up and sat down. His face was getting redder, and his eyes began to spin as if behind the exterior they were doing a washing machine load on a setting of forty degrees.

"Your round me old son. Come on get the f, f, fucking drinks in chap." I shouted a little too loudly. Boomer promptly fell off his stool again. Bang. Straight down to the floor. That was going to hurt in the morning. I shuffled off my stool and helped him up and back onto his perch. No sooner had I done so than he fell off again.

"Just give me some money I'll get the fucking drinks." I yelled. He opened his wallet whilst still sat on the floor and handed me a note just as someone who had been working behind the bar approached us. She had an unlit cigarette hanging out of the side of her mouth and had tight brushed back black hair that was styled into tight ringlets. She wore a shirt which if it had been an England Rugby shirt would have suited far better than the plain black number she was wearing. "Oi you. If you fall off your seat again then you're going to have to go. I'm trying to run a proper fucking nice establishment here right, and I can't have the fucking dipso clientele lolling about on the lino. It's not good for business." She bellowed. Boomer held up both his hands in his defence as an apology as he clambered up from the sticky floor. "It won't help, errr, happy, happen a, a, a gin, no, again." He mumbled. With a clink of adding more collected glasses from our table, the proprietor was away.

"Two triple vodkas and one tonic" I shouted over the sound of the jukebox. Within thirty seconds I had my bounty and wobbled back to the stools Boomer, and I located at the far end of the bar.

"Down the hatch" I said as I added a splish-splash of tonic to my clear liquid throat burner, face gurner. This time it didn't go down as easy as silk knickers like the last few rounds had. It took another two forced gulps to drink the meth like spirit and by the time I had finished my turps, Boomer had sadly fallen off his stool again. I picked up my black and decker body wrecker cocktail of stout and more vodka and downed it as I had a hunch the night was over.

The black shirt from behind the bar was over in a flash. "Look gents. I don't want to be fucking difficult, but you've got to go as in piss off out. It's nothing personal. I'll call you a cab and you can stay until it arrives but no more alcohol."

Our driver Mustaf from Dib Dab Cabs arrived within fifteen minutes in a blue car that had seen better days, but when needs must and all that.

Mustaf was decent enough to help me bundle Boomer into the back of the car. He was now so drunk that he was in and out of consciousness. This posed one problem in the fact that the only thing I could remember was he said he lived in Bracknell.

Thankfully, Boomer stayed awake long enough to give an address. I caught the words "151 Sutton" Something? Mustaf managed to decipher the rest from what he had said. He punched the info into his sat nav. It stated it was twelve miles from the site of the pub in Slough to Bracknell. We had such a good laugh tonight I thought to myself as the taxi driver reminded me again to buckle up. I just didn't want the evening to end. I was hoping that the guitarist from The Grunts who had been trying to show me how rock and roll he was had some booze and powder in back at his place.

The taxi set off and was moving towards the signs for the A332 and turned right at William Street. Within half a mile the vehicle had exited onto Windsor Street merging onto said expressway from the slip road.

Colours, shapes, and sounds came flying into my line of vision from all directions as the motor car built up speed. It was quite therapeutic. In fact, I became so relaxed that I began to drift off to sleep.

The taxi covered the twelve-mile distance in twenty minutes. As Mustaf pulled up outside 151 Sutton Street, he realised he had a problem. Both passengers in the front and back seats were fast asleep.

He surveyed the scene before him. Front seat had his head back as drool slid from the side of his mouth. Backseat looked like the easier option to wake for the driver. He was younger and the one who had given the address he had driven to, so he assumed he was the owner of the property.

Mustaf exited his vehicle and opened the back door. He prodded Boomer a few times and thankfully for the hapless driver he stirred. "Mister, mister, we are here. You need to get out please."

With Mustaf's help Boomer made his way out of the back of the car. He then got a twenty quid note out of his wallet . Mustaf made his way around to the front of the car and tried to shake awake John Leonard, but he wasn't stirring. "He lives in London. Brixton area, I'm quite certain he said earlier, or was it Chalk Farm?." said Boomer. "Take him there, yeah Brixton. Here's twenty for my t, t, trip and twenty for him." He stuck the crumpled notes in Mustaf's paw and headed towards the front door of his house. By the time Boomer had dropped the key, fumbled with it, dropped it again, got it in the lock and finally opened the door, the blue taxi was approaching the exit for the M25 to London.

I'm not sure what the fuck was going on, but I suddenly woke up with a start and my heart was beating swiftly. I looked out of the window and the car was bombing down some motorway. We must be still on the way to Bracknell I thought. I looked around in the back of the car and panic started to set in. There was no-one sat in the back seat. "Where, where, where is the bloke from the back. Did we put him in the boot?" I asked sounding like someone who had just learnt to speak English. The driver just looked at me as I looked at the meter which was on £40.50. Cue more panic!

"Whoa! Hold ya fucking horses mate" I cried out. "I haven't actually got any more money. Where are we going?" I quickly checked my pockets and pulled out a handful of coins which immediately spilled down the side of the car seat and some fluff from my jeans which didn't. Mustaf looked in his mirror and responded, "Your friend says you live in Brixton, London." I was confused and angry. "No, I fucking don't. I'm staying at his house." The meter hit £43.00.

Mustaf put on his indicator and pulled off the motorway onto the hard shoulder. "Tell you what I'll get out here." I foolishly offered and dropped some more of the coins I was holding onto the floor as I tried to put them into the hand of the hired driver.

The driver didn't remonstrate too much. I still wasn't sure where I was as I opened the door and exited the car. I stood motionless as the blue car pulled away leaving me stood rooted to the spot.

I hadn't got a fucking clue where I was going. How long had I been in the car? Where the hell was I? I started to trudge back the way I came but then saw a traffic sign on the other side of the road. I looked left and right and jogged over six lanes of empty motorway.

The sign informed me that Bracknell was only seven miles away. I became confused and disorientated then crossed the road once again and decided in my mind that I would walk back to Bracknell, and set off, even though I was now following the direction the taxi had just driven off in, which was towards London.

In my desperate state of two paces forward and three back, I decided that hitch-hiking was my best option. I began to stick my thumb out as I slowly walked / wobbled my way towards Bracknell (Actually London)

During my sortie, a number of cars had sounded their horns and honked at me but alas no-one actually bothered to stop.

It was only minutes later when a dirty yellow car pulled directly in front of me that I understood why I was being constantly honked at by passing motorists. I was actually walking down the inside lane of the motorway instead of along the hard shoulder. How on earth had that happened? I'll tell you how….VODKA FRENZY.

The yellow car that had pulled up had its engine purring. A youth got out of the passenger side door. "Oi mush" he shouted at me "Do you know you are walking in the fucking road you fucking muppet. Have you got a death wish or what?" At the time I hadn't noticed exactly where I had been walking. He continued to shout at me "Where you going dickhead?" I searched the confines of my mind, where was I going, and why was I here? Then I located the answer deep under the section of my brain reserved for football trivia "Bracknell" I gleefully shouted back as if the answer had just won me ten grand on a quiz show. By now the youth had the door open and the front seat pushed forward and beckoned me to get in.

As I approached the car I could see that there were two other youths in the vehicle. The driver and another one in the backseat. If I had to guess I would have put them early twenties and definite 'Meat Market' fans. I clambered into the back seat.

"You's is fucking mad man," said the driver. "I nearly hit you's. You soppy daft cunt. Where are you's going trundling along the inside lane of the motorway like a dippy fucking spackers three-wheeler? Did I hear you say Bracknell? Yeah we are going near there. I'll drop you's before an articulated does." Lied the driver, and with conversation over the yellow car pulled out of the hard shoulder at breakneck speed and headed along the A4 to London.

John Leonard started to drift off to sleep in the back. The youth in the front had lit a doobie and passed it to the youth sat in the back. "He's dozed off the fucking muppet." The receiving youth said to front-seat youth. "I'll wake him" said front-seat as he turned around and punched John Leonard square in the face.

I felt a bump to the head and awoke. "What, what was that?" I asked. "We just gone over a bump mate. You's hit ya head on the seat." The cackling front seat youth laughed.

I was then handed a dope stick by the back-seat youth to my right, and I reluctantly took a hit on the sweet-smelling weed. I really needed to clear my mind, and this was not the best way to go about it. I was just about to take another drag on the bifter when there was a loud bang of something off to my left outside of the vehicle. The car continued to move at high speed as I began to doze off again.

"Oi muppet. Wake the fuck up. Do you's know what that was?" asked the driver, who I was glad was using his mirrors. "No" I lamely croaked back. "We just gotta flat fucking tyre." The driver laughed as he then took a drink from a can of coke, pushing his bonce so far back he couldn't possibly see the road ahead of him out of the window.

Despite revealing the flat tyre to my left the car showed no sign of slowing down or stopping. Driver youth and front seat youth continued to laugh and talk to each other as the car slightly tilted to the left. By now you could clearly hear the clear sound of the rim of the wheel grinding along the tarmac of the road filling the car.

Drunk as hell as I was it didn't take Einstein to work out that I was most definitely sat in the back of a stolen car. The driver didn't give two shits that the wheel was grinding metal at high speed which would of course cause some serious problems to the vehicles undercarriage and wheel arch.

All of a sudden and without any warning the driver youth violently pulled the car into the hard shoulder with an almighty screech of breaks. "What the fuck…" Thankfully I had managed to fix in my seatbelt, or I would have been thrown around the back of the car like a rag doll. "'Ere you's go you's drunken cunt." The driver said then continued "That's Bracknell and the closest we're going to that shithole. It's just over there, beyond those trees." I looked out of the window and all I could see was pitch black utter darkness. Front-seat youth was now out of the car and had tilted his seat forward so I could get out. I tried to move forward but had forgot to unclip my seat belt. "What a doughnut" the driver shouted as he laughed at me being thrust back by the belt.

As I exited the car, front-seat youth posed me a question as he pointed to his crotch. "You could have gone to the town I've got here in my underpants." Before I had a chance to compute he blurted out "Staines" All three members of the stolen car gang burst out laughing again. "It's up the hill there to Bracknell mate" I heard being shouted from the car as two of the youths began hilariously pointing in different directions. I assumed the call came from the youth in the backseat and not the driver as the sentence hadn't ended with the word cunt. Foolishly, I took the advice and started to clamber up the grassy hill that was immediately in front of me.

John Leonard made it up the grass embankment despite a few stumbles and came to a large open field. He looked left and right into the pitch-black void of night. To the right was in his mind a number of waiting serial killers, vampires, and other assorted spectre waiting to do him evil harm. To the left he could just about make out some dim distant light. Hopefully, it was the light of salvation, Bracknell.

With left chosen as my preferred chosen destination I marched on the best I could. I slipped and skidded on items unknown underfoot and progress became dismally slow. By now any light that the motorway had to offer me had also disappeared. "Aaaaggghhh...Bollocks! Should have gone right." I angrily yelled to no-one.

With a slip and slide method of moving forward I somehow managed to reach a dry-stone wall. This obstacle was soon easily cleared, and I forged on ahead. Within minutes though I suddenly found myself trying to manoeuvre myself through some of the most intense brambles that I had ever encountered. A thought of 'Who the fuck owns this field and why hadn't they done some gardening and cut this shit back' entered my head. Progress was now negligible. Every four paces forward were hampered by five minutes untangling myself from the next bush I found myself entangled in. I was also getting scratched more than holiday mosquito bites. I was literally going nowhere fast.

This route wasn't working. I suddenly remembered I had my mobile phone with me and desperately searched all available pockets of my clothing until it was located, and I turned on the torch application. The illuminated vision ahead didn't make for good viewing. I had entered a vast shrubbery.

There was no way I was going to make it through all this dense looking bush ahead of me. I began to retrace my steps via the reverse method of spotting the torn threads of material that had been ripped off from my jeans and hoody which were hanging from huge thorns.

By now I could feel that fatigue was setting in. All I wanted to do was curl up and go to sleep but I had to get out of this forest, farmers field, serial killers trap, what-ever it was, or I was a dead man. Brown fucking bread. Despite my best efforts I just couldn't find my way out. It was as irritating as a fungal infection or Southgate after match interview.

My drunkenness began to subside as trepidation, dread and terror took over. Personally, I preferred the drunkenness. Thoughts now turned to the newspaper headlines, not that I was famous enough to attract them though. I checked my phone again. There was still no fucking signal on it. How was that possible in this digital age? As the crow flies I was less than an hour away from London.

I had now made my way out of the thorny bush field and had managed to circumnavigate myself around it, but I was getting tired fast.

There was nothing for it but to keep on walking and that was when I fell headfirst over two sheep.

Where the hell had they come from? The first I knew about this was when the sound of one sheep let out a bloodcurdling bleating sound which penetrated the night air. I tripped over sheep number one and had gone flying straight into sheep number two which thankfully broke my fall and sadly I in turn had broken its neck.

Leonard scrambled around on the floor trying to regain his footing as sheep number one dropped some poo pellets in fright and retreated away from the human invader in fear. Leonard then got back down on his hands and knees and carried out a professional fingertip search for his dropped mobile phone that the police would have been proud of. Johns blower had taken an aerodynamic route thanks to the sheep incident.

Once the phone was once more secure he switched the torch element back on and was left to survey the scene somewhat reminiscent of a horror movie. There was one sheep bleating loudly whilst the other was laying on its back with its legs in the air and blood dripping from its nostrils. Time to jog on John Leonard, sheep killer.

I felt bad about the sheep and vowed to go vegetarian for the next four weeks to make up for the death of the wollyback.

I have no idea how long it took but I finally managed to remove myself from the fields of Thorn Central and the poor deceased sheep. I stopped dead in my tracks and looked down at my white trainers which were white no more due to a combination of dirty grass water and cowpats. My jeans also looked like I'd been wearing them whilst mud wrestling.

I wasn't sure how long I had been out here now? Would I need a rescue? The sky was still charcoal clouded with no sign of daybreak. If it had any sense, daybreak was still in that Slough pub getting absolutely wankered. If only that idiot hadn't fallen off his stool in the pub. I couldn't even remember his name now. If only I hadn't fallen asleep in the taxi? What had happened? It was all a blur. 'Keep going forward' my inner voice kept telling me. I had to ask it to stop talking as I was getting a headache.

No idea how long it was before I saw the light again, but when it came into view it was sure brighter than before I had started this perilous journey. I started to pick up the pace to the best of my ability. There was an adrenaline surge throughout my body. The light was becoming clearer and nearer. I climbed over another couple of walls and jumped over a small stream. I was picking up quite a head of steam now.

Within minutes I could see rooftops. Yes! I was nearly there. Thank God, thank the lord et cetera. The rooftops then disappeared. Fuck your God, or your holy spirit. My internal demons battled each other again. I could hear female voices. 'Have faith you are being guided to the light.' The first whispered in a calming tone, before an evil sounding voice butted in. 'No ,don't listen to that bitch, it was her God who allowed you to get so drunk. Let Lucifer help you.' I put my hands to my ears and yelled "ENOUGH, STOP!!!"

Then at that moment I saw it. It was barely fifty yards away. It, my friends was a gate. Hallelujah, praise to God, never have I felt such exhilaration at the sight of a bloody gate, which even more importantly backed onto a garden. A garden which was at the rear of some sort of house. I broke into a big beaming smile, I would have sunk to my knees in deep joy, but I knew then that there was animal shit everywhere. After the smile I broke out into a full-on gallop and ran towards the property. Mirages don't appear in the cold right?

As I got closer to the building I could see that it was a farmhouse. 'Oh no, they're going to have a dog. I know they will have a dog.' I thought to myself. "What if they have a dog?" Chirped the angel sat on my left shoulder. "Good cuz were fucking starving. John son, if they have a dog, kill it, and eat it. What's another dead animal to you tonight. You've already offed a sheep." advised the impish rapscallion perched shoulder right. I ignored both as I pressed onwards.

It was the usual set up at the property. There was a long wooden fence that was covered in barbed wire with a rusting gate bang slap centre. Hopefully, it would just open, and I prayed it wouldn't be locked and I would be able to gain entrance to the back garden.

Once in the rear of the property I would need the escape committee to form and get myself out of here. Of course, I could just knock the door, but what if they knew I had killed one of their (More than likely) livestock would they call the 'Fleece Police 'to arrest me, if such a thing exists?

All of a sudden Colditz escapee 'Big X' appeared before me like a vision. He was in charge of the Allies escape committee from the World War Two German prison and was decked out in a khaki green military uniform. He spoke with a home counties English accent as he twiddled his long moustache. "Just climb over the back gate Leonard and then you are home free. I can confirm there is no dog. Here are your papers and remember, speak German only" I began to shake my head quickly to clear the vision. Bracknell, home (for the night) was just beyond this last gate.

The gate was locked. So, John Leonard took a run up and pulled himself up and over the eight-foot-high entry gate and landed in the garden. But Big X was wrong, intel had been incorrect. There was still one more gate to negotiate before he had the chance to escape fully to freedom.

I made my way to the back entry of the property. Thankfully, the door leading to that wasn't locked. Fate was finally turning my way. There were discarded buckets, some odd bits of fencing lying about the floor, a couple of used paint tins but just not enough room for a decent run up to help me vault the gate. 'Shit.' I should have just knocked the door.

It was probably ten minutes of staring at the last door to freedom when my mind was finally made up for me. A light suddenly came on in the upstairs of the property. I quickly placed two of the discarded buckets upside down and prayed they would take my weight. I needed them to get some extra spring and purchase to assist with getting over the fence and out into Bracknell, the mecca, the promised land of a bed for the night.

The sound of the upstairs toilet flushing pushed me to act fast and I ran full tilt towards the two buckets and hoped they were as sturdy as they looked. My left foot hit first, and the black bucket held firm, my right foot came down a fraction of a second later onto the second dark coloured bucket. Success, it gave me the springboard I needed to clamber up and over the gate, but I copped for a nasty splinter in my right-hand index finger. Oh, I also made a damn racket making my escape as the buckets went flying from the motion of my feet bucking off them. I also somehow tripped over a tin of the paint during my run up which in turn flew up in the air and hit the back of the entry gate with a loud whack.

John dropped down in front of the gate. He had made it over. Then more lights were switched on in the house and the reverberating blare of body movement from the window punctured the spooky silence of the cooling night.

I had cleared the fence and had landed in Bracknell, my utopia, but now I could hear people who would not be happy that I had invaded their evenings privacy and more importantly their home. I could hear German voices. "Good luck" one shouted as I took off and ran as fast as I could without making the mistake of looking back.

Leonard ran down along a grass pathway which in turn came out by a jetty which led into a side road where there was much more regular housing to be seen, which of course meant life.

Never have I been so happy in all my life to see bricks and mortar. I was ecstatic. Now I racked my brains for that blokes address I had spent the night drinking with. I still couldn't remember his name, but he lived on Sutton Road, Bracknell I seemed to recall.

John Leonard walked up and down various roads in the vain hope of finding the right address.

It was getting hopeless. I couldn't find the right road anywhere. How big was Bracknell though for fucks sake? Each road had looked vaguely familiar. I reached again for my mobile phone. I know I now had a signal but still couldn't fire up the internet connection on it.

Without thinking and especially as the cold had more than began to bite at my cheeks, I realised this was now a life-or-death situation, so I speed-dialled my manager Carlton Gooch at 3.47am.

Leonard recapped as much of the story of the last three or four hours to a perplexed Gooch. But since John had woken him up he felt he had an obligation to assist his old friend and employee.

A back-and-forth phone conversation went on for the next ten minutes. "Look, this isn't getting us anywhere old fruit. Find me something to work with here treacle." Requested Gooch.

Leonard sauntered up one street and ambled down another until he found a street name. "Brewer Street. I'm on Brewer Street" John slurred down the phone. "How apt." answered Gooch. Despite being given this address Gooch couldn't find any such road in an internet search of Bracknell.

John walked further on and reported that he was now on Tucker Road. This instruction also didn't help his cause, and then when he came to a bus shelter he finally understood why his friend and band manager was having such difficulty in aiding him to get to his bed for the night.

"Err….. Gooch mate, It, errr, says Staines Transport on the bus shelter. I'm not in fucking Bracknell. I'm in Staines. Where the fuck is that?" John meekly commented. "Stay put asshole. I will get my driver Bullock to come and pick you up. Don't damn well move you crazy gold-plated banana" Gooch cut the call. And he didn't move. John Leonard was fast asleep passed out on the bus shelter bench when Gooch's assistant and minder Bullock pulled up to collect him over one hour later.

The second of the two 'Bedding Festival' appearances had gone a lot better in Berkshire for Dutch Courage, but Gooch was still pissed off. He had since received word of an unpaid bar bill totalling some nine hundred odd quid from the Hypnos Hotel in Dewsbury, along with a claim for damages to some statue that was broken in the hotel saloon area. According to the angry hotel manager the piece broken was a rare artefact that was worth three hundred quid. Neither Mac nor Slam, who were accused of breaking the bust during a scuffle in the bar area could remember this happening. Gooch also had to fork out another one hundred and twenty notes for an old couples refund for their one-night stay in room 406. This was the room next door to Mac and Slam. Apparently Mr and Mrs Grimes had complained about the constant noise both 'Rock Stars' had made all night which in turn had stopped them from sleeping.

Add to this bill another fifty smackers for the Dewsbury hotel security to reset the room safe combination and a further eighty sheets to further reimburse the same hotel to return the one solitary item found in said safe, Mac's glasses. These were returned to 'Asteroid' via courier. Cher-Ching.

Gooch had already had to placate Mike Beavis the promoter of the 'Bedding Festival' to allow the band to complete their contractual arrangements in Berkshire. The first batch of grovelling had to be done following Gooch's learning of John Leonards off stage break into the headline bands 'Reserved' area. He also had to re-apologise for Leonards on stage melt down in Yorkshire and was also being billed further for one broken mic stand. Add to this the double time overtime that Gooch had to pay his minder Bullock for going out during unsociable hours to pick up and put up the lost drunk as a lord John Leonard.

To say that Carlton Gooch was fuming was an understatement.

Nocka Izzet was definitely 'Man of the Match' from the two festival gigs and the only one of the band to not get into any strife to date or cost him money.

THE WARMUP SHOWS

PRIOR TO THE DEPARTURE FOR the United States tour John Leonard had been booked via 'Asteroid' for an appearance on the BCB2 cult music quiz show 'Too Much Pressure' It was a simple formatted show where two regular team captains were joined by guests from the world of entertainment and politics. Carlton Gooch wasn't sure where Leonard fitted in with their booking policy but then again there was also going to be someone from the 'Green Thumb' eco-collective appearing. This group of eco-warriors were currently camped out at Gatwick to stop the expansion to the runways at the airport. 'Should have just invited them all onto the show' thought Gooch that would have cleared them all out easily from their underground tunnels they were holed up in without force or any cost to the local authorities.

Gooch was thinking about damage limitation and that wasn't a band on his books. Chaos and catastrophe seemed to follow John Leonard and his band 'Dutch Courage' about. Fair enough it seemed that Leonard had amazingly acquired something of a stalker on his case, judging by the amount of texts he had showed Gooch and the unsolicited pictures he had been sent via the snail mail from some American harpy. 'Had that been a close up of a part?' Gooch had asked himself when unsure what he had actually been looking at.

The Gooch needed to nip this chaos and stalking business in the bud before it cost his company more money and affected his own reputation in the entertainment industry. The Gooch reached for his intercom button and alerted his PA Dorinka Stupor to come in. "It is not one O'clock, I don't have nurse uniform on yet Mister Gooch. You early" She replied through the tinny intercom.

Carlton Gooch was going to put his best man on the job. He had his PA put a call into the best road manager and minder he had ever used during the last fifteen successful years of the 'Asteroid Agency.' Ex-army captain turned road manager Guy Ropes answered almost immediately.

The Dutch Courage guys had been warned to keep a low profile prior to going to the US. Any negative publicity or arrest could impact on their working visas that the 'Asteroid' Agency had secured for them at great cost.

It had also been suggested that in the time they had prior to flying out to the States that they be more productive and were advised to cut a single and play another low key warm up show in John's local area of Hungerton.

For once the guys abstained from anything other than focusing on three tunes that Gooch earmarked for quick release to be able to capitalise on the bands infamy before the World forgot about the anniversary of the bands involvement with the infamous ferry sinking and TV documentary that had been aired just a few weeks ago.

A couple of days later and John Leonard was once again heading to 'Asteroid' for the weekly ' business' meeting with Carlton Gooch.

Gooch's PA told me it was ok to go straight through this time, but I still knocked out of courtesy before I entered. Gooch was just sat there and seemed lost in thought whilst staring intently at his laptop screen. "Hey Carlton, it's John. What you looking at?" Without looking away from the screen Gooch answered, "I'm thinking of buying a club." Wow that is big league I thought to myself. "Which team?" I asked. Gooch responded immediately "Oh for the love of cheese. No, a golf club you dingbat. I'm not sure which one to get. The thick ended one or the one that ends with a thin metally bit. If it's a good enough game to play for the US President, then it's good enough for this land lubber, dig, amigo." He then confusingly warbled the words to some song about cricket before adding "I just love the clothes dear boy. I don't know why I hadn't found this get up sooner. Golf is the new black. Look at the sweaters on that." He drew breath, stood up and immediately started to scratch his meat and two veg.

I tried to block out his lower half from my vision as he continued to blather on.

"Ah JL, and to the reason for your visit today is not to show you golf sweaters. No. It is because I felt the need to alert you to the fact that I've set up two more warm up shows. It was 'felt' (Gooch said this word making quotation marks with his fingers) by the major heads and Buddhists that Dutch mark two needs a little fine tuning and it's also felt that another couple of low-key gigs wouldn't go amiss flower." There was more 'felt' than a cushion maker used in today's opening gambit. It was, however, difficult to argue against it though. He continued to yap as he began to run his fingers through his fine hair. "I want people to say that they go to a Dutch Courage record when they need a lift. Or the punters play one when they are having a good time or when people pass over to the other side. You know? It needs work Johnny boy. It needs to be slick, slick, slick. The only way that happens is by doing more gigs, gigs, gigs. We need to look at the pachyderm in the room Monsieur. I'm concerned and I'm sick of you lot fudging up every opportunity I get you finks. So, with that in mind and your previously presented American problem, I've kindly employed for you a road manager / security head, got you a couple of gigs and an interview with the newspaper 'The Daily Reflector'… Just wear anything with a red star on to that and a good write up will be secure. Is that Diggy doo with you-Hoo?"

The Gooch had pre-arranged two more low key London gigs for 'Dutch Courage' to fine tune their craft and both were scheduled to occur before the TV performance that John Leonard had been booked for.

The first gig was at the intimate setting of 'The Windmill' in Holborn, London. Prior to the gig Martin 'Mac' McCarthy called round for his mate John who was using a bolthole flat in London that Gooch / Asteroid had supplied him with.

John answered the knock at the door but wasn't quite ready to leave. "Come in mate. Just need to have a slash and to put my shoes on."

In all the years that Mac had known John he had never known him to be ready for anything on time.

John offered Mac a snifter and told him to help himself to the bottle of Bourbon that was present on the solitary table in the poky front-room. The bottle was stood towering above a pile of papers and band photos that looked like they had seen better days. Mac picked up the bottle and unscrewed the cap, he was just about to take a big gulp when he noticed that some of the papers had the words 'Dutch' ,'Courage' and 'Contract' splashed across them. Mac put the bottle down and had a read. It was the standard contract which Mac and the other pair in the band had already signed. He was just about to put it back down when he noticed an area on the page that included stuff about percentage points and merchandise. It also seemed that the payment on offer to John Leonard was for a significant amount of more money than he was getting, yet he was still writing half the songs and he had come to Leonard with the offer of re-joining the band. What was this skulduggery? Mac heard the toilet flush and hastily pushed the contract page back in amongst the other papers on the table and then took a hearty slug of the Bourbon. It seemed that Leonard had lied to him and negotiated a better deal with 'Asteroid' than he or the others got. He could understand doing that deal over the newcomers, but to cut him out of some much-needed green queens. What a bastard! Inwardly Mac was all a rage but outwardly he remained calm and knew he would have to pick his moment to have this out with the double-crossing guitarist in the near future.

Gigs at short notice. They are alright if you are in the top ten or are an established act on the tour circuit but for someone making a comeback like us I was a tad worried that no-one would turn up, I thought to himself.

Two people who did turn up at the London gig were Carlton Gooch who arrived with some guy who actually turned out to be called Guy, an ex-army bloke who was going to be looking after us on the road from now on.

Gooch bounded into our dressing room with this guy called Guy in tow. He was a well-built gent, wearing army fatigues and had slick black hair with grey highlights. Gooch made the introductions. "Buddhists, gather ye, gather ye" (We were already all in the confined space of an exceedingly small dressing room) He blathered on. "This fine upstanding citizen I have with me here will be keeping you on the straight and narrow from this moment forth. I am putting my man here Mr Guy Ropes in charge of you cretins, sorry that word isn't directed at you Enoch. He will be travelling with you to the US and ensuring that things start to go like clockwork around the world of the Dutch Courage. You dig amigo's?" Guy moved out of Gooch's shadow and addressed us. "Right, thank you Mr Gooch. Let's have a look at you 'orrible lot. Hup two, three, hup two, three. Leonard, McCarthy, and Slam I will be paying awfully close attention to you. Understand? Hup two, three, hup two, three, Izzet as you were. Lovely to make your acquaintance all. I will see you all after the show for a debrief. Have a good gig."

I looked at Mac. He looked at me and we both mouthed 'WTF' to each other. I gave him half a smile, as I knew this was coming but in return got a total grimace from him. This was like getting a child minder for forty-year-olds.

The intimate London gig was a lot of fun. I also really enjoyed 'The Hi-Jinks' a two-piece group with a drum machine who supported us. They sounded fresh and young with a bit of Geordie charm and humour thrown in. It was a shame that no-one in the audience could understand a word they said. Guy Ropes had stood with me by my side throughout the whole of their performance.

Whilst we were on stage later in the evening my mind began to wonder. It didn't affect the performance; it was the crowd that I was looking at and the types of punter that you get at gigs these days. A lot had changed in the twenty odd years since we started playing to paying customers. Most crowds today though seemed that they could be made up of the same types, which in my mind are thus.

1) A) The Mobile Phone Enthusiast: This is someone who pays the entrance fee and then stands in the same spot all night and watches the whole of the gig through the small screen on their mobile phone whilst videoing what later turns out to be moving pictures of other people's heads backed by a cacophony of white noise. What is the point of that?

B) Additional Mobile Phone Enthusiasts: These are the people who feel the need to take five hundred pictures of the band. These pictures include a number of selfies with friends in front of the stage whilst the 'act' goes about the business of doing their thing. We, the punter have paid to see the band, not you and your grinning bozo mates. It is also rather belittling for the 'act' to have to see this as they go about their trade.

C) Additional, Weird Mobile Phone Enthusiasts: One person stood to my right at the show spent the whole gig on a face-to-face call with some bloke. She danced and he watched her, or she turned the phone around so he could see the stage and watch the show. Now unless you are a head in a jar and are fit and able then get to the gig! Mobile phones are killing every part of society as it is, and they are now infecting the music scene.

2) The Slobbering Couple: It nearly put me off my guitar solo. There's always a couple who are all over each other and swapping spit all through your set. They are usually kissing and groping each other right at the front of the stage. Oi!!! Get a room! No-one wants to see it.

3) Speccy Fanzine Seller: This person needs to pick their moment. They go around the venue hassling punters to buy their homemade paper zine whilst the band plays on. No-one can hear what you are saying. Sell during the interludes. Surely with the advent of the internet this sort of print died years ago with other glossy music magazines.

4) Mortal Drunk Annoying Twat: The doors to the venue have only been open thirty minutes yet there is already someone present at the show who is drunk as a skunk and getting on the nerves of everyone they approach or go near. This is normally a solo attendee. You can guarantee that bitter farty smell that hits the atmosphere every so often near where you are standing is from them.

This person will throw the devil horns at you every time you look their way, or they see you, which was probably only just two minutes ago. It doesn't matter where you try to move to in the venue, this person and their stench will follow.

5) Stage Diver: Normally only seen at the smaller end of the gig going fraternity. This person feels the need to constantly get on stage, dance and then dive off when / if security decide to intervene. This person is usually male and the size of a rugby player who casually takes out half of the front row of the audience when security try and fail to detain this dude from jumping star fish into the crowd. Tsunami!

6) The Obsessive Fan: This person will be wearing the latest twenty-five quid tour tee shirt and most likely be carrying a plastic bag which usually

contains a copy of said bands latest vinyl long player to sign. They also stand at the front and shout the words to the songs. Oi mate, I have paid to hear the band sing them, not you. Such a person stood next to me during the support band who played at our intimate gig. He was wearing a 'Dutch Courage' bucket hat which I didn't even know existed. He also didn't even realise who I was even when I tried communicating with him to button it.

7) Bar Fly: These are the many people who just seem to hang around the bar at gigs ignoring the bands playing and chatting loudly to friends (If they have any) or to random passing punters. Their hand will have a constant half-filled glass of alcohol in it. This type of person contributes greatly to the between song chatter that you hear these days that nearly drowns out the band. A lot of unnecessary hugging of punters and handshakes are also common practice with the bar fly.

8) Chatter Box: Why go and see a band if all you want to do is talk all the way through the show. Another talker. These people always stand near the front. Normally it is a couple having a conversation they could have had on the way to the gig, at home et cetera. They talk through every song. Noise annoys. If you just wanted to chat STAND AT THE FUCKING BACK!

9) The Tall Guy: This bloke will be over six feet tall and is usually located stood in front of the smallest member of the opposite sex that is in attendance. Also, it doesn't matter where you move to, they inevitably will still end up stood in front of you again within moments. Picture the scene, you have a good gig watching vantage point, the house lights go down, it becomes pitch black in the venue, the band come on, lights go up and this guy has somehow manoeuvred his way in the dark to be stood directly in front of your line of vision. Despite the fact that you only just moved away from him a couple of minutes ago.

10) Drunk Guy Comatose on the Floor: Does just what it says on the tin.

TOO MUCH PRESSURE TV SHOW

'TOO MUCH PRESSURE' WAS A popular music quiz show made by the world famous BCB TV. This programme would be aired on the trendy, youth wing of the company via their BCB 2 channel. It was hosted by overtly gay comedian Rich Flavour. I had no problem with the fact that he was gay, what annoyed me about him was that all his comic punchlines were double entendres for anal sex. Words failed me as to why he was so popular amongst the demo graph who watched this show or even why I, John Leonard was booked to appear as a guest. Still in for a penny in for a pound and all that and the appearance money offered was quite a good few quid.

The brief was simple. Recording was held on a Wednesday night at the BCB studios in the glamourous town of Watford, a place situated some twenty miles from my bolthole in London. It was then to be broadcast on the forthcoming Friday night.

If all went to schedule, the show would take around three hours to shoot and it was shot in front of a studio audience, a bit like Alison Ward and Adam Parker were in 2015 by Lester Leigh O'Flaherty. If you didn't know him he was a sacked television cameraman who gunned down both Ward and Parker live on air at a TV station in Virginia, America. He had been dismissed from the job he loved due to rape allegations that were hanging over him. Legend has it on the day he got the bullet he waited for the news show to start then returned to the studio and ensured his ex-colleagues got it too. He then turned the gun on himself. I would definitely buy the DVD of that show.

The best bit of news for me about the work I was about to undertake was that I could get the train there and back from my on-loan flat in London which meant I would be able to take advantage of the notoriously good BCB hospitality I had heard about. 'Bang on' I thought.

I reasoned that I would be safe to walk from the train station to the television studio, but questions soon entered into my head in what you would classify as the 'Who, What, Where Why' category, and that first question was why Watford? Was it cheap for the broadcasting giant to operate in? I mean It was a run-down place that the governing authorities had forgot existed. It was all concrete and dog shit littered streets. Did they even have a football team?

Too get to the studio I had to run the gauntlet of a number of baseball cap sporting black clad hoody wearing urchins who were stood around on the streets doing nothing but trying to look menacing whilst some rode about on bicycles.

I managed to avoid the hooded idiots bar one extremely helpful young hoody wearer who not only pointed me in the right direction of the studio , but he also bagged himself a sale of some cocaine which I bought at a reasonable rate. Bingo, full house everyone's a winner. I was sure they wouldn't have sniffer dogs at the studio.

He had told me to take a left, then a right and I was now on a road that had one shop in amongst many terrace houses. The shop looked like it was an off licence.

The only person on the street was an old bloke walking a three-legged grey coloured greyhound. The streets were quiet but only for the next thirty seconds or so.

Out of the off licence came some skaggy looking woman who couldn't have been seven stone wet through. She crossed the empty road without looking and immediately began to confront the old man with the dog.

I stopped walking and watched the 'cunt off' unfold. Their conversation went as follows with all words pronounced in their local dialect.

Skag Head (SH) "You Kant"

Dog Walker (DW) "No, you Kant"

SH "Kant"

DW "You Kant"

SH "No you Kant."

DW "Kant"

This flow of single insult carried on for the next two minutes until finally the skag head woman changed tactic.

SH "You paedophile"

This change seemed to throw the dog walker as he was stuck for something to say in reply. There was thirty seconds of dead air as the cogs in his brain whirred around and then he came back with the killer blow of…..

DW "Fall over"

SH "Paedophile"

DW "Fall over"

SH "You fall over."

The three-legged dog then attempted to walk away and pulled on the lead, the woman sensed the dog wished to move on, so without another word she herself just walked away. The dog walker then moved on to get on with his day as if nothing had happened.

On the brick wall behind the two arguing was some graffiti which ranged from the apt 'WATFORD IS SHIT' to the curious 'ELTON IS A WANKER' (Did they mean John or Ben, but I'm sure the one slur covered both?) and there was a huge yellow daubing advertising 'THE KINGCROWS – KINGZ OV PUNK' I made a mental note to check them out when I got back home.

The place where the show was being made was underwhelming to say the least. It seriously needed a lick of paint, and it was such a small premises that I nearly walked past it at one point. 'This can't be it' I thought to myself, but it was. State of the art, it was not.

Once inside though it was a whole different ball game. The commissionaire on the door, a helpful old geezer called Noel signed me in and I was immediately collected by the studio runner, another chap, this time going by the name of Pip. He led me to the green room and on the way told me about the studio's health and safety policy (Didn't listen) and the wrap party. (Ears pricked up) "I'm well ready for the wrap party." I informed him as I patted my right jeans pocket and the hidden plastic packet of white powder that was tucked away in said enclave.

My first disappointment was when I was taken to the green room, and it was painted mustard yellow. Why the hell is it called a green room? I still don't know and neither did any of the guests who were already ensconced in the room, a room that only had a makeshift bar and one large potted plant in it. Maybe that's why it's called a green room I thought to myself as I stared at the potted plant.

The other guests on the show were already present and were all drinking booze which was a good sign. In one corner was author, TV personality, professional cockney geezer and street punk rocker Larry Muscle, who had now sold out his punk cred by writing for 'The Pun' national newspaper. Still, who wouldn't? We would all take the gold to climb the slippery pole if offered. Still, he had at least tried with his style of dress tonight and looked most dapper in his black pin stripe suit and tassel waggling matching black loafers that he was sporting.

Then there was an unlikely alliance formed in the far-right corner (Where else) of the room. Sat at a table enjoying a chinwag was former disgraced right-wing Tory MP turned TV celebrity chef Wellington Botham-Brown, who once did six months jail time for swindling his MP expenses a couple of years ago and legendary protester 'Shrooms' Whose real name I was to discover was Quentin Quicksilver-Green. So, it seems they had more in common with each other than they thought. Both had ridiculous double barrel names with colours in the title.

The last person present but most definitely not the least was 'Demi,' the female lead singer of the heavy rock beast called 'Motabike' She hadn't bothered to make any effort with her attire. She was dressed in regulation tight black denim jeans, white cowboy boots and a t-shirt of the band 'Little Whores on the Prairie' which was giving the shows director some cause for concern. (Thanks again to Pip for that titbit) 'Demi' had just been in the national news claiming she had had over a thousand conquests in the bedroom. Couldn't quite see the attraction of her to be honest but at least her band was appropriately named. She had an open bottle of 'Jack Orff' Canadian whisky, so I made a move to sit at her table.

I approached Demi and found that I couldn't look her in the eye instead focusing on her tattoo of the name and emblem of British punk band 'Fatal Dose' which was on the inside of her left arm. I braved it and spoke. "Hi I'm…" "Fuck off." She hastily said whilst in turn cutting my conversation off with her at the second word. Behind me, Larry Muscle started laughing hysterically and loudly. Seems he had watched me walk over and waited for the inevitable (to him) crash and burn.

I turned on a six pence and heading for the sound of Larry Muscle who was holding a pint of brown foamy looking liquid aloft in a cheers style salute in my direction.

That just left the host of the show and the two regular team captains to show their faces, but according to Pip they were in a production meeting finalising 'jokes.'

Muscle offered me a seat. "Cor blimey apples n pears mate. She doesn't have a nice smile like the old Queen Mum did huh, god bless her cottons. Still, you got further into the conversation than me my old China. I only got as far as 'Hi' before she told me to Foxtrot Oscar. Bloody lumme."

It was going to be a long night, so I got myself a drink. There were only two choices at the bar. Watered down piss coloured looking stuff or watered-down brown looking stuff. I opted for brown and made my way back to where Larry Muscle was sat.

He took one look at my pint "Blimey son beam, love a duck. That looks weaker than the alibis of the geezers at the Great Train Robberies trial. Stroll on son. It looks more like army and navy, though I wouldn't spoil my Sunday roast pouring it over. The bottle stoppers really ought to raid this gaff. Any road, we all need to make some bees and honey right. That's why I'm here. Are you working on set…Sorry how rude of me guv. I'm Larry Muscle. Who are you by the way?" I finally got a word in and introduced myself but then Muscle was straight back bumping his gums at 100MPH. "Oh, the ferry disaster bloke. Talking of which have you heard Roxy Music's new single. I panned it in The Pun in my 'Flex Your Muscle' newspaper column. You read it right. Good boy, good boy of course you do. Anyway, Ferry, he got his Alan Whicker's right in a tizzy over it. I mean I gave it five out of ten which means I liked half of it, and that half I liked was the cover. Cor blimey, it had some brass who was painted blue with her thruppenny bits out. WALLOP! I'd have given her one, two, three and four but five was a fair mark. Ha-ha" This guy didn't pause for breath before he was on another tirade. "You been on here before? Or you an FNG?" "A what?" I interjected. He lent back in his chair and began to fiddle with his red braces. This guy was too much! "FNG. A fucking new guy. I'm usually on Brinsley's team. You know that annoying singing turd. Usually have a good time here geezer. Got some port in a tin in my skyrocket. We'll get on it and get cattle trucked what do you say. You say yes, I should cocoa."

My head was now spinning. I needed to extricate myself from this position quickly and get on the snort. I made my excuses and went in search of the toilets blaming the watered-down booze for my prompt lavatory retreat.

The BCB studio was a bit of a maze with little in the way of signs unless you wanted to get to Studio one, two or three. I tried a couple of doors which were locked and then on the third I struck gold, ok, gold was probably over egging the pudding. Let's say bronze. I found the canteen and there sat on his own having dinner was television personality Den Leslie. He was the host of such TV classics as 'Family Forfeits' and 'The Price is Shite' which was a clever game show where if you didn't win the one and only star prize by guessing the cost of things like cars, houses, or holidays, then you went home with a lump of dung in a box shat out by the resident studio pig 'Pricey.'

Autograph claimed, he even thanked me when I pointed out he had spilt curry down his sweater, I returned to the green room to find that everyone was now in conversation with the show's producer, a bloke called Byron, who had a long ginger beard and was wearing the brightest red jumper I had ever seen. He was also wearing shorts, at work, and he was at least fifty years of age. He was flanked by the two regular team captains, the aforementioned comic Brinsley, and General Burnout, who was the lead singer and guitarist in an off the wall punky / goth band called 'The Dimmed' Who hadn't had a hit or been relevant for the last twenty years in my humble opinion. Though it must be said he had the most amazing frizzy hair which had covered and hidden the entirety of his face.

"Ah, John Leonard I presume" Byron called out and everyone turned to look at me. "Nice of you to join us. I was just going through the rules of the show for anyone who isn't familiar with it." I nodded and held up a hand in apology for my tardiness.

The show was the music equivalent of 'Truth or Dare' You were asked basic questions which you had to answer before the on-screen egg timer ran out and if your music knowledge weren't up to scratch and you got it wrong then the opposing team could ask you for a truth or make you do a dare. Cutting edge television.

I was paired with 'Demi' and Larry Muscle and was going to be on the team of Brinsley Austin. We would be up against Shrooms, Wellington Botham-Brown, the General and one other who wasn't yet present. Where the hell was the missing body? We were due to start recording in under forty-five minutes and Pip had been in to advise that the studio crowd was now filing in.

Larry and I ordered two more pints each from the makeshift bar. Just as we sat down a make-up artist who was introduced himself as Boyd George (Did no women work at this diversity driven, woke, snowflake channel I thought to myself.)

"Oh Larry" Boyd said whilst intently scanning Muscle's face. "I just need to touch you up."

He then bent down and expertly dabbed a sponge with one hand and flashed a brush across his 'boat' before setting to work on me. "Oh, I've got my work cut out here." He said standing back from me. "You're on in thirty minutes. I can't make a silk purse out of a sows ear. The things they make me do."

Larry Muscle put his pint on the table and got my attention by waving. He then kept the base of his hands together, along with the thumbs and little fingers. He then allowed his index, middle and ring fingers to slightly open and pushed both hands down, and thus made the international language sign for calm.

I let Boyd George do his worse and then he went off to see 'Shrooms' who still had remnants of dirt encrusted in his face from a recent underground protest at Gatwick Airport. Good luck with that one Boyd.

Not only was his hair a tangled greasy mess but he also refused any make up until it was confirmed that all contents were ethically sourced.

I turned my attention back to Larry who during my quick makeover had returned back to the bar and had just about covered the length back to our table with two more pints of dishwater. At least they were Freemans. "So, who is the mystery guest then Laz. Any ideas?" I asked. "I've got a good idea" he said but before he could say anymore he picked up his pint and drained it in one go. "Well?" I pushed for an answer. "What is your good idea?" Larry burped and wiped some froth and dribble away from the corners of his mouth. "Oh, it was to drink that." He said with a cheeky grin. He then reached into his suit jacket and took the lid off a silver hip flask that I could plainly see the inscription 'My Dad is as Hip as This Flask' He then took a huge gulp and then handed it to me. I was beginning to like this guy.

The coke, Ching, Charlie, freebase, pebbles, I don't care what you want to call it was beginning to infiltrate my blood stream. I was beginning to feel alert and full of confidence, power, and energy.' I think I'm going to enjoy the show,' I thought to myself as I took a huge glug of Larry's offered drink. Christ on a cycle. It actually was port he had in there. Who on earth drinks that these days bar Santa on the twenty-fourth of December? It was rank.

Larry continued to chat, a lot. I actually wondered if he had also bought some laughing gear off a Watford hoodie. "Don't get too Elephants John Boy. Your eyes are looking glassier than the Sistine Chapel. They'll ply you with plonk if you get a dare cocker. Have you not seen the show? Your loaf has gone all red. Is your Strawberry beating something chronic or what guv? Simmer down. Right, here's that Pip. He'll be showing us into the studio. Get up on your scotches Lets go make some giraffes."

Pip, the runner (TV technical term) asked us all to follow him to studio two, where I could hear the anticipation and buzz of an expectant crowd. There was a warmup guy talking to them. "Can anyone tell me something useless?" he asked of the audience. "Appendix" shouted someone, "Manchester football teams" yelled another. "How about the Tory government?" the man on the mic had yelled back and got a roar of approval. Mr Warmup then changed tact as he noticed a light above the stage change from red to green. The man with the mic began to introduce us guests, the team captains and finally the host of the show Rich Flavour to the stage.

The crowd began to whoop and applaud wildly. Rich took a bow, and the guests all took their respective positions which were marked in the bold lettering of their names at each team desk.

The other team to us were still one member short and there was a larger than usual space and chair opposite my seated position where they would be sat. It was obviously for someone huge. I suddenly remembered I was about to be on a television recording, so I removed my glasses and placed them on the desk in front of me. I wanted to look cool. I then noticed than there was a ledge just below the top of the desk and Larry had three more pints lined up on it.

Rich Flavour finished his bow and was handed a portable microphone. "Thank you for attending everyone and thanks to Gus Guzzler for warming you lot up huh, let's hear it for Gus." There was a liberal sprinkling of clapping. "Right, you may notice that we are one team member short tonight. Before you get excited (Which was Rich's catchphrase), and the crowd as one shouted back "We're excited Rich, we're excited" Flavour continued. "Let me assure you it isn't gonna be any of you shit munchers filling in. But you're in luck, you can tell your friends you were there on the night 'Too Much Pressure' rolled out the red carpet. Or should it be pink. We have an incredibly special guest ready to come on. So, folks, pals, and everyone in between..... Here he is ready to bring home the bacon..... Please put your trotters together for our final guest, it's only the legend Pricey from 'The Price is Shite' Go mental!" A huge pink pig then waddled onto the stage led by a lead held by Pip and true to form, it crapped on the floor within thirty seconds of being on set, and it fucking stunk. Never work with animals or children, right?

The host Rich Flavour took his position and began to read from the autocue. His first task was to introduce the two team captains. "Well hello citizens and welcome to the first in a new series of 'Too Much Pressure' The music game show that has gone down (O-errr!) in the anals……… (Rich puts his finger to his earpiece as word comes through from the show director in the gallery) upsy-daisy Ha-ha… Let's try that again. That has gone down in the annals of rock music history. Yes we're back. Just when you rockers thought it was safe to go back into the studio. Right, before you get excited" (The crowd all shouted, "We're excited Rich, we're excited.") Rich continued his patter. "I'm afraid we have bought back the same two captains that we have had for all three series so far. We just can't get rid of them. Please say hello to Brinsley Austin." The crowd whopped and hollered. "So, what have you been up to since we last saw you Brin?" asked Rich. "Well Rich" said Brinsley in a slow neanderthal drawl "I've found that music gives your soul to the universe and wings to the mind of imagination. That and I've got well into crotchet and extreme ironing" "Yes" replied Rich. "I think we can cut to a clip of you trying to iron a shirt whilst skiing down Ben Nevis." The crowd began to lose their collective minds laughing. At what, I wasn't quite sure as the shirt he was donning tonight was wrinkled to fuck.

We didn't actually see the clip in the studio so I assumed it would be added in on the edit. The compere continued to introduce our team. "So, we also have joining Brinsley's team this week motormouth Cockney geezer jack of all trades, but master of none, the don of Fleet Street, Mister Larry Muscle, (Slight applause) Next to Larry is Motabike lead singer 'Demi' Demi claims to have bedded over a thousand blokes, and according to 'Cool Slang' magazine is the hardest woman in rock. 'Motabike' also has a new single out called "Face of Mace" Sounds like a lovely ditty dat Demi? The biker tossed her hair back and just uttered the word "Yeah" "Anyway, welcome to the show." Flavour continued his introductions "And we also have John Leonard from wet indie band Dutch Courage. Wet because they literally once sank from the charts without trace" The crowd howled their collective laughter and applauded. I went to speak but Flavour had already moved onto introducing the other team.

"Back again thanks to some good drugs from the NHS is the good General. It's General Burnout, everyone. I'm sure he's under there somewhere." Rich said referencing his wild mane. I now realised that the Generals schtick was being utterly non-communicative, and he just let his frizzy hair do the talking. This was still getting a laugh three series in. Unbelievable.

"Also joining the General is someone who is used to facing the music and also use to being on the opposite side of the pigs, is disgraced former Tory MP, Wellington Botham-Brown. He served six months in a London jail and now serves up celebrities at his restaurant in Kent 'The Big Legrillski' Now Wellington, you have a lot of dishes that you make out of insects and invertebrates." Botham-Brown nodded and confirmed with a simple "Yes Richard" Flavour went straight into the punchline "So you could say you served in Wormwood Scrubs, and now you have to scrub up to serve worms." The gathered throng found this hilarious and laughed heartily and even threw in a round of applause.

Flavour was in the groove now and introduced the final two of General Burnouts team members. "Next we have celebrity, eco warrior Shrooms. Shrooms is not keen on expansions or erections on green land...." The crowd was ahead of the joke as they burst out in fits of giggles. "Normally he's the dirtiest on the show, but tonight he has competition. It's only the co-compere of 'The Price is Shite' it's Pricey everyone." A section of the crowd known as the Pig Pen went ape. "Pricey, it's true your favourite music film is the Sex Pistols Rock and Pork Roll Swine-dle?" "Oink, Oink" responded Pricey.

"Ok, let's get stuck into round one, which is General Knowledge. Ok, General? If you answer your question wrong though, you will face the ultimate in Truth or Dare. Right, I'm going to play some music and the first to buzz in and correctly identify it, gets a point."

Some brass led instrumental music began to play. I knew the answer and hit my button before anyone, but nothing happened. There was no sound or anything and amazingly Pricey's buzzer sounded. Rich Flavour went straight to Pricey. "Pricey, your answer?" "Oink, Oink" went Priccy. "That's correct. It was indeed 'Pigbag' and a hit from over thirty years ago with Papa's Got a Brand New Pigbag. One point, well done. I bet you weren't even born thirty years ago hey Pricey?" The pig oinked again, and then let out a massive fart.

And so, it went on with more emphasis on the pig and everyone laughing along whilst John Leonard was getting more and more frustrated at not having yet said a word.

Demi had also yet still to utter a single word. Yet she was riding high in the charts. Flavour would use that as his next insult. "Demi, shame your surname isn't God. Did you ever think about calling yourself that. Anyway, keep consistent and don't answer this." (The crowd fell about laughing) "Your new single is riding high in the charts and according to the tabloids, you're riding everything with a pulse. Hetty sex….Yuk, it makes me shudder, a bit like heavy metal does. It's so loud. The authorities should play that when Shrooms buries himself underground to stop the expansion at Gatwick." More laughter rained down from the proles in the seats. Demi just hunched her shoulders let a forced half smile appear on her lips.

"Don't go giving them ideas." Butted in Shrooms with an accent so posh that it could have gone to Oxbridge University itself. The only other time I'd heard someone speak like that was at public school or the Labour Party conference . Rich Flavour picked up on it straight away. "Shrooms. Nice accent that love. You speak like you have a plum in your mouth. Get yourself cleaned up and shaved and you could have two later." Rich winked at him and the sheep in the audience clapped and hollered their approval at the latest celebrity put down by the show's host.

We were losing seven points to nil, and I had finally answered a question even though I got it wrong, and my dare was that I had to run around a pole five times and then drink a pitcher of beer as the forfeit. Forfeit, well I say forfeit, but it was actually better than winning a poxy point.

The downside to the dare was that if I were to use a record playing turntable analogy, I would say that my head now had revolutions of 78 per minute instead of a steady old 33 and I really should learn to keep my mouth shut when I feel like this.

Rich Flavour was poking fun at chef Wellington Botham-Brown. "Look Well. If I came into your restaurant and asked for you to bake me a cake. What kind of cake would you knock up for this old girl huh?" Botham-Brown thought about it a little too long before answering. "I, err, I don't really know you well enough, are you allergic to anything, some people don't like raisins…." Flavour flicked his hair back in a very camp manner and mocked a stifled yawn. " Boring. I'm going to throw it open to any of you. If I got Wellington to make me a nice big fluffy pink cake, what should he cook me. I said cook me, calm down you animals in the pig pen." I finally saw my chance to get involved. I knew Flavour was gay. Most of his jokes and conversations alluded to the fact. I buzzed in and answered. "A fairy cake Rich, or maybe a fruit cake. How about even a rainbow cake or just some fudge" I sat back smiling with my response, but then the audience started booing, someone even shouted 'Homophobe' at me. I sensed hostility and for some reason just shouted "I vote Labour" several times to try and win the crowd over.

Larry Muscle seized his chance for some potential airtime "Love a duck. Hasn't the Queen got a lovely smile. You're a diamond Rich. A rich diamond. We're getting thrashed so much I feel like I play football for Derby. Leave it out Mr Flavour. Give us an easy one my old China. Or at least ask us for truth instead of dares, we're getting mullered on them dares over here. Cor blimey, hit the frog and toad Jack."

Suddenly without warning it all too got much for 'Motabike' singer Demi. She just grabbed her microphone and yelled into it "Fuck this show." She then ripped it off and threw it to the floor. Demi then got up out of her seat and left the set. The director was making all manner of hand signs to Rich Flavour to carry on as they were still rolling as they say in TV land. "Oh, Oh, I hope Demi hasn't come over all queer. Though I myself have come over queer quite a few times…" The crowd was suddenly again pissing themselves laughing.

"We can see you sneaking out" I shouted, echoing a football style chant pointing to the door where Demi would exit from the studio . No-one joined in. "Don't mock women you cunt" another distant voice cut through the atmosphere. Had I been entirely sober I would have taken that person to task on their choice of words and indeed turn of phrase to put me down. "We love you Demi" shouted another person who had probably been laughing at her only seconds earlier. A spontaneous round of applause broke out and the crowd slowly stood up chanting "Demi, Demi" I shook my head in disbelief as a girl on the front row of the crowd who had her dyed blonde hair in bunches and was wearing a green/white harlequin style cardigan yelled "Sexist pig" in my direction. The bright lights glinted off her teeth brace as she spoke which almost blinded me. "That's no way to talk to Pricey" I responded as quick as the flash I had just had off her metal tooth brace. I looked over to the pig, but he was being fed. His snout was in the makeshift trough that his agent had brought. Pricey's agent had also put an eiderdown over him to keep him warm, so he literally was a pig in blanket.

The crowd was seriously getting on my case when one distinctive lone voice shouted out unequivocal support for me by yelling; "I love you John." I recognised the American accent that had pierced the strained atmosphere immediately. I cast me eyes to the crowd but couldn't see a thing. I then removed my glasses from their latest resting position of being in my denim jacket inside pocket, put them on, and cast my eyes back to the crowd. At this point, my number one fan / stalker Erika Puck was stood up waving frantically at me.

Someone then shouted at her, I assumed it wasn't nice as the comment was followed by a can of drink flying in her direction and it spilled over others as it locked onto her position like an Exocet. By now BCB security had to act and did so by removing Erika and another woman who I couldn't quite make out as she was sat in the shadows of the seats in the studio.

The crowd had already begun to turn ugly and then became hostile and the last thing that I clearly remember was thinking that they'll cut out all this bollocks in the edit and the last thing I recall seeing was the director coming on set to appeal to the audience for calm utilising the international hand sign for it.

The cameras started rolling again and the last thing I remembered hearing was the jeering that accompanied all my answers to the remaining quiz questions. In fact, I was jeered anytime I opened my mouth to speak. Even when I cracked what I thought was a woofer when asked "What my favourite tree was?" and I replied "Aintree" It was met with cat calls and boo's.

The show was broadcast on the forthcoming Friday night as an uncut double length season starting special, where in fact it was cut and edited to make things look worse than they had been.

Despite professional cockney geezer, man of the people and guest Larry Muscle telling me he was on my side on the night and that he 'One hundred percent' agreed that by giving the pig the limelight it was demeaning to the rest of us on the show. So, it was a surprise that he only went and produced a hatchet job on me in his latest newspaper column. This slagging appeared in his 'What to Watch' section that was printed in 'The Pun' newspaper weekend television pull out guide that accompanied the Friday edition of that arse wipe. To top it all off they even gave 'Pricey' an interview, and this included a photoshoot of him adorning some high-end fashion suits, even a top designer Ted Bacon one. Den Leslie had even been quoted by Muscle saying that I had intimidated him whilst seriously intoxicated as he tried to eat his vegan Falafel and houmous dinner in the BCB restaurant. The bastard had been eating chicken curry for fucks sake!

Carlton Gooch was less than impressed with the ham-fisted approach by the tabloids to my appearance especially as the name of his business 'Asteroid' was tagged to the word 'Haemorrhoid' with the headline reading 'John Leonard Haemorrhoid' The review went on to say that I was harmless enough but would cause pain and that I should return to the rectum I had just crawled out of. There was also an online poll which was running at 93% of voters who wanted me sacked and took off his books. (I wish to take this moment to personally thank the 7% who loyally stood by me. Respect. It means a lot.)

The Gooch was going to have to put out the fire and for him, getting me away and out of the country couldn't come soon enough. This was just as well really, that our impending trip to the United States of America was only forty-eight hours away from take-off.

DUTCH GOES TO AMERICA

SAN FRANCISCO

THIS WAS ONE OF THOSE pinch me moments in life. Just like being on the television had been before, but here we were in the departures lounge at London's Heathrow Airport. The day had so far gone smoothly, and with the exception of Nocka Izzet setting off every alarm he passed through at security we were finally all ensconced around a table keeping an eye on the bright blue departures screen by the bar. This screen was constantly changing and requesting passengers to move to this numbered gate or that numbered gate so the big white winged bird could fly them to Hamburg, Hanoi, or Helsinki.

True to form we were going the scenic long way round as it was no doubt cheaper. So, our day would consist of a flight from London to Philadelphia and then onto San Francisco which was to be the scene of our first ever US gig.

We were flying Americana Airways - AA (I'm sure Carlton Gooch had booked this airline on purpose as we had it drummed into us the no drink / no drugs mantra) No drugs….Ha! Every time I looked in my hand luggage I come across my blood thinners and cholesterol tablets, but I know this wasn't what he meant.

We still had time to kill before the off and I fancied a pint or two to calm my nerves. I hadn't left the country since 1999 and now I was about to head off to a city that according to the guidebook I had read on it had been hit by numerous earthquakes (1989), fires (1906), tsunamis (1960) boating disaster (1955) and oil spill (2007), the only thing it hadn't yet suffered was a plane crash. This information hadn't helped me one bit.

I slipped away from our seated position and piled up hand luggage and ventured into 'Johnny Harps' the airports Irish Bar. There was only one person working behind the bar, but he was amazing to watch. The bartender was like one of those circus performers who spins plates as this guy kept pulling half full pints of Guinness and then topping up others to keep the queue moving along. I had just ordered a pint of the black stuff myself when I felt hot breath on my neck and then a familiar voice.. "Hup. You don't really want that Mister Leonard sir. Two, three. Remember we have to be sober for our passage through American Immigration later today. Let's leave here and re-join the others. Hup two, three, hup two three." I was just about to tell Guy Ropes our moustachioed chaperone to 'fuck off' when the plate spinner requested the ridiculous sum of eight pounds and ninety pence for the pint of ordered frothy black stuff. "Yes, you're right." I lamely turned and said to Ropes before declining my part in the transaction by walking away without adding a word to the circus performer behind the bar.

Two hours later and we were in the air. I have never been a good flyer and I usually like to have the captain put me at ease with his/her plummy welcome and posh English tones. What I hadn't anticipated was being greeted over the intercom by a Geordie. "Wey aye man. I'm reet glad ta welcome you's aboard this flight to err... America. Take a seat canny lads n lasses. I'm ya captain Bobby Dazla and today this B6969 Turbo Nutter Bo Class will be flying fast man. We will be flying at about 33,000 to 45,000 feet and the tab light is on so nooo smoking." It was at this point I swear I could hear the clink of Brown Ale bottles ; I was sat with a subdued Mac who despite having remembered to bring his bass guitar with him this tour, was being continually sick into a bag. Nocka, Guy Ropes and Brandon Slam were sat two rows behind us.

Stage one, the eight hours, and fifteen minutes to Philadelphia had been noneventful. We landed and Guy Ropes had herded us across the airport to make the connection to our San Francisco flight which was to provide us with another six hours and thirty minutes in the air. Fan-deep vein thrombosis-tastic!

On plane one I had stretched out the best I could with the room I was allocated in cattle class. Flight two had the same seating arrangements but less leg room as it was a smaller plane, so I was once again sat with Mac.

The air stewards were not so generous on the second flight as for inflight food we were given a cheap plastic bag which in it contained an orange drink that didn't taste of orange with a straw that tasted of synthetic flowers (Don't ask how I know), the smallest sandwich I had ever seen (Still unsure of what meat it contained. Maybe Pork butt) and a sachet that contained precisely 27 apparently salted peanuts.

We had around an hour of flight time left when Mac handed me his latest sick bag, got up out of his seat and headed down the aisle for the toilet. Whilst he was walking I noticed a guy with striking orange hair further down the plane also get up out of his seat. I shook my head in disbelief. It was Mr Orange again. He moved out into the aisle as Mac passed him. This time Orange was wearing a peach-coloured tee shirt and shorts for his trip to warmer climes. He started to stretch in the aisle. That was how cramped it was between rows that even a ghost had got stiff. I looked down at the tour itinerary that we had for the 'Prepare to Die a Thousand Deaths Tour' We would be going to San Francisco, Los Angeles, and San Diego on the West Coast before traversing back to the East Coast for shows in Boston and a brace in New York with a band who were if I heard Gooch correctly a bit of a cult.

I had read up on our tour partners 'Frog Splash' They were a hair metal band who hadn't released a new album for over twenty years a bit like us. They were fronted by two ex-professional wrestlers but other than that I couldn't find out much about them on the internet which was a bit odd.

We were also being joined on the tour by another Brit by the name of 'Chelsea Bird' a one hit wonder from London who now lived out in California. Decades previously he had a massive hit with "It Takes Two to Tango" which was taken from the film "Play Mates" where he had played the lead role of Kane Mates. That song was number one for much of the Summer some years back, the film didn't fare so well though. Apparently Bird now resided in LA and was back out on the road to help fund a forthcoming sex change operation to literally become one. I looked up again and the orange phantom had disappeared, and saw that Mac was on his way back down the aisle looking rather red faced and unhappy.

The petit Asian woman politely unbuckled her seatbelt and moved into the aisle to let Mac return to his seat in the middle of us. He dropped down into number twenty-seven B with a thump. "What's up with you?" I asked. "I really need a shit John. But it just won't dislodge itself. I never normally have this problem. Maybe it's because we are forty thousand feet up in the air. I don't know, but it won't come out. I huffed and puffed but it's stuck." The Chinese woman had thankfully popped her headphones back on and was watching some film on the back of the seat in fronts headrest.

That was more or less the last thing that we had said to each other during the flight even when the Captains voice came over the public address system and advised we take a look to our right to get a glimpse of the famous 'Golden Gate Bridge' during our descent into San Francisco International. The view was spellbinding. Nightfall was upon us. I had no idea what time it was back home or was here to be honest. This was a sight though that I wouldn't forget in a hurry.

The plane landed and came to a slow halt. The Captain changed the seat belt sign from on to off and people began to stand and push towards the exit door. Why? They weren't going to get out of the airport any sooner than anyone else. I looked out of the window, and spied a yellow-coloured bus approaching the plane which was no doubt going to take us all to arrivals.

It took another fifteen minutes to get the exit door of the aircraft open so the passengers could finally begin to disembark from the transport. The air con was off, and I began to sweat like a sixty-year-old radio DJ who had just learnt that the Police Forces Operation Dewdrop had started.

I finally reached the exit myself and took in my first breath of California and got back a nose full of diesel. I looked around from the top of the stairs and all I could see for miles were planes. This airport was like most things they said about the US that everything was 'Much bigger' Judging by some of the passengers holding blue US passports the people definitely were, and I wasn't judging them in height.

As soon as we disembarked from the plane Mac got the urge for the bog and was hit by bad stomach cramps. Guy Ropes had asked him to hold it in until we were through immigration but had no idea how long that could be. I knew from the look of Mac that he was at 'Def Con One' and he scuttled off to the nearest toilet block as soon as he saw the international toilet sign pointing the way.

Mac entered the toilets. What he saw nearly took his breath away had it not been for the smell taking his breath away. There all in a row were some thirty cream-coloured cubicles. He had never seen so many in all his days. Mac picked the second loo from the left as that appeared to give him some distance between the next habited bog.

Mac was beginning to regret wearing his skeleton onesie at times like this. He was desperate to unload his previously consumed inflight meals and he had more than one belt to unbuckle. He pulled the zip down of his costume and planted his arse on the seat in relief. 'Any minute now' he thought it would be 'bombs away' He looked to his left and grunted and heaved. At the second heave he noticed the unnaturally large gap at the bottom of the toilet cubicle. "What the..."he found himself saying out loud as the gap between Formica and the toilet flooring was large enough for Mac to see straight along the whole toilet line. From his current vantage point, he could see two other people who both looked to be having a dump but neither person was sat directly on the toilet like he was. Both men who's faces couldn't be seen were hovering their arses just over the toilet drop zone. 'What devilment is this?' Mac thought to himself before uttering aloud 'This is a perverts paradise' with a few too many decibels than was necessary as his hearing had still not 'popped' following the plane landing.

The bassist was brought out of his deep thinking by the sudden surge of waste departing from his body. His relief was short lived as the answer to his prior question was then answered.

Four doors down, hoverer number one had finished doing his business, wiped, and then flushed, and as he pulled on the flush handle this caused all the other toilets to simultaneously flush in sequence. Mac looked down in unexpected horror as his own toilet unexpectedly flushed. This action caused the water in the bowl to rise to the surface bringing the contents of the pan up with it. The rising water cyclone hit an unsuspecting buffer (Macs arse), which was impeding the flush cycle before all contents would be sucked down the loo with force and replaced with fresh water. The blocking arse caused water and excrement to push itself through the gap between Mac's arse and balls, past the pair of spindly white legs and down onto the floor and gathered clothing. If anyone was looking in It looked like a small dark barrel going over Niagara Falls.

"Oh bollocks!" cried Mac as he desperately began the clean-up operation with his bare hands. He picked up a flaky corn infused lump of turd and dropped it back down into the toilet bowl. He wiped his fingers clean on the pristine white door of the cubicle.

Three minutes later Mac soggily re-joined his band mates and waiting tour manager who had all been loitering just outside the toilet block for the last twenty minutes. A cleaner shouted his annoyance as Mac continued to leave a slime trail as the party finally made their way through to immigration.

Immigration was cleared despite Mac giving off a sweaty stench of margarine and shit. He was asked one additional question of "Are you nervous son?" by a huge Latino Homeland Security Guard named Julio before his passport was stamped and he was cleared to exit.

"As soon as I get my suitcase I need to get changed out of this wet stuff." Mac stated the obvious, and of course the obvious then happened. Everyone's case was there for collection on carousel 27 at baggage reclaim with the exception of Mac's.

Outside of the airport and having successfully collected most of the bands luggage and with one suitcase reported missing it was time to put road manager Guy Ropes to work to sort out transport. He soon commandeered two available cars.

Ropes split Mac and myself up and I got into a car with Brandon and Nocka that was going to be driven by a middle aged portly African American chap who had salt and pepper coloured hair, a golden earring, and a bright yellow shirt to match his happy persona. I immediately noticed that his shirt wasn't buttoned up correctly but that just added to his charm. He had clearly skipped a button. I pointed this fashion faux pas out to our driver, but he just let out a large infectious laugh.

"So, who you guys fly high with today?" he asked. "The last flight was with Tommy Cook" I replied. "Snakes alive. They have an airline called cock... seriously?" he replied with a question and another rumbling belly laugh. It was at this point I realised that I didn't think he understood half of what I was actually saying. After putting our luggage into the boot / trunk he got into the driver's seat on the left-hand side of the vehicle. I had now taken residency in the front with the other pair climbing in the back.

I wound the window down slightly to let in some of the nights warm air. "So, guys, did you have a good flight?" He asked again but didn't stop to wait for any answer as he started up the car, signalled, pulled out and started to drive us away from the airport. He continued to speak. "So, my name is DeJohn, and it is my pleasure to welcome y'all to San Francisco and be your driver tonight." The passengers in the back of the cab seemed non-communicative so I attempted to strike up some sort of rapport with our overtly smiley driver. "Hi DJ. Glad to be here." Before I could add anything further he had once again taken over the conversation. "First time in the Bay huh? You'll love it here. There's just two things you need to know bout old Frisco. One....Stay out of the area called Harrison and two, stay out of the part of the town they call Tenderloin. You do that and a good time will be had be y'all. Now where is DeJohn to take you guys on this balmy night?"

John fumbled in his pocket for the name of the hotel the travelling party was booked into as DeJohn steered the car onto Highway 101. He had only just looked at the name of the place as well, but it hadn't stuck. It was a nice-looking property on the corner of streets Rose and West.

I looked out of the window and saw so many green direction signs with famous and familiar names. The Mission District, Alcatraz, Oracle Park, I looked at a large white pick-up truck that pulled out to overtake us and there sat in the back was Mr Orange who looked over and waved at me as the truck accelerated away from us but then cut right into our lane of traffic. "Yeah man

I surpass your ass at the next lights" shouted DeJohn as he sounded his horn at the pickup truck driver.

"Say my man, what's da name of your hotel?" DeJohn asked again. "Oh, sorry man" I responded and pulled the paper with the details of the hotel again from my pocket. "It's the Renoir Hotel. Do you know it? It's on the corner of Rose and West." The cab driver raised his eyebrows. "Oh, good lord. I know it. That's in the Harrison District." Despite delivering this potential bad news to me he still let out a laugh as the half-opened window next to me suddenly automatically raised to a close. "And what brings you to the Bay? You here for Pride?" "God no." I said a little too quickly. "No mate, we're a rock band called Dutch Courage, not Butch Courage. We're here to play a gig at Slims Music Hall, ever heard of it?" I asked. DeJohn's eyes left the road and settled on me as he let out another hearty roar before delivering the knockout punch. "Ow man, yeah I know that sucker, heh heh, that place is in Tenderloin. Been nice knowing you ha-ha" I tried not to let these two pieces of bad information spoil my arrival. "We're doing a gig there with a band of wrestlers. Ever heard of a group called Frog Splash?" I asked in hope. "Nope can't say I have. Fog Dash, what do they sing? And what is a tessellar?" DeJohn inquired again having not correctly heard fifty percent of the words I had said. "Wrestlers mate, wrestlers!" I reiterated before reasoning with myself that whilst I was in the US I was going to have to talk a bit slower and enunciate words properly if I ever wanted to get through a conversation. "A rest home" DeJohn said as he looked at me gone out. "No, no, the other band we are touring with are wr-est-lers." I reiterated somewhat slower letting the incorrect name of the band go. This time the driver got it. "Oh, wrestlers ho-hum, that sport is such bullshit man. Ever notice how they never have any falls or knock outs during the advert breaks when it's on TV? That shits more fake than a ten buck Ho's orgasm dig." I was beginning to like this guy despite the fact that he couldn't understand most of what I was saying.

Our car passed under a brick subway which had been covered in graffiti as the provided streetlight went out, until we came out the other side. As we did I could now see the bay and the shiny Pacific Ocean and then a sign came into view that informed all and sundry on the road that San Francisco was only four miles away.

Ten minutes later and DeJohn pulled over to park on a stretch of road that was adjacent to a car lot. "Ok brothers this is as far as I go. The hotel you want is just down there. That last building on the end of the block. You'll have to walk the last bit. I'm slightly sorry about that y'all."

It seemed that our taxi driver didn't want to venture any further into the area they called 'Harrison' Before I could remonstrate, he was out of the car and on the street as the boot / trunk was automatically opening. Soon he was moving our luggage out onto the sidewalk where I noticed that our parked vehicle had attracted some unwanted attention. There was still no sign of the other vehicle carrying Nocka & Ropes, but across the street I swear I saw Mr Orange stood there laughing giving me a double thumbs up sign.

With DeJohn paid and tipped (What the hell is all that about huh?) We continued to walk towards the Renoir Hotel which was easily visible from our position on the widest sized street that I had ever seen in my life.

We carried or pulled our cases along slowly. It had been a long flight, it was night here, but we were seven or eight hours ahead in time from the United Kingdom. My body wasn't sure where it was, and fatigue was beginning to dampen my original excitement of being here.

"Don't look now" said Slam "But it looks like we have a tail" I couldn't help myself. He might as well have said stop what you are doing and look behind you, as I stopped dead in my tracks and turned around to look behind me. It seemed that a small collection of dossers, street people, hobo's, whatever you want to call them were following us. We picked up the pace, but it was like one of those cartoon chases where it didn't matter how Bolt like, say Scooby Doo ran away, the ghost who moved at walking pace was always just two steps right behind him.

"Keep moving we are nearly there" I said to the others as perspiration dripped from my brow and into my mouth. All around us in the street was eerily quiet, there wasn't even any cars on the roads which I found strange. 'Thanks again Carlton Gooch for booking us into the hotel equivalent of 'H Block Prison' I found myself cursing.

We inched ever closer to the Renoir Hotel. It had been touch and go but we had just got the edge on the walking dead that were following us. I tried to fathom out why they hadn't broken into a trot if they were in the mugging business. If they were, they weren't particularly good at it.

We could all now see the entrance to the hotel and relaxed a little bit. The safety zone was in sight. Slam couldn't resist turning and shouting some abuse at our pursuers. I glanced at his beaming sweaty features just as Nocka reached the entrance which is when we saw it.

The card at the locked hotel door read 'If arriving after 8.30PM please use entrance on Rose Street.' Oh bollocks! This meant that we were going to have to walk back the way we just came in, or go the long way around the block, possibly running the gauntlet with good knows who or what?

"What now?" said a panicked Slam. The gaggle of people on our tail continued to walk towards us at a pace reserved for funeral marches. "Fuck it, just go around the block." I said sounding braver than I felt. We rounded the corner and tried to make a run for it. Nocka luckily stumbled across a discarded shopping trolley. He cleared out the junk and plastic bottles from it and lifted his suitcase into it. As soon as the first items of the cleared-out debris hit the pavement was when we realised the stuff that had been in it wasn't actually discarded. A small grubby naked man with a bushy beard popped up from beneath a mound of cardboard and old dirty bed sheets. "Hey stop motherfucker. Stop thief." He had the audacity to shout as he jumped up and down and then began searching the trash, his makeshift bedroom for some item of clothing to put on.

All three of us broke into a run of what felt to me like I was trying to pass SAS selection. My muscles ached and I felt the burn as I lugged my suitcase along as thoughts like 'Did I really need to have bought that jacket, that much underwear, and three sets of trainers' ran through my brain much quicker than my legs were going.

Three minutes run time felt like five years. How the hell do people run marathons for three hours? I was completely blowing after one hundred and eighty seconds. Still, it paid off as we reached the open entrance to the hotel on Rose Street unharmed. 'He Who Dares' and all that.

Mac discarded the shopping trolley, and we entered the hotel all jostling for first position to get through the revolving door. Thankfully, there was no sign of the people who had been trailing us or the beardy naked guy we had woken up which was a bonus.

The hotel looked exquisite. It had a lot of marble features and a gold banister leading all the way up the stairs. It felt as if we had travelled back through time to the thirties.

Slam was already on his way to the Reception desk. Nocka and I were not too far behind him. The night porter who was about to address us had a name tag attached to his white shirt which indicated that his name was Seymour. Suddenly there was the sound of a gunshot. We all ducked as Seymour smiled. "Don' be alarmed... Tha' vas a car back fi-wing." He alas had a short tongue. "You ah the west of the Wope's Party, yesh?." We then learnt that Guy Ropes and Mac had beat us here by & I quote Seymour 'free quarters of an hour.'

We hurried through the check in procedure, allowing copies of our passports be taken and made for the safety of our room on the sixth floor. On entering I chucked my suitcase on a vacant bed and looked out of the window and down on the street below I could just about make out a gaggle of people who seemed to be stood stock still staring back up at me.

Despite having been on the go for over twenty-four hours, my need for sleep had subsided by being freaked out and had been replaced by the need for adventure and more importantly some alcohol. But I wasn't sure that I fancied venturing out just yet. Slam and Mac felt the same, so I switched on the TV and watched the news as the other two took turns using the bathroom facilities.

Having never been to the US of A, or hardly anywhere in the last twenty years no-one can really prepare you for the thing they call 'Jet lag' We had been in the hotel for over two hours now, had a few dollars burning a hole in our pockets and couldn't get to sleep if you paid us despite the three AM time that luminated from the rooms digital clock.

We had all taken to our beds some time ago, but my brain was still ticking over. I still couldn't believe I was here, had been on national television twice in the last six weeks, had a new single coming out on Compact Disc, Vinyl, MP3 and AK47 download file or something. My happy thoughts were then crudely interrupted "I can't fucking sleep." Mac eloquently shouted out. "I'm still awake as well mate." Slam responded. I acknowledged both that I too was still wide eyed, and bushy tailed. "Maybe someone should switch the tele off." Was an idea I floated but had ignored. "We are being so fucking lame here. Where's your head at? I mean where's your head at and where's the mini bar?" yelled Mac as he sprung out of bed all excited like he had just invented the lightbulb or something. This is when Brandon Slam, the third column amongst us suddenly came clean. "There isn't one lads. Look you're good blokes. But some of us have been instructed to keep an eye on you two and keep you off the wanker juice. There is no booze in this room."

It was nice of Slam to come clean and admit that he had been keeping half an eye on us for Carlton Gooch. It was hardly the world of the KGB or Mossad but even so. He went on to advise us that he had found it more difficult as time went on as he could see that Mac and I were just a pair of clumsy morons when it came to drink and drugs and that we just unluckily found ourselves in dumb situations.

We didn't have a gig for two days so what harm could be done? None of us could sleep and there was bound to be a bar open somewhere probably down in the hotel lobby right?

Wrong. The hotel bar was closed. Seymour watched with a wry smile as we ventured out of the revolving door. "Left or right?" I asked my bassist and singer colleagues. "Gotta go left right?" said Slam. "Who do you think you are Guy Ropes? Left, right, left, right." The three of us burst out laughing on the street. It broke the silence.

We chose left and headed towards where we thought the sea and beach were going to be. I couldn't believe Mac was still wearing his shit infused onesie in this heat.

Less than ten minutes later after a few lefts, and the odd right, we weren't sure where we were and more importantly we hadn't yet found a single bar or food outlet open.

I detected we were close to the sea now as I could hear the crashing waves. It was still pitch black and we still hadn't seen another person on our travels.

A mist or fog that you normally only ever see in horror movies had started to come in off the sea and that's when I heard something.

It sounded like the sound of someone on roller skates and suddenly ahead of us I could see outlines of a figure in the fog. The roller-skating sound started getting closer and then we all saw him, out of the banks of mist a guy dressed in a bright coloured purple suit and sporting a purple pork pie hat skated towards us. He pulled up by right next to Mac by utilising the T-Slide stop. It was impressive and would have scored at least a nine out of ten from me had the guy not looked like an overly aggressive seventies pimp. In his left white gloved hand, he was holding a baggy which to the naked eye looked like it contained pills of some variation. For some reason Mac held out his hand awaiting his approach as if Mr Purple had put him into some kind of deep trance.

Mr Purple was also wearing a mask that was the outline of a skull and more importantly covered his entire face. He had probably been drawn to Mac, who was wearing his skeleton onesie (Well he didn't have much choice as his luggage still hadn't been located) … which became illuminated at night. If he had bought that mask adorned by Mr Purple he would have been complete as a skeleton. Mr Purple thrust the baggy into Macs outstretched paw. "Forty dollar." Mr Purple Train hollered. Mac looked open mouthed at the contents in his hand. "Look numb nuts. You have my merchandise. You now have a contract with Purple Train. SOOO…Gimme my motherfucking green, white boy" Mr Train pulled open his purple jacket to reveal a purple waist band just above his trousers that had a gun (Not purple) of some description tucked neatly into it.

I think I had got this straight. If we paid Mr Purple Train forty green motherfuckers then he most certainly wouldn't blow our heads off with the gun he appeared to be showing off. I didn't know about the price of ammunition, but could we have negotiated? What was the price of three bullets? Surely it wouldn't be financially viable for him as it might take one or more bullets to 'Off us' so to speak. I was thinking about entering some sort of counteroffer when Brandon Slam handed over two 'Jacksons' at a speed only a magicians hands could move. Mr Train snatched the dough and tucked it away in his pocket before beginning to start 'rexing' on his wheel footwear which I was to learn was a backwards manoeuvre on the skates. (Thanks Brandon) He then completed a salchow before spinning and dipping and then he was off like grease lightening into the fog from which he had initially appeared.

In the distance we heard some glass smash and raised voices then flashing lights began to penetrate through the fog, we backed up a few steps, turned around and started to walk away from the noise of the commotion. We had only managed to walk a few hundred yards when the familiar colours of police red, white and blue lights beamed through the air. A cop car then pulled up right beside us with a screech of breaks as it halted. The window of the passenger side was already down. "What the fuck are you guys doing down here at this time huh?" It had been a reasonable question which Brandon Slam gave a reasonable answer in the poshest accent he could muster. "Hello there officer. We are looking for a quiet bar for some ample refreshment. We have just arrived in your fine city and…" "Shut the fuck up you Limey prick." Officer Marv Gorman said as he exited his vehicle with his hand hovering above his holstered gun. To be honest I wasn't enjoying San Francisco as this was the second firearm I had seen in the flesh in under three minutes. I gulped so hard the sound was evident. Thankfully, the police officer didn't deploy his weapon when he realised he was dealing with some right weapons in the shape of three hapless Brits in the guise of holiday makers. "Look you guys. You're a long way from home right and you're all from London yeah?" (Why do all Americans who enter into any random chat with Brits think all people they encounter are from London? Is it because they don't know anywhere else in the country? If so that's not entirely fair is it? I mean these days I can walk into any British supermarket, hit the clothing section, and can purchase hoodies or tee shirts bearing such diverse US locations as Los Angeles, New York, Miami, even Chicago. Now I was in America I assumed I could visit any supermarket here and find the reciprocal shirts for Scunthorpe, Norwich, Rochdale, and Hull.)

"Yes we are from London." We collectively mumbled whilst nodding our heads politely. Officer Gorman was now stood by the rear door of his vehicle which he then opened. For a moment panic set in. Mac still had about his person the drugs that he had only moments earlier purchased courtesy of forty bucks from Slam. Was this a shake down? Were we going back to the station? Or The big house? Were we going to end up in Alca-fucking-traz less than twenty-four hours after setting foot in the god damn state? "Get in guys." Gorman indicated to the back of the vehicle before adding "Which hotel are you staying at?" "RENOIR" three positive responses came back in double quick time. "Ok, we know it." Gorman said to the back of Macs head as he was last one in and closed the door.

The cop car pulled away from the kerb at slow speed. Officer Gorman continued his lecture. "This part of town guys, sketchy. The only stuff that happens at the Wharf when the mist comes in at four in the morning is murder and drug deals. You don't want to be caught up in any of that bag." We all nodded our agreements at him very quickly.

Our free ride pulled up outside of our hotel. Officer Gorman exited the front seat and opened the back door to let us all (hopefully) out. We stood on the street, but Gorman wanted to see us off the sidewalk. "In you go then gents." We shuffled towards the revolving door with the policeman's eyes burning holes in the back of our heads. "And enjoy Pride whilst you're here." He added with a smirk as we re-entered the Renoir Hotel.

The following morning at breakfast and Guy Ropes was planning our day ahead over black coffee and a lightly buttered croissant when I wearily dragged my aching carcass into the dining room for breakfast. "Ah Mr Leonard, hup two, three, hup two, three. Is Sir all bright eyed and bushy tailed ready for this present morn?" He didn't wait for my answer and didn't get one as I had only three hours kip. He beckoned me to sit and join him at the table, just as Nocka appeared carrying a yoghurt of some flavour I couldn't fathom from the picture of a woman sitting by a tent on the pots panel picture and a single piece of toast, unbuttered. "Of course, you are ready Mr Leonard. You were born ready Sir. Please fall in. Take a pew, hup two, three, hup two, three. At ease now. I think as we have a free day prior to concerto number one that we should take in the sights and sounds of this delightful city, what do you say Sir?" I struggled to nod my approvement as my half shut bloodshot eyes gave away how I was actually feeling. Ropes turned to study Nocka. "Fall in

Mr Izzet. Now relax, hup two, hup two. Fine choice for breakfast. You want to be match fit but the first show. I commend you Sir." Nocka sat and replied. "W, w, well y, y ,yes. But it was what you told me to have." I half smiled as a waitress approached the table.

"Good morning Sir, I'm Cindy your waitress today. Is there anything that you fancy…" Not half I thought as I looked her over. She was probably in her early twenties, with neat auburn hair tied back into a ponytail and she had a bust every bit as big as a 40-million-dollar DEA sting. We're talking thirty tonnes of a find. She finished her sentence as my mind returned from the blue planet…."From the breakfast menu?" I looked her square on. "Yes please Cindy" I said pretending to look at her name tag. "Can I have the Blueberry pancakes, with links, bacon, eggs, sunny side up (What-ever the fuck that was I thought to myself, but I had always wanted to say it. Using that terminology in 'Cecil's Café' back home in Hungerton had never appealed.), French toast, a cinnamon roll, hash brown, Belgian waffles and coffee and orange juice please." "Ok Sir. Do you realise you have just read the whole menu to me in order, so you want one of everything?" I shook my head. "Err…..No the pancakes and eggs sunny side up with coffee will be just fine." Cindy stomped away wobbling in all the right places.

"Your concentration please Mr Leonard. Hup two, three, hup two, three. We are here after all to work." The annoying fucking Sergeant Major road manager reminded me. As if I could forget with him sat there watching me like a hawk. "Where are Messer's Slam and McCarthy?" he enquired. "Well Slam is having his third shower since we arrived." I informed Ropes. "He is most definitely not the right person to bring to a hot dry state that has been in a drought." as California had for the last four years according to the News on Foxx 1 that we had seen before our walk about the previous evening.

My breakfast arrived and I felt I had smashed the stereotype of the British person for the Americans as.

1) I had arrived in the dining room without wearing a bowler hat or pin stripe suit.

2) I had failed to say please, cheers, mate or thank you during conversations with hotel staff at least four times.

3) I had farted, swore, spoke with my mouth full and burped loudly through the eating of my enormous breakfast.

Breakfast…It had been more like a banquet. I was going to have to at least knock having the syrup on the head going forward. Far too many calories. But then again I was just on my holidays, sort of, so it didn't matter too much right?.

Slam soon joined our merry band at the dining table and advised all sat listening that Mac was still fast asleep. Between us we agreed on a day of sightseeing. All the usual haunts were listed. Alcatraz, see the sea lions at Pier 39, Twin Peaks, and a trip to Oracle Park the home of the Frisco Giants baseball team. I also demanded that we visit the steps at City Hall where I had seen ' Old Dirty Harry' troupe down them many times in film. We were all on board for the trip out, but for Mac McCarthy still in the hotel room, he would be undertaking a completely different trip out for the day.

John returned to his room with Slam and tried to roust Mac into getting out of bed. "Piss off" came his diplomatic response. He simply wasn't interested in, and I quote, 'Doing tourist shit' I wasn't sure Guy Ropes would allow to leave him to stay home alone I joked with him. No sooner had the words of our tour manager left my lips than there was a knock at the door, and the hand doing the knocking belonged to the aforementioned Mr Ropes.

Amazingly it was agreed to leave Mac in the room to 'Come round, two, three, in his own time.' We arranged to meet him later in the day at Pier 39 which was easy to find by all accounts along the sea front. "Just head the way we went last night." I jokingly instructed Mac after Ropes had extricated himself from our room at full military marching pace.

John, Slam, Nocka and Guy Ropes had left the Renoir heading for the first port of call, which was to be Twin Peaks, leaving a jet lagged Mac behind at the hotel still lying-in bed. Mac was in turmoil with his body clock fighting over whether it should be asleep or not at this current time of day.

Out of the blue Mac suddenly sneezed and in the involuntary spasm that his body made as it omitted a semi-autonomous, expulsion of air as foreign particles in the room irritated his nasal mucosa he knocked the top pillow of the two-tier pillow system he was operating in the bed for head rest to the floor. As Mac sat up and looked around the room sheepishly, his eyes desperately trying to focus against the bright sunlight that was cascading through the windows.

The streaming sunlight was causing a glint off of something on the floor that was remarkably close to where Mac was sat. It didn't take Sherlock to quickly work out the cause as Mac looked down to see that the sunlight was bouncing off the plastic baggy of pills that he had put under his top pillow the previous evening / incredibly early morning for safe keeping.

Mac was torn. He didn't want good drugs to go to waste, but he had no idea if they would be any good. He had also signed a contract vowing to not take any, but that prick Carlton Gooch was miles away back in Britain and his henchman Guy Ropes was off out on his field trip with the others he smiled to himself. He stretched out his left hand, scooped up the bag and exited the bed in one fluid manoeuvre.

There was only four pills in the bag so they couldn't be much good at ten dollars a dollop thought Mac. He moved into the bathroom and poured himself a glass of water and took a pill. Sixty minutes later and he still hadn't even got a buzz off one, so he foolishly took another and that's when Mac went out on a trip of his own.

Mac flew down the thick carpeted stairs forgoing the lift at the Renoir. He suddenly felt claustrophobic in his room and needed some fresh air. What the fuck had he taken he thought to himself as he got the drug sweats.

After a couple of extra revolutions and false starts with the hotels revolving door, Mac Suddenly found himself out of the streets of San Francisco. Here he was seeing beautiful colours and images of rabbits, golden halos, and birds with human heads flying by. He was suddenly guessing that the tabs weren't your bog-standard E pills but possibly mind-bending high strength LSD, and he'd just necked two of them.

It was in fact the correct assumption by Mac. He was indeed just commencing an acid trip whilst the other members of the band trooped around some deserted and dilapidated prison on a rocky island.

The hallucinogens got to work. It was a pretty easy job for them once they arrived in Macs head as there wasn't too much in the brain area in the way of obstacles to overcome. They soon got to work to disrupt the communication between brain chemical systems and the spinal cord. Once that was done they moved forward like a small invading army into his neural circuits that used serotonin, which is a neurotransmitter. This is what causes changes in perception.

Macs brain tried to hold off the foreign parties attacking. It was a gallant rear guard action, but they were essentially fighting a losing battle. It was all a bit like Custer's last stand.

"Are you staring at me" shouted some hallucinogens towards some hardy brain cells that were being resistant. "We're Millwall" they then chanted as they continued to cause carnage inside Mac's mind and the brain cells soon scattered for safety.

The hallucinogens continued to march forward until they caused impact on the part of Mac's brain called the prefrontal cortex, which also plays a role in mood, and rational thinking. The rampage in his mind continued as they affected the next port of call in the brain which was responsible for arousal and responses to stress levels, and once they had taken that,... Mac was fucked.

Mac floated down the street and he passed cocktail bars, a lush park, and a beautiful rooftop restaurant to which he was totally oblivious. He saw a sign directing traffic to an area of the Bay called 'Nob Hill' and he spent the next thirty minutes stood on the same spot of the sidewalk laughing to himself.

Shoppers, the general public, and parents with kids on the street wisely gave what they thought before them was a lunatic wearing a thick black onesie that stunk of shit a very wide berth.

Mac regained some sort of composure and continued to roam wherever his feet led him. It was a warm day, and he was sweating profusely in his black onesie as his heartbeat banged against his chest like it was attending a rave with some of the other organs in his body. As he stopped and unzipped his black clothing down to the waist he noticed a bar on his side of the street called 'Finnegans' He was about to go inside when he noticed a gaggle of sorry looking dossers all sat against a wall by the entrance to Union Street Metro. There was hordes of them all sat in a neat line.

A silver-coloured butterfly started to fly and then land on everything in Macs line of vision. He tried desperately to get it to fly onto his fingers but eventually gave up. He suddenly couldn't remember what he was about to do. He looked at the bar. 'That's right' he thought to himself 'I was going to go and speak with that bunch of sorry looking individuals that were littering the pavement by the train station.'

Mac approached the people all sprawled out along the wall that led to the metro entrance. On closer inspection many were dressed in rags, and some looked like they had seen better days. He headed for the one vacant space in between a punk looking dude and what he thought was possibly a woman? It was difficult to tell as all he saw was a mass of greasy knotted hair peeking outside of a blue boiler suit. There was no face visible.

Some of the people were begging and had homemade signs. Some were blatant lies 'Vietnam Vet. Please spare some change' said one which was being held by what looked like a kid in his early twenties. Others were a little more honest 'Why Lie. I Wanna Get High' read another. Mac's favourite was 'Give me the Fucking Money' by someone wearing a Geldof mask.

'This looked like a nice way to spend the afternoon' thought Mac as he made another grab for the fluttering silver butterfly. 'Fuck cultural attractions, this is the real life right here in this town' he added as an afterthought.

Mac approached the punk. The punk got excited as Mac got closer as he thought he was going to click for some money. His hopes were soon dashed as Mac asked by nodding at the gap if he could join him in the vacant space next to him to beg.

"It's a free country dude." Said the punk. "By the way. My names Cody dude."

The Dutch Courage bassist dropped to the floor and immediately set about removing his shoes and socks. He then spotted a nearby discarded drink cup and got up and retrieved it. Mac still hadn't spoken a word. He suddenly felt cold and zipped his onesie back up and pulled the hood up to cover his head.

"I'm Mac." Mac finally said to Cody after a few minutes. "Am I doing this right?" "Well, what you trying to do dude?" asked Cody. "Beg. I'm begging,

begging for a better life, yeah?" "You need a sign dude to attract attention. Put something honest and heart-warming on it dude. Say why you are doing this man; dude are you really homeless? You look too clean dude." Cody then had a strong waft of excrement and margarine come from Mac's direction. "I'm not sure Cody?" replied Mac. Cody reached into a dirty brown backpack that he was using as a cushion and fished out some grubby paper and a sharpie. "Here dude. Use this." He said as he offered the items to Mac. Mac took them and began to scrawl out his own beggars notice. 'Will Fuck for Crack' read Macs sign.

For the next hour Mac sat with his head bowed which was covered by his hood as his white feet began to obtain a degree of sunburn. He also collected many insults, three French fries, a free bus ticket to leave the area along with the sum of eighteen cents from the commuters who had been coming and going into Union Street Metro.

All of a sudden a hand tapped Mac on the shoulder. He looked up to see a woman, dressed head to toe in black. She had spiky dyed yellow hair and a huge smear of the brightest green snot that Mac had ever seen across her face. It must have been there a good while as it had set. "Excuse me but you are in my spot" said Yellow Hair in a polite soft-spoken voice. "Huh?" responded Mac. Yellow hair spoke again in mellow, quiet tones. "Excuse me Sir, but you are in my spot. I normally sit here." she said again whilst pointing indicating to the position Mac was sitting in. Mac immediately jumped up to his feet "Well where have you been? I've been here for well over an hour." Yellow Hair took a step back but wasn't fazed by Macs outburst and nor did any of the other homeless people look over or even bat an eyelid. She continued to address Mac. "I've been on my break." Mac chortled before letting loose a maniacal laugh, and then he launched into a tirade at Yellow Hair . "On a break, on a break, on a fucking break, you're a fucking beggar, you aint got time to take a fucking break." Mac moved away from the wall and kicked his collecting cup to the floor and by doing so its bounty scattered around the floor close to the feet of the woman who looked like she had just returned from her half days holiday break.

The disgruntled and heavily out of it British bass player began to shuffle away from the street people when Cody walked after him. "Hey Dude. Are you fucking high or what? What's your story man? You should not be an asshole but be kind to these people dude, some of them have not got shit right. Do you get that. You know some of these crazy mother fuckers will do anything for money." Mac stopped dead in his tracks and turned to face Cody. "Yes Cozy, I'm high as a kite, what was the other question?"

Cody opened his mouth to repeat his speech when Mac continued "These people will do anything for money you said? Piss off." "Dude, what the fuck, where do you get off. Trust me. Some of these poor bastards haven't got a choice man. They live on the street." Cody then beckoned over a small guy who he had addressed as Noah who had been sat by broken billboard which was displaying a torn yellowing poster which judging by the age and state of it had advertised a since long finished double header concert of bands called 'Thrill City' and 'The Deploied' at somewhere called Sidney and Orpah's House, in the East Bay.

Noah slowly limped over. He was dressed in a once white dirty tee shirt, two right footed flip flips (Maybe that accounted for the limp? But there was no need to ham it up I wasn't from the Welfare thought Mac) and green shorts that had more holes in them than a Stephen Seagull action movie script. Cody addressed the newcomer. "Dude, tell this man what you will do for ten bucks homes?" Noah looked Mac up and down before answering. "I do anything for ten dollar."

Mac's head was now spinning. He wasn't sure what to do, he should in truth have just walked away from the conversation. What he definitely shouldn't have done was unzip his onesie and piss in the drinks cup that only moments ago was being used to collect his begging donations.

Mac held the cup aloft to the sky like he had won a trophy. It was the one trophy you honestly didn't want to drink the spoils of victory from. Inside the cup was a full to the brim amber coloured shade of strong urine. A nice froth had also formed, and a couple of pubic hairs had dislodged around the rim of the cup for good measure. "Drink this Noah and you just made yourself ten bucks" offered Mac with a huge shit eating grin as he waited for Noah to drink his piss. "Lemme see the green comrade" replied Noah. Mac fumbled in his bum bag and pulled out a couple of fives. Noah reached forward and grabbed the cup from Mac and bolted the drink down as if was a hot Mojito. Mac handed over the money as Noah was wiping away the remnants of the drink from his lips. He hadn't even flinched whilst knocking it back. He laughed and shouted "I would have done that for five" as he snatched the money from Mac then continued to walk away; destination unknown. Mac turned on his heels to depart from the scene himself.

Cody shouted after him. "Hold up dude. You want some company in getting fucked up in this town, I'm with you dude. I know all the holes." Mac stopped in his tracks, turned, and beckoned Cody to join him.

The two staggered around the streets, trying to avoid any police and the countless number of irritating joggers that were about. To Mac it was like completing some Olympic slalom event just to get a bloody drink.

Whilst sat in 'The Hip Joint' Cody assessed his meal ticket as he took his time with the latest booze that Mac had supplied him with. It looked the same colour as the one he had paid street guy Noah to drink but thankfully this one was ice cool. "Man, dude, you got green, so what are you doing hanging out with us bums?" Mac just shrugged and then put his hands in his trouser pockets. Within moments he had located and placed the small plastic bag with a couple of pills left inside it onto the bar table. "Fuck man. What is that shit? Do you wanna get high or higher? Ok dude, I'm in all the way. Let's get twisted brother. Let me show you the sights and how this town can eat you whole dude ha-ha!"

Mac used the beer to aid him necking his third tab of the day, not that the effects of the other brace still rocking and a rolling in his system had yet worn off. Cody popped his after a long stay in the 'Bathroom' Which was American for the toilet, and bizarrely didn't feature a bath in it. Whilst he was in there he also proceeded to give himself a bit of a wash in the sink.

The pills soon hit their mark and were quicker working this time, and both guys were soon living in a parallel universe to everyone else around them. Cody and Mac left the bar and went walkabout in San Francisco. They made their way down Fell Street which proved to be quite apt for Mac as he tumbled over a huge bag of discarded trash that had been left on the sidewalk and gashed his elbow. Some nearby young kids laughed, Mac just picked himself up and called them 'Wee cunts' in a loud mock Scottish accent before aping the actions of a chimpanzee and then charged at them making monkey noises.

The pair of them continued to head in a south-western direction along Market Street. They passed by the anarchist book stall. Mac retreated and went inside. Behind the counter was a young man dressed in green army camo trousers, red neckerchief, and a Che Guevara tee shirt. "Oi. Have you got Mr Angry Anarchist by Roger Hargrove?" yelled Mac laughing at his own weak joke. He hadn't even got the authors name correct. Using the surname of Hargreaves might have made his Mister Men joke move one percent funnier.

"We don't sell books that use pro-nouns like that" replied Mr Che Red Neckerchief.

Mac left the shop in hysterics but confused as the Yank and Brit ambled to the end of Market Street which then turned onto Haight Street, and the area of Haight Ashbury, the once drug, and hippy counterculture capital of the United States.

"Where the fuck we going dude? Isn't it time for another beer?" Cody mentioned, his own voice to him sounding as if he was ten feet underwater. Mac ignored him and continued walking in a haphazard style with no direction. He turned down a small road which was actually a dead end. Sat at the end of the road just in front of a number of trash cans, some of which were lying upturned with garbage spilling out onto the sidewalk was a man. This was no ordinary man. This guy was sat alone on the rubbish strewn pavement in the double cross position. IE He was sat with his arms and walking pins both cross legged.

This guy looked like he was going for the standard Jesus look as he was sporting a long thin black beard to go alongside his long dark lank and greasy hair. The one thing he had in contrast to JC was that our lord and saviour never wore denim dungarees. Out in front of the Buddha like positioned Christ was another handwritten sign (San Francisco loved a handwritten sign) and to the left of that was a dusty looking baseball hat that had the words 'Forty Niner' emblazoned on it. Mac approached the guy for a closer inspection.

The sign in front of the guy who didn't move, speak, or even acknowledge Mac's presence simply stated, 'ABUSE ME FOR A DOLLAR' Mac was ready to play and inserted a dollar coin into the hat, and then broke out into the infamous English football chant of "You're shit, and you know you are, you're shit, and you know you are, you're shit, and you know you are, you're shit, and you know you are." Mac then doubled up laughing. By now Cody, who had been slightly hesitant in following Mac down what looked suspiciously like ambush alley had caught up and joined the chuckling Brit.

Mac reached into his pocket and this time pulled out a green note. You could just make out the crumpled features of Abraham Lincoln as the money dropped down into the hat. Mac was going to take his time over this put down. He stared intently at the man still sat stock still on the floor. He hadn't moved or even blinked as far as either of the drugged-up duo could ascertain. Mac knew he had to make this count. He tried to dredge his memory bank for something suitable. It took several seconds but then he had it. He took a step or two backwards realising that he needed to take a run up for this particular put down. He cleared his throat, spat out the contents onto the floor, then looked at his victim front on, glassy eye to eye. Mac then commenced his four-pace dash forward towards the man sat still on the floor. Left foot forward, right foot forward, left foot forward then right foot forward and he was there in position to deliver another bit of prose from the world of football. "OoooooooooooooooooooooooohhhhhhhhhhhhhhhhhhhhhhhH, You're shit, AAAAAGGGGhhhhhhhhhhhhhhhhhhhhhhhhhhhhhhhhhhhhhh!" yelled Mac bringing his head to a stop two inches from the seated guys nose.

The man on the floor was still unmoved. Cody backed away as if this was some kind of voodoo. He had literally no idea what was going on? Was this really happening or just a figment of his imagination thanks to the pill that he had necked over an hour or so ago.

Mac was perplexed. This guy couldn't be human. He was vigorously checking his bum bag and available pockets for more change or small notes to have another ago when a fourth man came out of nowhere and joined proceedings. He must have been watching events unfold from nearby.

The fourth man had a shaved head and handlebar moustache. He was wearing a blue Gingham style shirt which was tucked into short blue jeans. His look was completed with red braces and oxblood coloured monkey boots. His arms bulged thanks to huge biceps. He didn't look like the type to fit in with the areas hippy clientele.

"You're doing it all wrong" said the fourth man to who-ever was listening to him as he flexed and stretched his fingers. He then cracked his knuckles and released the nitro bubbles in them which sounded more like gun shots.

The fourth man then dipped his hand into his back pocket and brought out a tanned wallet. Cody stared intently and began to quiver as he saw the bulge of notes contained within. The fourth man opened his wallet and selected a ten spot. He returned his wallet to its original starting position with his left hand and then folded the crisp ten-dollar bill in half, bent down and placed it inside the crusty cap to join the other collection of coins and notes that were already in there.

He took a step back from the guy still sitting in the street who after all this time still hadn't even moved or acknowledged anyone present or said a solitary word. The fourth man then clenched and unclenched his fists, took the one step back from his original starting position and then moved forward quickly and punched Jesus in denim Dungarees square in the face four times in lightening quick succession.

By the third punch the static Jesus was rocked and had blood spurting out of a now wonky looking nose. He still hadn't made a noise though. After punch four had landed, The fourth man addressed a stunned Cody and Mac. "That's what he means by abusing him. You get it? And that's how you do it." The skinhead looked down at the bleeding Jesus and spoke. "See you tomorrow Brody" Mr Skinhead then turned on his air wear heels and left the scene.

Mac and Cody didn't want to hang about either. Cody had lived on the streets of San Francisco for years, but this had creeped him the fuck out. "Let's get out of here dude" he remonstrated to Mac whilst tugging vigorously on his arm as Mac stood spellbound at the scene he had just witnessed.

Cody pulled on Mac's arm again and finally managed to get him to move along thanks to the distant sounds of police sirens.

"Fuck this voodoo shit dude, let's get a drink homes. You know what I'm saying? This is way too creepy for me down here. Come on let's go bananas."

To Mac, things were already going bananas, but not in the sense that Cody meant. Bananas was actually a happening bar and club down in the Chinatown area of the city.

The sun was now going down on Frisco Bay and the vibrant scurry of the regular Joe and holiday makers on the street was slowly being replaced by a completely different kind of person. The street people, hustlers, gang bangers and dealers were now prevalent everywhere as tourists, shoppers and workers had slowly disappeared. It was if Cody and Mac had somehow travelled to a completely different city.

Mac and Cody were now looking for somewhere to have a drink before hitting their final destination of this mad day which had taken a turn for the worse in Haight Ashbury for both the bassist and the homeless hobo.

"So, bro dude, what do you do when ya not pretending to be homeless homes?" asked Cody. Mac burst out into laughter. He wasn't sure what he did or why he was even in the god damn state or country. After some deep-rooted thinking he had an answer for the punk dosser. "Oh, yeah, I'm a musician. I play the bass. Yes that's it. I'm a mean mother bass-tard from the planet Muso. Rings, rings, I got rings on my fingers. I'm here to play bass bro mate."

Cody hadn't been paying proper attention and only partly heard what Mac had said. "You play basketball?" Mac put him straight. "A musician." Oh, bro dude, that's super awesome man, totally rad punk rock dude." Cody started throwing the horns and peace signs as if it was some kind of musician solidarity.

The pair had been sauntering around the busy road and could have picked anywhere to drink but they settled on a small bar they saw down an alleyway called 'The Rusty Nail.'

Cody was instructed to order the drinks as Mac needed to visit the bathroom, washroom or whatever other name the locals had for toilet.

Mac strode towards the corridor where the toilet / bathroom was situated. He hadn't noticed that the smattering of people gathered in the bar were all male.

He reached the facilities which were behind two red painted doors. Red door to the left had a picture of a cartoon head of a cock which to Mac indicated the male side as the equally red graffitied door directly next to it had the cartoon picture of maybe a hen on it? Was it a hen? Mac dithered about which side to go. He looked at the pictures again. Yes the door to the right was a hen, maybe after it had been hit by a tractor, but he was sure it was a hen though it was a tough call. Mac grabbed the door handle to the left and expected it to open and lead to urinals and cubicles. What he hadn't expected was it to open directly into the bog and him to have to witness a half-naked man pleasuring himself in what was a single occupancy toilet. The man stopped what he was doing and turned to Mac with his stork on. "Finally. I didn't think anyone was going to come and give… me… a… hand…" he said as he looked down at his erect penis. Mac slammed the door shut and hot footed it as fast as his body would allow back to where Cody was sat, just as two halves of some brew were placed upon beer mats at their table by a waiter. Mac staggered back, red faced and picked up both drinks and necked the brace instantly. "We're leaving NOW." He shouted a little too abruptly at Cody.

The two men exited the bar, with shouts of protest coming from behind them as they had failed to pay for their alcohol as Cody had set up a tab.

It was now hours past the meeting time that Mac had agreed to meet up with the rest of the band and tour manager Guy Ropes down at Wharf 39, along the Bay sea front. Countless text messages and calls had been put into Mac's mobile phone that he had been given to use for the tour and all had gone unanswered. The reason for that was that the phone was still ringing out sat on the small table next to Mac's bed in the hotel room which was the direction the other four men who had been waiting for Mac were now heading.

Guy Ropes was not a happy bunny. In fact, he was raging, but his military training didn't let it show. Deep down he knew that Mac and Leonard were the two on tour that could not be trusted to stay out of trouble or do as they were told. He had got John Leonard onboard and now realised he had made a schoolboy error of judgment by not insisting that McCarthy got his arse out of bed that morning and joined the others for the days excursions.

The other three members of the touring party had been good as gold and had even enjoyed the boat trip around the Bay and all the other tourist locations that they had visited as far as he could tell. Now It was time to get back to the Renoir Hotel and locate the missing man who was most definitely in action.

Guy Ropes' walk turned more into a march. 'Hup two, three, hup two, three' he called out to himself more than anything as the band members hurried back the way of their digs looking like a small platoon out on manoeuvres.

Mac had of course lost all track of time, reality and more or less his mind. Mac meanwhile was happy to follow Cody to where-ever he suggested and more importantly for Cody for him to pay for everything they did.

As they sauntered along a busy street they both heard a heavy metal version of Abbas "Dancing Queen" penetrate the air and they both followed the sound to a bar called 'The Fuzz Buzz'

Up on a small stage which was situated about a foot off the ground were four figures dressed in white suits that were splattered in blood with a huge banner behind them declaring that the band were called 'Abattoir.' "I like the look of this joint" said Mac stretching his head around the place at the door. "This joint looks even better dude" laughed Cody as he held a perfect freshly rolled number in front of Macs nose. 'Wow' thought Mac. 'How did he manage to roll it so good?' If Mac's mind weren't already blown by a heady mix of drugs and alcohol then seeing a perfectly rolled spliff without dirtying the papers by a dirty street guy who sported peeling, half stuck plasters on some of the fingers of his right hand and a blood-stained bandage wrapped around his left hand most certainly would have done.

Cody and Mac staggered up to the bar. Mac got the attention of the bar keep. "Hey up chap. I want something strong. What do you suggest?" The bar keep turned around and pointed at a list of shots that were clearly marked on a blackboard. "Well for you friend. I would recommend the Kennedy shot. It'll take your head clean off." Four Kennedy's were duly ordered and consumed.

In the next bar 'The Handsome Knave" Mac suddenly remembered something that Cody had said a couple of hours back. "Cozy, you said something about bananas." Cody lifted his head off the bar table his eyes drooping as slobber dripped down his chin. "Yeah dude, bro. You got the greenbacks homes? I got no bread, no wad, no cheese you know. You got the clams to spot me til I get some cheddar of my own? You need bacon to go Bananas, yeah? But dude, I assure you if we can make it there you will have the life of your mother fucking time. It's just I'm struggling homes. Me got no coin." Mac turned to face his newfound punk friend. "What the fuck did you just say? You haven't had any money all day. But It's all right. Get us there. I've got something that I think I can use to gain us access." Current drinks were downed, and onward plans were hatched.

Back at the Renoir Hotel Macs phone had long since been discovered in his shared room. Other than getting Poirot on the case it was going to be a case of playing the waiting game for Martin McCarthy to reappear. A plan of action was made, and drinks were ordered in the hotel bar. "So where are you when I need you Mr Orange?" John muttered to himself as he took a seat and then a sip on his 'Orgy on the Beach' cocktail. (So called as it contained four shots of all ingredients to 'Sex on the Beach')

Back out on the streets, Cody and Mac sidestepped ladies of the night, pimps, and the hustlers to join the bohemian throng walking the length of Valencia Street. Mac momentarily lost Cody but then somehow picked him out of a crowd. He stopped moving forward and retraced his steps. Cody seemed to have acquired another rather long cigarette and was sucking the life out of it with the velocity one might expect of some person removing poison from a loved one after a venomous snake bite.

Mac took the bifter baton from Cody who couldn't even smile at this stage, but the passing of the joint had been something that the US Olympic relay team would have been proud of. Mac took a deep toke of the sweet-smelling herb and almost immediately regretted it. He instantly coughed frantically as his limbs began to feel heavy, and he became lethargic and confused. He hadn't put anything other than some chips into his digestive system all day and the ones he had consumed had been a bone of contention. Mac had become annoyed and complained aggressively when the portion of chips ordered earlier in some random bar had been delivered cold, when he really wanted something hot. Despite everyone in the transaction speaking English,

Mac received what he would have described back in Britain as crisps. He hadn't noticed at first and had even poured a gallon of vinegar all over them.

The lack of solid food meant that the smoke had quickly bypassed his digestive system in record time and had joined the race with the alcohol and LSD in his bloodstream as to what was going to put him down to sleep for the day. So far, Mac was just about holding his own.

Before vagrant and bassist knew it, the cigarette was down to the grubby roach. "Where now Columbus?" asked Mac. "It, it, it, it, it's not far dude. St, st, stay close homes. It's getting busy tonight." Tonight, was just about to turn into tomorrow.

Despite the fact that Cody and Mac looked like they had come straight from the drunk tank, the two bouncers at the single door of an innocuous looking twin storey building stood aside to let the pair in after Macs credit card payment had been accepted. He hadn't expected to have to sign his name on any bills. They had stopped that kind of caper in Europe.

It had taken two attempts. The first looked nothing like his name and on closer viewing the cashier had told him that he had just written something that read RATIN FART instead of Martin McCarthy. Mac lifted his glasses up onto the top of his sunburnt and freckled head. The sale was cancelled, and he tried again, this time getting somewhere closer to the correct looking signature that looked like a dead spider that was scrawled on the back of his card.

With entry to 'Bananas' secured the duo slowly made their way up the stairs to where Mac could hear the dim sound of a Hammond keyboard coming from.

They opened the grey double doors, and some bright rainbow coloured flashing lights welcomed them inside. Mac looked around and could see again a mostly male clientele sat scattered around the venue.

Cody picked a seat for them close to the front of the stage and the two men slumped down into hard seats. Cody just burst out into spontaneous laughter when a waiter dressed as a bunny girl joined them. She looked at Cody, but he just pointed at Mac. By now the piano-based music had stopped. Mac looked up at the woman who had repeated the words "Can I take your order?" In Macs mind all he saw before him was a large white rabbit in pink hot pants.

"T, T, two beers" he stuttered waving a peace sign at her just in case she hadn't heard.

The waitress was back with the beers in a flash. "You're a long way from home. Are you British?" Mac nodded as Valerie Kobe Chung the waitress plonked the two green bottles on the beer-soaked table. "You want a tab?" Mac nodded again, as Cody moved slowly to pick up his bottle just in case it disappeared. "You from London?" Another nod from Mac. The waitress continued to make small talk. "I thought so. I got a friend there. Her name is Maggie Hall. Do you know her? " This time Mac shook his head. "Oh, I love the way you guys say spoon over there. Can you say spoon for me? Just one little spoon. Come on. I find it so sexy." Mac tried to oblige but the word kept coming out wrong. 'Moon' had been the closest he had got to it after a couple of false starts, which considering the state of him, was not bad as he had only been a couple of letters out.

The lights suddenly dimmed, and the waitress took this as her cue to leave. A man wearing a Tuxedo strolled onto the stage. "Hey, how's my people?" he shouted down the microphone. 'It's a mic not a yoghurt pot' thought Mac before the silver butterfly which had been missing for the last few hours returned and landed on his nose. He tried to remove it and flick it away which to onlookers looked like he was slapping himself in the face.

Mr Tux continued to tell a few lame jokes and ended his last one with the punchline "So I said do these genes make me look fat?" He then asked how his people were once more before going on to ask for a big hand for "Wendy" A large African American woman bounded onto the stage as naked as the day she was born. She already looked like she had large hands and everything else.

"Banana's, say we going to have a good time tonight?" A slight mumble of agreement went up from the meagre crowd. She started to repeat her opening line more slowly.

"A-R-E W-E G-O-I-N-G" before stopping for a moment as she had run out of breath "…. To have a good time tonight?" A slightly better cheer went up.

Wendy then went into some spiel about needing some musical accompaniment for her act. This was the only time in the last five hours that Cody suddenly came alive and began to shout. "Here, this dude. He's in a band" The spotlight was turned on Cody who was pointing out Mac who just sat in his chair gormlessly smiling.

The onstage performer left the stage and ventured out in the crowd where she grabbed Mac by the hand and with one yank pulled him straight out of his seat. "Come on sugar. I need you to keep the beat for me tonight." Mac slightly stumbled behind Wendy back onto the stage. As she let go of his hand she bent down to pick something up that was partially hidden behind a chair but kept it hidden behind her large back. Mac somehow stopped himself from falling down in a heap. Wendy was now holding the microphone in one hand and teasing the crowd about something held behind her back in the other. She turned to Mac. "So handsome, what's your name?" Mac suddenly had a mental block. What was his name? He tried to remember it but couldn't so said the name of a distant friend he had. "Graham, Graham Pinder" "Yes honey. GraHAM (Big emphasis was made on the Ham part of the false name by Wendy) What a lovely name. GraHAM Pinner. Let's have a round of applause please for GraHAM. Ok GraHAM sugar, I need your help here tonight." By now Mac had broken out with sweats and shivers as carnal visions of what he might be expected to perform entered his mind. "I hear from your friend that you are a musician?" Mac suddenly looked like a rabbit caught in the headlights. He was quickly put out of his misery as Wendy presented him with a set of bongo's that she had in her hand behind her back. She then placed the mic back on its stand and lowered it, so it was at the height of Macs waist. She then pulled the lone chair from the back to the front of the stage and sat on it legs akimbo. "Play for me GraHAM" she demanded.

Mac looked out into the darkness and could only make out the shape of one man who's arm was moving quickly across his body to his groin area. Wendy had now picked up a over ripe banana and was putting a condom over it. She turned her attention back to Mac. "Play something sugar" Mac started to hit the bongos as the banana disappeared from sight into the performers vagina which for Mac was thankfully hidden by midriff flesh.

Mac was now sweating so much that he thought he was hyperventilating but being a good bassist as he was he had locked into a decent beat. Wendy had finished inserting the banana and had peeled it and stuffed it in Mac's mouth. The crowd had tittered.

A tall balding thin white man had now ventured onto the stage, and he had been introduced as 'Mr Brillo' He was ugly as sin but packing more tackle than a fishing retailer.

A once cream coloured mattress which was now filthy and stained had been dragged onstage and Brillo and Wendy had started to engage in sex acts upon it. Mac was still playing the bongos and had tried to play "Ebony and Ivory" as the duo bonked each other lovelessly.

It was the following morning and John Leonard was sat alone having breakfast at the Renoir Hotel where there was still no sign of the missing Dutch Courage bassist. All of a sudden he was joined at the table by the spirit of Baz Oakes AKA Mr Orange.

"You called mate?" The ghost said. I rubbed my eyes. It was true then, the visions I kept having were real. I looked around the dining area to ensure that nobody was in earshot, but I still kept my voice low "I called on you last night Baz. Where on earth have you been? Mac is missing." Mr Orange laughed. "It doesn't work like that John. You can't just summon me." He responded. "Then what is the point of you appearing now?" I asked. Orange looked directly at me. "Look this is a trip of a lifetime for me as well you know, and I intend we all enjoy it after what happened last time I went away somewhere with you." (Orange mimed the slitting of his throat to indicate death) John Leonard nodded and looked around again to see if anyone else in the hotels dining area was paying him any attention. "So, this is really happening. You are here. You are really here? Why now? And where were you when I needed you?" whispered John. "Ok, ok, if you must know I was at Stamford University hanging around the girls showers in the changing rooms. After that I materialised at a porn shoot in Silicon Valley. They can raise the dead there all right. Can you fault me for that?"

John shook his head with a smirk. "No, but it's our first US gig ever tonight, and Mac is fucking AWOL. Can you not help at all?" Orange pondered before answering. "Get me an item of his clothing and I will see what I can do."

"That's what sniffer dogs use." I said just a little too loudly, but Orange had disappeared again, and I was left with two casually dressed potential holiday makers on the next table looking at me gone out.

That same morning over at Skid row, in a ramshackle tent community by an underpass, Martin McCarthy was passed out sound asleep, having torn his favourite onesie and lost his bum bag, watch and glasses. His feet were bloodied and red raw from walking bare foot all day/night and there seemed to be no chance of him waking up anytime soon. The only thing he had left in his pocket was a keyring with the logo of somewhere called 'Bananas' on it.

Mac had now been missing for over twenty-four hours and 'Dutch Courage' had to meet their tour partners 'Frog Splash' and soundcheck for their first Stateside gig at 3PM. Guy Ropes was contemplating ringing law enforcement to report Mac as a missing person.

On the last tour Dutch Courage had done in Europe in 1999, Mac had turned up to go on the road having forgotten to bring his bass which other than his passport was the only thing he really needed to remember. Twenty years on and this time the band had lost the actual bassist, or more to the point he had somehow lost himself. The curse of Dutch Courage was again rearing its head.

There was no leads. (Guitar pun intended) I sat alone pondering what could have happened to him as the steam from my coffee rose into the ether. No-one had seen him or had any idea where on earth he had got to. For all anyone knew he could be lying somewhere with a bullet in his head. But of course, that was worst case scenario. I'm sure he was still alive, I could sense it, or surely Mr Orange would have bumped into his spirit one assumed on the 'other side.' Still, the show must go on.

'Slims Music Hall' was a grand old red brick building in the Tenderloin area of San Francisco. It had been hosting gigs for bands who could or thought they could pull twelve hundred souls to it since the sixties.

Despite the fact that Martin 'Mac' McCarthy was still Absent Without Leave, Guy Ropes, wanted to set a good example and ensure his charges were at the scheduled band meet at the venue for 3PM. 'Dutch Courage' and their entourage would be in the company of headline band 'Frog Splash' and annoying one hit wonder 'Chelsea Bird' for the next eleven days as they traversed states, hit five cities, played eight gigs, and travelled across country with them.

The tour itinerary had been clearly laid out.

Day 1 – Gig. Slims Music Hall, San Francisco, CA.

Day 2 – Travel Day

Day 3 – Day Off / Meet with Nobbled Knee Management

Day 4 – Gig. The Bourbon Chorus, Los Angeles, CA.

Day 5 – Gig. The Bourbon Chorus, Los Angeles, CA.

Day 6 – Gig. The Bourbon Chorus, Los Angeles, CA.

Day 7 – Gig. Rock Box, San Diego, CA.

Day 8 – Airport / Travel Day.

Day 9 – Gig. Club Fusion, Boston, MA.

Day 10 – Gig. BCBE, New York, NY

Day 11 – Gig. Argyll Plaza, New York, NY

Day 12 – Airport / Home

John Leonard was sat in the back of a white people carrier. What did we know about the band and future touring partners 'Frog Splash?' he thought to himself once again whilst also scanning the streets through his transport window for any sight of the unaccounted bass player.

The answer about the Frogs was nothing more than he had already found online. Just that they had been a bit of a deal twenty years ago when they caused something of a splash (Pun intended again) on the rock scene with debut album 'Mandible Claw' (Whatever that meant) They were fronted by two lead singers who had also both been pro wrestlers for 'The Wrestling Association Troupe' (T.W.A.T) Promotion, but both had since found God and religion. There was far less information to be found on the internet for one of their two singers, the one who answered to the name of 'Budge.' For this guy you couldn't even find any mention of his real name, whilst the other singer Walt Donker had streams of info about his personal life and the several released solo albums put out during the last two decades. He sadly hadn't had much success to write home about though.

We arrived in good time at the venue and had loaded our gear in and were sat in the designated waiting area along with fellow ex-pat 'Chelsea Bird' who had arrived with his band (A backing tape) in his backpack. We patiently awaited the arrival of our touring partners and their 'Nobbled Knee Inc' management who wanted to talk to us / Lay some ground rules.

Just as I was about to go to the toilet in they all strolled, looking like they expected applause from us. They even had brought a hype man who was carrying a portable handheld mic. He didn't even say hello to any of us before he sprang into action. "Ladies (There wasn't any…yet, but Chelsea was working on it) and Gentlemen (Debatable), back in the house for the first time in over twenty years, please go bat shit crazzzzeeee fooooorrrrrr, (He was now on his knees) the band that the Gods broke the mould making, the venue filling, top billing, bone shaking, history making, men who swapped the Suplex for spandex, the one and the definitely only, yessssssss everyone it's….FROG SPLASH' (The hype man fell forward from his on knee position into a heap)

A motley collection of guys who were much older than I thought they would be shuffled into the room. Guy Ropes burst into applause and looked at us to do the same thing, which of course we half-heartedly did.

Then a much younger geezer stepped forward and picked up the handheld mic from the clammy hand of the prone hype man. He looked around the room, beamed a fifty grand smile and then began to address us as the older guys who I assumed were the band went over to a table (That had a 'Reserved' sign placed on it) that was situated in the corner of the room and started opening ice cold bottles of water that looked quite inviting. We, however, weren't offered any. Some Christians huh!

The young guy looked at us as we in turn looked at him. He was wearing a blue Hawaiian shirt that was adorned with bright yellow flowers, straight cut blue jeans, brown leather shoes, and introduced himself as Mister Joshua Hoffman, the Frog Splash manager. He then in turn made the introductions of the band. As each name was read out, Arlo Carter on drums, Virgil Banta on bass, Rick Troutbeck on guitar, Keeler Rockpantz, drums and your boys Budge and Walt Donker on vocals, the requisite band member waved nonchalantly. Some even waved with their backs to us. The band even had their own Doctor who was introduced as the brilliantly monikered 'Medical Bill.'

Hoffman then more or less proceeded to read us the ten commandments for being around 'Frog Splash' during the tour. For example, there was to be no swearing in their presence. He, and the band would appreciate us using alternatives like ''Sugared Hot Iced Tea' instead of S,H,I, and T. 'What the fuck!' I thought to myself. It seemed that Walt and Budge had apparently seen the light in recent years and had become committed Christians, so Hoffman spent over fifteen minutes telling us that we mustn't have alcohol in their presence, drugs were out, and absolutely no groupies were to be allowed backstage. There was also to be no blaspheming. After removing those options, I couldn't really see a reason to be out here. It was also revealed that the tour was in support of their new forthcoming album "Jesus Wept" which ironically were the first words that came out of my mouth after Hoffman had finished his speech. I raised my hand and asked if partaking in a round of golf would be ok? But the sarcasm in my question was lost in translation. "I'll get back to you John, you are John aren't you, is that all right?" Asked Hoffman. Yes I was John. Mad fucking John. Not John the Baptist but John the angry Bastard. The Gooch had stitched us up like kippers. Again! What fun was this going to be on tour with a bunch of dull boring God botherers.

By now (Early afternoon) Martin 'Mac' McCarthy had woken up and was feeling like a broken man. He had no shoes or socks and had little recollection of what had happened the previous night and worse, had no idea where he was or what time it was either. He already knew that he had no money but thankfully his credit card was somehow still in his inside onesie pocket. He knew he had something to do today, but that could wait until after he vomited. Barf!

All Mac could see through half-closed eyes was miles of roads and concrete white bridges. How had he ended up here? Where was his pal from last night, he couldn't quite recall how the night ended. The instrument of the bongos kept flashing before his eyes. What did that mean? He could just remember someone lighting a fire for warmth as it got cold. Again, he tried to fathom out where on earth was he? Also back was a niggling thought in his brain that he had something extremely important to do today, but that could also wait until he vomited again. Double barf!!

Mac eventually sobered up enough and prepared to leave Skid row on foot. He had now recalled he had a gig to perform today, though he couldn't swear to it. "Which way to the city?" he asked this crazed looking woman who was sat stroking a child's toy dolls head of hair with her fingers. She looked at him and smiled a toothless smile and reached down for a teethless hairbrush and started to brush the dolls hair again instead of answering him.

A lone voice with a heavy accent penetrated the sound of the roaring cars that were flying by on the freeway. "Quieres la ciudad?" Mac turned around to see an old Latino male who was wearing a once yellow T-Shirt that proclaimed 'Money Can't Buy Happiness' sat on a rock. 'Money couldn't buy happiness, that's true thought Mac, but it could buy you a way out of this hellhole.

"La ciudad es por ahi mi amigo" the Latino said as he pointed left. Mac hadn't got a clue what he was saying but decided to follow the pointing finger, just after he had ralphed up for a third time. Triple barf!!!

Mac looked down at his puke. 'Where was this all coming from?' he thought to himself. All he could remember eating yesterday was a peanut. There's no way he had green beans or what looked like straw amongst the technicolour yawn that he left by the cardboard bed he had used for shelter the previous night. "Fuck. I hope this isn't anyone's bed they lent me." He said to himself before he hobbled away, to try and find a way back to the city or at very least the hotel.

Mac tried his luck at hitch-hiking and reasoned that he would need a late fitness test for the gig he thought he was going to play later that night, which actually in essence was due to start in under ninety minutes.

Dutch Courage hit the stage at Slims Music Hall at precisely 8PM sans le bass. The venue was only half full when they played and that was as good as it got attendance wise all night.

Post gig and John Leonard and Brandon Slam were sat backstage in their dressing room, when Frog Splash's Doctor 'Medical Bill' popped in to see the band and let them know that he enjoyed their set. "Hey guys, loved the show. Forgive me though. I've forgotten the name of the band." "Dutch Courage" answered Slam in his finest spoken English. "Ah yes, 'Duck Curry.' Love the name and it rocked balls. You know. Balls. Anyway, if any of you need a little pick me up later on in the tour." Bill tapped his right index finger to the side of his nose.

John was about to request a menu when Slam grabbed his arm. "This could be a test John. You could get us thrown off the tour."

Leonard stood up and walked the ten paces over to the Doctor who was already holding out a bag of what very much looked like amphetamines. "This is as strong as I go. Our little secret. I can also put my paws on some herbal remedies if you know what I mean, I can get you synthetic cannabinoids, methylphenidate, purple pin balls, cosmic Mother Riley's door knockers, donkey dust, piperazines, Biz bombs, liberty caps, mephedrone, propylphenidates, rubella tap dancers or a bunch of Cletus Wonk… but if you just want a long night of it, then this is the best and most efficient Billy J. Whizz this side of California. This will get your juices flowing. It'll rock your balls. Shall I set you up a tab? No drug pun intended heh-heh." Asked the medic. The Brits just stared at him open mouthed.

Fuck the ten commandments. I had come on tour for a good fucking time, and I wanted that, even though our bass player was still lost / lying dead who knew where?. Everybody gotta die sometime though. I took the bag from Bill and took the whole lot in one sitting and waited for the buzz of that choppy sour tasting white powder to kick in. I had a beer with Bill, yawned a couple of times and then made myself a cheese sandwich from the stuff on our rider as he left to check on his charges. 'A rider' I thought to myself, we had never had one with food on it before.

Bill returned as Slam exited to show support for 'Chelsea Bird' who was about to go on stage. "Have you known the band long?" I asked Bill. "Yeah I met Nathan, oh sorry Budge in San Quentin about a dozen or more years ago now." Bill immediately brought his hand up to his mouth. "Oops. I shouldn't have said that." Whispered Bill.

San Quentin. The name rang a bell. "Wasn't that a prison?" I innocently asked. "Keep your voice down. I shouldn't have had that beer. It's gone straight to my head. Loose lips sink ships brother. Yes, it was a prison, but forget you ever heard the name. You know nothing, you know less than nothing, right? I've clearly said too much. Look this is going to have to be our second secret, ok?" I nodded and didn't think much of it. "So, are you an actual Doctor then Bill?" Bill laughed shaking his head. "God no. But it sounds better than gofer Bill right? But I do take care of the medical side of things for the band. I also have the defib by the side of the stage with me at every gig. Take Budge. He's got something of a weight problem in that it, his weight, is a bit like the price of living in California, it just keeps going up massively. You know, I took him to the Doctors for a medical recently and the outcome was that he was advised to exercise more. What's good for that? He asked. Doc replied swimming, but, nah he don't like that. Running, that's just not possible in LA baby, do the math brother, so riding a bike was the number one option. He likes bikes. So, you know what he did? He went out and bought one of those motorised pedal cycles. He now goes everywhere on it thinking it's doing him some good. He just sits astride it with his legs up .That's not quite what the good Doctor had in mind for him but at least he tried you know. This Christian thing is new for all our asses. Now we have to watch our P's and Q's and all the fun of going on the road is out. But I still need to earn some greenbacks, dig? I'm about the only brother left from the old days when we use to tear it up you know. Forty date tours, fifty dates, hot chicks, HA! they needed drugs then" Medical Bill got up to leave and left me to my sandwich wondering what that was all about?

The next thing that happened to me that evening, happened about two hours after my chat with Medical Bill. I opened my eyes to see Guy Ropes shaking my arm, trying to wake me up. He had found me asleep in a chair whilst still in our dressing room as Frog Splash played. So much for Medical Bill and the best speed in California, that stuff he sold me put me to sleep and was more like slow.

Dutch drummer Nocka Izzet had just left the club to board the waiting people carrier for the return trip to the Renoir Hotel. He left via the back entrance and on making thirty paces he was approached by an attractive girl who on first glance to him looked Asian / Latino with big rosy, red lips. "Hey handsome, are you in Dutch Courage?" Nocka walked further into the light so she could she him clearly. "Y, y, y, yes miss, I, I" But as he answered Erika Puck was already retreating back into the shadows putting her hands up to her face in defence of her mistake.

As the people carrier drove us back to the hotel, Guy Ropes read us the riot act. He suspected that we had been on the booze and had been disrespectful to 'Frog Splash' somehow. I'm not sure how he came to this conclusion as I could hardly keep my eyes open.

Back at the Renoir a sheepish Martin McCarthy was found alive and well, actually that should be not so well but alive in his bed in our hotel room.

"I guess I missed the gig then?" he stated the absolute obvious as I entered the room. I would have been overjoyed to see him had I not felt so tired. I looked directly at his sunburnt face and into his bloodshot eyes "Fucking hell Mac. The last time I saw something this wrecked was Lady Di's car in France. Where the fuck have you been?. Everyone has been out looking for you. I've even seen Mr Orange, and he's been looking for you as well. I knew you weren't brown bread."

Mac glared a thousand-yard stare back at John Leonard and the word 'Fuck!' ticked over in his mind. He thought he had done a lot of drugs in the last twenty-four hours but what the hell had Leonard taken? What was this Mr Orange business' thought Mac to himself as he also struggled to keep his eyes open.

The next morning, we were leaving for Los Angeles which was a three hundred- and eighty-one-mile drive away. This blew my mind. That was about the same distance between Hungerton and bloody Scotland. We didn't have a gig scheduled for that day as 'Frog Splash' were going to be making a video at some church in Oakland to break up the journey. For Dutch Courage it was going to be two hundred and ninety-three miles along the Interstate five south. It was at this point of tour proceedings that I missed our old drummer Chester Rataski and his spicy reading matter. Reading was probably a bit too strong a statement for it; naked picture book was probably a more accurate description for his on-tour porno collection.

Chester Rataski I thought to myself again. Old big space hopper sacks himself. In a strange way I was looking forward to meeting up with him in New York. He had apparently declined the offer that Gooch sent him about taking up the Dutch Courage drum school. Then again, I suppose winning two hundred and fifty thousand dollars on the lottery helped make up his mind. The lucky bastard. Just think how many jazz mags he could buy for that. Though one thing I felt for sure was that he probably still didn't get his round in.

As Dutch Courage approached the halfway point of the bus journey to sunny Los Angeles, Macs luggage was delivered by courier to the Renoir Hotel in San Francisco where the departing party of Brits had of course left no forwarding address whatsoever.

LOS ANGELES

LIKE MANY KIDS GROWING UP in mainland Britain, the thought of seeing palm trees, constant sunshine, and endless beach babes / boys (Delete as applicable) and the legendary world renown Hollywood sign in the flesh were zero. These things might as well be on Mars. Never did this boy from Hungerton ever think that he would one day set foot in the city of angels, the city of light, Los Angeles.

Granted our American tour had got off to a weird start having had to appear at our first gig as a threesome, but with the word threesome on my dirty mind, I began to think if that dream would happen on this tour then it would happen here, in this town right? And if it were to occur here in La La land then this time I had to make sure I got the ratio right. IE I didn't want two dicks in the scenario.

In LA we had been booked into a cheap chain of motels called the 'The Dunne Inn' The one we were staying at was situated in the San Pedro neighbourhood of Los Angeles on a three-mile-long road called Campbell Street.

San Pedro was a nice seaside area with a huge international seaport that was situated by the biggest bridge I'd ever seen that led to the city of Long Beach. But the only seamen I could think of doing some unloading didn't work down by the docks.

I looked up at the huge glowing orb in the sky as another plane was leaving a vapor trail from its recent take off and ascent into the clear sky blue from the nearby LA X Airport. Why would you want to ever leave here? I thought to myself and then when we went out to put the sweat back in, so to speak, we found out why?.... It was seven fucking dollars for a bottle of beer, (About a half pint in British money). Jesus! (Apologies to 'Frog Splash' for the use of this term) I got it. This place was as I was about to find out, damn expensive. (Apologies once again to the Frogs....)

We had been remarkably let off the leash by Guy Ropes and allowed to go out and see landmarks or go shopping with the understanding we were back at the digs for one o'clock sharp as 'Frog Splash' manager Joshua Hoffman had kindly offered to take us to a must visit vineyard in his hometown.

As we walked the streets which in turn got us a few strange looks, possibly as Mac was still wearing his bedraggled shit-stained skeleton onesie with holes in it we came across a young skinny white guy who was bizarrely wearing a black beanie to match his sun absorbing matching black tee shirt and shorts. He was stood at a street intersection with a huge sign that read 'GIANT SALE' which had a large finger pointing across the street to a clothing store that the guy was obviously working for. As we walked by him he quietly uttered the words "Giant Sale" at us. Mac stopped in his tracks and began to engage him. "But where would I keep it if I bought one? How tall are they?" Mr Beanie was utterly confused and didn't understand what Mac was getting at, so we just carried on walking and laughing at Mac's gag.

There wasn't much we could afford in the way of good clothing or any stuff until we came across a rundown Army Surplus shop called 'Chucks War house' (See what they did there?) which was situated on Burke Street. Mac needed clothes and he needed them quickly.

Now this place was the ticket. Nocka and Slam weren't interested in it and went for a boring coffee at a nearby diner called 'Chux Up,' but Mac and I ventured inside and bought some Vietnam Vet medals, US Sniper Division T-shirts, and a very apt shirt (for him) that just had the US military acronym 'FUBAR' (Which stood for 'Fucked Up Beyond All Repair' if you were wondering?) printed in bold black capitals on nice camo green nylon. I even managed to stretch to purchasing an eighties era white sailors uniform.

We thought long and hard about trying to purchase some bayonets but realised that it wouldn't look too good when they showed up on the airport X-ray. It was a nice haul anyway, and we had only spent just over one hundred bucks between us Mac was soon wearing his brand-new second-hand US army shirt and shorts.

Amazingly, 'Gus' the storekeeper even took cash. In fact, he was utterly insistent on it.

We walked back to the motel, and it was quick showers in our room for Mac and me. We then got ourselves ready for the trip out with Hoffman.

As we met up in the lobby of the motel I could hear Guy Ropes talking as I approached. I was the last one to present myself. On greeting the small, gathered touring vineyard party, I noticed that Mac and I were both wearing the same 'US Snipers 101 Division' tee shirts that we had just purchased earlier in the day. It was a quality black shirt which sported on the front of the garment a huge cartoon pigs head and a rifle with the gun crosshairs motif emblazoned on it in yellow print. Across the back, also in yellow print was the sniping division motto 'Suffer Patiently and Patiently Suffer MF.'

Joshua Hoffman pulled up in his black, 2019 plate people carrier. Our own cars back in the United Kingdom would look like roller skates in this city I thought to myself. The window to the driver's side wound down silently and Hoffman removed his dark reflective sunglasses to reveal pale blue eyes and then started to address us "Sorry I'm a bit late Guy and guys. I went to the other motel just down the block by mistake as it's a four star. I realised the error of my ways when I drove past and saw you guys stood outside here as I literally passed the Dutch Courage on the left-hand side" He snorted at his own eighties referenced 'musical' joke.

The back door to this huge car opened automatically and Hoffman spoke again. "Please get in when you're ready guys." "Come on chaps, hup two three, hup two three." Guy Ropes shouted at us.

We drove out of the city heading to the countryside. "You're going to freaking love this" an excited Hoffman had repeated over and over whilst talking to Guy Ropes who was sat in the front passenger seat which was still bizarrely for me on the right-hand side of the motor.

Our vehicle passed the tallest buildings I'd ever seen in my life, we then hit the most gridlocked traffic jam I'd ever seen but finally after a travel time of ninety minutes plus we were out in the suburbs, the LA, USA equivalent of the UK's sticks.

The automatic door to Hoffman's car was opening after his vehicle had ground to a halt at a vineyard called 'Montrose' that was situated in San Bernadino County. The sign advertising the destination indicated a twenty-dollar cover to obtain entrance which entitled the purchaser to five tastes of the different wine that was on offer. 'Five...That's not going to touch the sides I thought to myself.' From the look on Mac's face, he too had clocked the same sign and we didn't need to be telepathic to know he too was thinking the absolute same as me.

I looked around to take it all in. The scenery was beautiful. There was acres of green space with more perennial vines planted than I could count. The grapes were either beginning to start to ripen in the sun or were ready for plucking. The west was indeed the best.

"Lead on boys" Hoffman said to Mac and me, who found ourselves at the front of the pack. We walked down a long gravel pathway towards the vineyard entrance with the paths tightly packed white stones crunching under foot as we walked. The place seemed to be doing a brisk trade.

As we approached the entrance, we could hear chatter and laughter coming from inside the wooden building structure where I assumed the tasting activity took place. As we got closer an old lady appeared by the door. She was short in stature, under five feet tall and wore a name tag that said her name was Grace. Despite the heat the name tag was fastened to a grey cardigan which was buttoned up to the fourth button of five. She was wearing said cardy over a lime-coloured frilly blouse.

Mac and I were the first to the door. We had marched on ahead of the others in excitement of getting stuck into the wine despite orders from Guy Ropes to the contrary. Grace removed herself from the wooden pine stool that she had been perched upon by the entrance. We were both clutching twenty bucks a piece entrance money.

All of a sudden Grace saluted us. "Put away your money, it's no good here, not for our brave boys off the frontline." For a brief moment I was confused, and then it dawned on me. Mac and I were both wearing 'US Army Sniper Division' tee shirts. We had a split decision to make. Option one: Tell her the absolute truth, that we had only just four hours earlier in the day bought the shirts second hand and we were for all intents and purposes holidaymakers or people on vacation. Or option two: Run with it and save us both twenty bucks. We could put on a phony American accent and blag in no doubt to the ire of Guy Ropes and Joshua Hoffman our host.

I went for option two. "Thank you Mam. No need to salute us though. We are only regular GI's back from the Nam." (I couldn't help the Nam bit) I said. Grace grabbed a hand of each of us and led us inside just as Hoffman and Ropes arrived to witness our Hollywood performances. (No Oscars forthcoming apparently) "Hey everyone. (Grace clapped her hands together) Anything our brave boys want is on the house. You hear me?" And she then presented us with a wine goblet each which looked a tad bigger than the other regulation glasses that were on display. "Scuse me Mam. That is very generous." I said to Grace. She slapped me hard on the back. "Anything you want boys. No drinks limit for my brave boys here. Have as many tastes as you care to take. Welcome to Montrose and enjoy yourselves." "Surely this place should be called Mont-rose' I joked in my best southern state put on accent. "Ha-ha what a sense of humour" laughed Grace as she clapped her hands together again. "Enjoy yourselves my brave boys" This statement was like a red flag to a bull. And was.

A taste was the equivalent to a small to medium sized glass of Vino in a standard British pub. I didn't think I liked wine, but it seemed to like me as I literally went through an A to Z of the stuff by just going down the tasting line and helping myself like the good woman Grace had said. I 'tasted' 'Alicante, Barbera, Biz Bastardo (Had to have two of those), Cabernet, Dolcetto, Fuchs, Gamay Beaujolais, Huth Noir, Kante Red, Malbec, Mahrez, Nebbiolo, Pinot Blanc, Okazaki Orange, Ranieri, Ruby, Sangiovese, Simpson Red, Syrah, Tinto Madeira, a Vardy and finished off with a Zinfandango or something or other. I then found I needed to drink water as I was becoming dehydrated quickly. Mac followed me from the letter B onwards as he discounted 'Alicante' due to the fact that it reminded him of Benidorm in Spain. A place he hated with a passion for some reason.

Guy Ropes approached us. Now I knew he was partial to a glass of wine but was he partial to having twenty-one glasses like I just had. I was all red faced and I tried to blame it on the sun. "You're undercover. There is no sun shining in here" he had quite correctly pointed out. "How many have you had Leonard two, three?" he asked me. "Cups, two, three, no Four" I lied.

I looked around to see Nocka asking if he could get a Coke or at the very least some sparkling water. Brandon Slam and Joshua Hoffman were in conversation, and I noticed Slam was taking swallows of the grapey nectar and was swilling the wine around his chops and then spitting it into a bucket. Not sure what that was all about? Total waste though. I hoped they didn't recycle.

Mac too was beginning to get in a state as he continued to neck the wine like it was OJ.

After an hour word went around that it was time for us to depart. Mac and I said our goodbyes to Grace and her wonderful staff. We had got truly annihilated for Freemans thanks to our early purchase of two eight-dollar t-shirts from the Army Surplus store. Result.

As we led the way back to the car I suddenly had some watery sick come up and fill my mouth. It was totally unexpected. My acetaldehyde levels must have become too high. My liver had decided that it couldn't cope with what I had sent down there and had voted with both feet to send some excess alcohol flying back up into my mouth.

I swilled it around in my mouth as I formulated a plan to try and get rid of it without anyone noticing.

My head started to spin. Wine is rather potent. I began to feel nauseous again. Then I had it. The idea to remove the puke and keep my manly cool. I pretended to sneeze. "Achoo" I went and stupidly moved my hand to my mouth to keep in the number of fake germs that I didn't really have in my mouth. In my mind I didn't want to give anyone influenza even though I wouldn't.

Unfortunately, this action caused the gathered vomit in my mouth to spray in a number of directions. Thankfully Nocka was the only one close enough to get a splattering. I put my hands up to apologise.

By now, we had arrived back at the car. From seemingly nowhere Joshua Hoffman had sent the electronic signal from his key fob to open the back door of his people carrier. I got in and slumped in my return seat ready for forty winks as did Mac.

The front door of the huge motor vehicle then opened remotely and Hoffman himself got in, he turned to face the two Brits in the back. "Wow. Did you enjoy that guys? Great vino I think. Ok just two more to visit."

My mind whirled. What did he just say? Hoffman started the engine with the press of a button. "Let's see what Martha's Vineyard has to offer next. Better than a foamy pint of that dark Bitty stuff you guys drink in England huh." Two more vineyards to visit. Why had no-one informed us we were going to more than one on a vineyard crawl. Mac and I were already utterly wrecked. One word entered my subconscious, and that word was 'Fuck!' Things were going to get messy.

After two more vineyard visits and exclamations of 'Holy Sugared Hot Iced Tea' Hoffman dropped us off at Santa Monica Pier. Mac and I were now as drunk as lords. Brandon wanted to leave us to have a go on some big white painted Ferris wheel whilst I made for the sandy beach to watch the sun go down. I made for a set of three vacant single white Formica chairs that I hoped were where I thought they were.

It was bizarre that someone had left three and I assumed they had been left by some distracted sun worshipper earlier in the day. The wind off the ocean was making the air feel cooler and the hairs on my arms were erect. I sat down with a bump directly onto the sand having missed chair one and looked up at the cloudless sky. How had that happened? Oh yes I was mortally drunk that's how. I got back to my feet and decided to not try seat two and picked out seat three to sit on. Typical! That wasn't really there either. Third time lucky I sat down on the one chair on the beach that was actually there. Wow, it was so comfortable.

I tilted my head back and felt sea spray across my face. I glanced around and found that I was actually now on a tugboat that was on the ocean. I looked behind me, was that starboard, no idea I was a land lubber. I knew I had got drunk earlier that day but not remembering getting on this boat was a stretch even for me.

The other lads must be on here somewhere. I called out to each of them as I walked around the small boat. I looked over the side of it and saw by the anchor that there were four faint white letters painted on it. A C R O. I was looking at them back to front. ORCA. The boat was named ORCA.

I started to shiver. It had suddenly got very cold and then something hit the boat with a great thud. Had it run aground? BANG, something struck it again, and Mac appeared on deck wearing a denim coat and shorts. "Fucking hell its cold out here" he shouted. "You're going to need a bigger coat" I called back and then I saw it, in the water, a huge white fin. Typical. It looked like it belonged to a shark. I'd had enough of water disasters in my life and could do without another one.

By now Nocka had joined us. He was pointing to the ocean and trying to say something. "Sh, Sh, Sh, sh." I pre-empted him. "Shit Nocka. Yes we are in the shit mate."

Brandon Slam appeared next and was bizarrely dressed not for a boat trip but for a magic show. He reached down into a big black top hat he was holding and produced a white rabbit from it which he promptly threw overboard. I was about to remonstrate with him when…. BANG!

I opened my eyes to find Slam and Mac dropping the chair I was asleep in from a height back onto the sand on the beach. "Wake up you prick. There's a bar up there by the Ferris wheel. Come on John youth, get it together. Let's go and have one for the road and laugh about when you put your nob in that woman's wine goblet earlier at the last vineyard. She nearly had a coronary ha-ha!"

I felt terrible and unsure of where I was for a moment as my eyes opened and I looked down and noticed the tide had come in and soaked my training shoes. I felt like some kind of Kind Canute or in this instance King Canewted.

The chair Leonard was seated in was lifted and dropped back down once again to the sand for good measure by his two band members to ensure he was wide awake.

This was no way to run a business and I learnt it took five hundred dollars from Guy Ropes to calm the woman at the vineyard down after 'Penis Grigio Gate.'

The next day was a gig day, and we were on our way across town in the people carrier to the 'Bourbon Chorus,' a venue situated on the famous or should that be notorious Hollywood Sunset Strip.

As the next three gigs were home comings of a sort for 'Frog Splash' all dates there were sold out.

We arrived at the venue, and it was everything I had hoped. It reminded me of the Tardis. It had police all over it. The place didn't look like much to see from the street but inside it was beautiful. A nice sixties style décor and even a seated area where the seats were made of crushed red velvet.

Guy Ropes who had torn a strip off us following the wine tasting debacle yesterday was watching us like a hawk. He also probably realised that his failure to control us meant that his job with 'Asteroid / Carlton Gooch' was very much on the line. Like we gave a toss. He continued to treat us as if we were in the army. He wanted us to get up early. Hit the hotel gym (If they had one) I for one and Mac for two were getting a bit sick of him.

Mac and John were both dehydrated following the big day out on the vine and for once were sticking to just drinking the water supplied in the cramped dressing room of the nights gig.

Dutch Courage played and for once everything had gone to plan. Even the crowd seemed to dig it, despite mutterings, that the crowd couldn't understand half of what the band from Australia were saying between songs and wanted subtitles or someone to sign for them.

LA gig day 2 and Mac and John are woken by an alarm call to their room for breakfast.

Mac shot straight out of bed and headed for the toilet. As I stretched, I could hear his urine hit the water and then every so often it would stop, he would then fart and then restart and sneeze. I'm sure the ferocity of the sneeze would cause him to miss the target. I made a mental note of not to walk around the toilet in just my socks.

Mac exited the bathroom with both hands placed inside his boxer shorts rearranging himself. "Can't believe how many police were knocking about that club last night. Inside and out." He said. I just yawned, and then he removed his hands from his boxer shorts and sniffed them. "But I still managed to get this." He half said, half laughed as he held up the plastic wrapper in his left hand. "Fancy some breakfast dear boy?" "Whoa, where did you get that you sly bastard?" I asked of him. "Like the good Colonel of fried chicken, I got my special sources. Do you fancy a quick snort before we go and grab coffee? Let's call it some Behind Enemy Lines, lines" I nodded my reply to him instantly.

Mac was just chopping two fat lines of what I was to be informed was pretty decent coke that he had scored in the venue the night before. He confirmed that 'Medical Bill' hadn't sold it to him, and he had looked at me strangely when I asked that question. He then confirmed that it wasn't cheap crap.

He chopped two big looking lines over by the sink when all of a sudden there was a knock on the door. 'Bang, Bang' "Shit, who on earth is that?" The knock came again. "Just put a dry towel delicately over it for a minute" I said as I motioned towards one of the two white crumpled bath towels that were lying discarded on the kitchen room floor.

I got up out of the bed and opened the door as Mac began to put on his wardrobe choices for the day. "Good morning, two, three. I just wondered if you'd care to join me for breakfast. Saying no isn't an option. I would like to pump you for a debrief on last night's performance."

John remained cool as a cucumber and agreed to join Guy Ropes and Nocka for breakfast but unfortunately for the 'Septic Siblings' Ropes and Nocka didn't depart the scene and waited for Leonard and McCarthy to join them immediately.

"Put some clobber on then man. Hup two, three, hup two, three." Ropes barked at me from the doorway whilst staring at me intently.

I pulled on a plain blue t-shirt, added a yellow hat then slipped on some green flip flops and finished my selection with a pair of purple shorts and joined Mac (Who was already standing outside the room on the landing with the other pair) I felt cool in my garb. I was ready to crash headlong into this day. I pulled the door of our room to a close. Guy Ropes looked me up and down. "Heavens above man. You look like a walking Pride flag son. We aren't in Frisco now boy, two, three, hup two three." In a brutal thirty seconds of chat, I went from a man to a boy. We then departed for breakfast which at 'The Dunne Inn' would be a choice of one type of cereal, half burnt toast and scolding hot tasteless coffee.

An hour later and Mac and I managed to extricate the pair of us from Guy Ropes and Nocka by stating something about needing showers and shaves. Ropes had been satisfied with the gig the previous night. There was some confusion in the mark he had placed on our performance. I still wasn't sure if it was hup two, three, or four? Still, he was actually pleased that for the first time since we set off for this country that we hadn't shown ourselves up. Just who did this prick think he was though?

"Just who does that prick think he is?" Mac asked as we walked back to our motel room. He also clarified that last night's show was given a three out of five by Ropes. "That's just what I was thinking." I acknowledged. "Anyway, come on, let's go and have our proper breakfast" Mac said giggling before adding a cheeky wink as he tapped the side of his beak.

We got back to our room on the second floor of the cheap motel in record time, but something wasn't right. When I opened the door, the first thing that I noticed was that the other white towel I had left on the floor was no longer on the floor, and that my bed cover had been pulled straight.

Mac bulleted across to the sink, where there was no longer a white towel covering some expensive white powder. Then we heard from the room next door, the sound of the hoover. What the hell. The fucking cleaners had been in! They'd either filled their boots or Mac's expensive cocaine was nestling in the vacuum.

The day hadn't got off to the best of starts, however gig 2 at the same LA venue would be a different proposition.

John Leonard had a bottle of Brandy smuggled into the venue and was holding court in the bands dressing room after the band had finished playing in between downing neat slugs. Nocka and Slam had once again taken up positions by the side of the stage so they could watch 'Frog Splash' perform, and Mac had ventured out into the crowd, where he had been accosted by someone who looked a little familiar to him, but he couldn't place the face or decide where he recognised them from?

"I love your accent." The short mocha skinned beauty with the rosy, red lips said to him. "You have real style and grace on stage." This slightly took Mac aback. Where was this chat going? This woman seemed to be about half his age. "Shall we get a drink?" she asked. "Can you get me backstage?" Mac was about to bail as his brain had sent the instruction to decline and say 'no' with an added warning, when his mouth accidentally propelled out the words "Yes, lets."

Several hours later. Mac groaned. He could feel the heat of the sun on his face. Last night had been another blur. That girl he went out after the show with had looked familiar, but Mac still couldn't place her. The drinks had kept coming and he thought / hoped that at some point of the night he would! For now, though, she was gone. What had she said her name was. Was it Erin or Corinne or something like that he thought to himself. What-ever it was, it had left his mind and it seemed that she had left him. She had asked a lot of questions about John Leonard though which was slightly unnerving. He could recall that, as he had got pissed off about it and asked her to stop talking about that dickhead at one point when he was totally loaded.

Hold on a minute, pondered Mac. Why could he feel the sun on his face? Before he got any further with this train of thought, Mac felt an annoying itch on his head that he needed to scratch but found he couldn't as his arms wouldn't move. He opened his eyes as he unsuccessfully tried to pull first his right hand towards the irritant and then tried the left. Neither hand would move more than twelves inches and then as his senses gradually came back he could feel the cool steel of handcuffs around each wrist. Hold on a minute, handcuffs! Mac went into panic mode.

His eyes darted around taking in his location. On the plus side he wasn't in the basement of some deranged sadistic killer. On the downside he wasn't in bed with some cute looking fit bird who was into S and M.

The sound of Macs mobile phone ringing emerged from his shorts pocket. Also unknown to Mac, the cause of this sending of a high voltage alternating current was a fuming Guy Ropes.

Macs phone was making a caw, caw, caw, sound as the ring tone had been set to the option mode of 'flock of seagulls.'

'How the hell had this happened?' Mac mouthed to himself. His phone stopped, but within five minutes it started again. He had no idea what time it was or even where he was, again? He looked around as his eyes finally fully opened and saw blurred grass and trees in his line of vision. Ok, he was on a park he reasoned. It was early morning as there wasn't any people about, thankfully.

Mac tugged at the chains that bound him to the railings. Nothing doing. He moved his hands from side to side but couldn't acquire much purchase in what he was trying to do which was somehow wrench his hands free.

Time dragged. He knew he was stuck fast and then his phone started to ring again. Now concentrate, he told himself, about last night. Mac dredged his mind to try and recall what had happened. Visions of glasses of Gin and Vodka, plus bottles of beer filled his mind, then having some snort in a cramped toilet stall. There were questions, many questions from the girl, he remembered leaving the club with, then a bar somewhere, then another bar, a sex on the park offer, surely that wasn't some type of bloody cocktail was it? Had he got his wires crossed as he reckoned he was onto a sure thing. Think harder. He told himself and conjured up the image of another bar with flashing lights and a huge parrot emblem, and his Uncle Pete. Hold on, why was he suddenly thinking of him? He couldn't have been there? Uncle Pete had been in prison for the last three years doing a seven stretch for armed robbery, the knobber. Had he been let out early for good behaviour? Mac tried to focus and think again, harder this time. Vodka, snort, girl, questions, beer, laughter, he got to the sex offer and just when he thought he was getting somewhere in piecing together what had happened to him during the night the urge and need to urinate came on strong.

Mac tried to refocus. Each time he did he would get as far as gin and vodka in his recollection of the previous night and then his phone would start to ring again or the desire to piss would come back stronger than ever. This was proving intolerable for him.

He tried to give it one more shot. Oh yes, shots, he had forgot about those. Add Tequila to the mix. Lots of them. That girl, red lips, John Leonard, Is he married?, What's he like? Money. He's all about money, he's not my friend...he's a fucking snake. Mac broke his concentration. The urge to pass water had now reached fever pitch. All Mac could think about now was a dripping tap, the pacific ocean waves, Niagara Falls.... No!! Why was he thinking of those for god's sake. He tried to think of something mundane quick, like every day boring things. He thought of golf, people who took photos of their food and shared it on social media, British royalty, especially Prince Barry and his wife Peg Sparkle who despite being dull as ditch water were everywhere in the news at the minute...Oh no, he had thought of ditch water..... This time there was no holding back and the compulsion to remove waste fluid from his body became overbearing and he couldn't stop the need, his tensed muscles relaxed, and he pissed himself.

It was another twenty minutes before the first jogger of the day saw him shackled to the metal railing just by the park's entrance and it was only ten minutes after that, that the LAPD pulled up and two officers arrested him.

Mac was cut free from the railing by one officer and then immediately handcuffed again by the other. Despite his protests he was bundled into the back of the cab after a plastic sheet had been put down on the back seat for him to sit on.

Mac was driven to a nearby police station where he was charged by the arresting officer, who was Officer Gonzalez, whilst in the presence of the community police station watch commander, AKA Officer Ashmore.

Officer Ashmore went through the usual routine asking Mac if he understood the charges, why he was being detained and if he was sick, ill, or injured.

A phone call came through to a furious Guy Ropes who became more incensed by each passing second. Brandon Slam was sat watching the drama unfold during breakfast as Ropes face went redder and redder until he thought he might actually explode.

Slam correctly guessed that Martin Mac McCarthy was the cause of the rush of blood to the head for Ropes. He listened in as he blew steam off his second cup of coffee of the morning. "Arrested.... Lost...... Trespass....... Bail....... two, three, bail two, three....... County Jail,..... you're an IDIOT!"

Ropes cut the call and looked over to Slam. "What have I done to deserve this?" he asked aloud.

John Leonard knew his old mate would turn up again like the proverbial bad penny. The problem now was could Guy Ropes get the ten grand bail money or a lawyer or what-ever else they needed in time to spring Mac for that nights gig?

There was one bit of good news, Mac's luggage had somehow turned up at reception and needed collecting. Guy Ropes put this bit of information to the back of his mind.

Back in the United Kingdom Carlton Gooch was woken by the sound of his personal mobile phone ringing. He opened one eye, sat up in bed, put his hand through his hair, leant over to the bedside table and switched on the antique gold lamp that sat there. He picked his phone up and squinted at it. It was 5am. 'Someone must be dead' he cheerily thought to himself. He answered and braced himself for bad news.

On uttering a feeble 'Hello' the voice of Guy Ropes began to bark. "Sorry to wake you Mr Gooch Sir, but we have something of a situation over here two, three."

It would have been better news if someone had of died. Gooch thought to himself on hearing that he needed to airlift in ten thousand dollars to get Dutch Courage bassist Martin McCarthy bailed from LA County jail. "What the French am I paying you for Guy? You've been in war zones Buddhist, trained some of the world's most elite soldiers and yet you can't handle two middle aged fat balding dossers from an obscure indie band. Tell me why I'm paying you the big bucks again bwana? I mean if I wanted a shoddy job doing I would have left those bozo's to go and look after themselves. The French! Do I need to get myself out there? I mean I'm a reasonable person and a charitable man, with a heart of gold but…. This is ridiculous poppet. Am I making myself clear as crystal? Broken Fondu set with unused out of date cheese….Deal with it man!"

Carlton Gooch had promised to have the funds sorted and calmed down slightly when he heard that according to the lawyer Guy Ropes had spoken to in California, the ten grand would be refundable as long as the suspect didn't abscond and returned for the court hearing. It was also reported that more than likely that McCarthy would just get a thousand dollar fine and potentially six months in the Los Angeles big house. (Lawyer speak for County Jail) This pleased The Gooch no end.

With all the commotion of the bedroom lights going on, and an angry raised voice shouting down the phone, the girl in Gooch's bed 'Cookie Crumble' had awoken. Her sultry tones punctured the silence after Gooch ended the early morning trans-Atlantic call. "Morning Mister Carlton" Gooch looked over at the woman whilst pacing around the bedroom with his mobile stuck to his ear courtesy of his right hand whilst the left hand re-arranged his crown jewels. She looked a picture as her lacy scarlet coloured negligee which offset her liquorice-coloured skin perfectly. He also noticed the skimpy garment was struggling to hold in her huge bouncing assets. Gooch put his hand through his hair and spoke to her as he waited for his next call to connect. "You might as well go deary. Get your clothes and get out. I've got business to deal with here" "But Carlton darling, what about our business, your nine O'cock?" Asked Cookie." "Just give me a credit back on my account. Use the phone downstairs to call yourself a cab." By now Cookie Crumble was getting angry herself. "But it's only fucking five AM honey, I's never going to get a ride this time of day nor it seems at nine in the god damn morning. Come on Carlton honey bunch, have a heart. The girl needs to earn." The Gooch already had the door open and was pointing towards the exit "That's the way the cookie crumbles." He said as she walked past him to leave.

With Guy Ropes away sorting out getting Mac released from jail, John Leonard decided to fully embrace the full-on rock and roll lifestyle at Dutch Courage's final Los Angeles show and the second of three American shows that they had played as a three piece.

Before the show John had spent some time in the company of Budge one of the singers of the headline band 'Frog Splash' when he accidentally walked into their dressing room holding onto his cock through his jeans opened fly zipper whilst desperately looking for a toilet.

Budge went mental as Leonard commenced passing water in the John.

"Get me security. There's a John in the John. Hey, this is not a hotel. Will someone get that guy out of the can. What is happening here?"

John Leonard flushed the toilet and re-entered the main dressing room and arrived on the delivery of Budge saying the word 'can' Leonard sneezed and then gobbed out some hard phlegm onto the floor. "Wow that water wasn't very holy. It was the colour of rust" He blurted out before he launched into a tirade against sport or to be more accurate, the holy grail of American sport.

"Basketball…Is for people with an attention span of three seconds" he had said before he moved onto American Football "Boring as hell…. Does anyone really watch a whole game. It's just one long fucking advert?" and finished off the triumvirate of insults with his Baseball observation "World Series…but only teams in this country play it. Are you having a fucking laugh? And don't get me started on Jesus. How can anyone…." Before he could insult his hosts any further, two security guards took him by the arms and frog marched the drunk as hell guitarist out of the 'Frog Splash' dressing room to more tuts and shakes of the head.

'What did I say?' thought John to himself as his feet returned to terra firma after being thrown out the door of the huge dressing room by two large henchman. Leonard stood shaking his head as he stood outside of the now closed door to 'Frog Splash's' dressing room. 'Communication breakdown' he decided. He gave it some more thought and decided it must have been using the use of the word 'hell' to describe how fucking dull American Football was in front of a group of Christians. 'That Budge guy is well read though. Some of the Shakespeare quotes he was coming out with, deep stuff.' John thought to himself as he wobbled back to his bands dressing room and more importantly the remaining half bottle of 'Feral Quail' Bourbon whiskey that was sat squawking at him atop his guitar case, just waiting to be hunted and shot down.

Show time. John was halfway through his guitar solo on the track "Fruit of the Poisonous Tree" when his eyes locked on another set as he looked out into the crowd and saw her. Erika from America was in attendance, and she was positioned near to the front of the stage mouthing the words 'I love you' from her red, rosy lips to John Leonard over and over whilst picking petals off a bunch of flowers that she was holding. What on earth was she doing here? John's mind when into overdrive and then he realised he was still soloing and Slam and Nocka had finished the song. "Thank you LA" Slam shouted out as lukewarm applause floated towards the stage. John moved stage left to his amp and opened the small bottle of water that had been placed next to a bottle of beer and poured the contents over his head. He looked again at the spot he had thought he had seen Erika, but she was gone. However, Mr Orange was out in the crowd, stood with his arms crossed shaking his head at how bad the performance had gone.

It was the next day when John Leonard was woken up by banging. It was two people going at it in the room next door. They sounded more like rhinoceros's shagging as they crashed around. He got out of bed to close the window in the motel room to keep out the din.

In closing the window, he had to open the single curtain that was by the patio door and that despite its ragged appearance was doing a terrific job in keeping out the fierce Californian sunlight.

The light hit Leonards face and he groaned and immediately looked for his sunglasses. He couldn't see them where he thought he had left them, so he staggered over to the fridge to get a drink of water. He managed to down two big slugs before he spat the third over the floor along with some hot dirty evil smelling brown vomit.

Christ what had I been drinking last night? I felt terrible.

Leonard got back into bed and pulled the cover over his head and drifted back off to sleep.

A little while later and John Leonard was awoken by banging once again. This time it sounded like the bloody feds were at his door. He looked at the clock that was situated on a small chest of wooden drawers in the room. He had been in bed exactly twelve fucking minutes since the last time his sleep was interrupted by some hardcore sex banging noises.

John slowly got out of bed as the banging on the door intensified. He opened it to find Guy Ropes was stood there with a very embarrassed looking Martin 'Mac' McCarthy. "Come on Leonard, hup two, three, hup two, three. Departure to San Diego is in ten, two, three." Mac just smiled, entered the room, gathered up his things that were mostly scattered around the floor into a plastic bag and left again.

'What's his problem' I thought as I stumbled around trying to get some clothes on as I hopped continually on the spot for a good minute trying to force my left leg into what turned out to be the right leg of my jeans.

Finally, after moving as fast as his wrecked body would allow, Leonard was packed, though he hadn't double checked under the bed he had occupied for his stay where he left a pair of yellow skidded boxer shorts for the next occupant to find.

The boxer shorts were in good company. Joining it left under the bed were a dust encrusted green coloured left footed flip flop, a tub of half full KY Jelly with missing lid, a crusty copy of a well-thumbed, creased gay porno magazine and two discarded water bottle tops. It was a hard job being a cleaner on minimum wage.

SAN DIEGO

During the one-hundred-and-twenty-mile drive from Los Angeles to San Diego along the US 101 South Freeway, other than Guy Ropes throwing out complaint hand grenades there was total silence in the Dutch Courage van.

Ropes wasn't happy with Leonard and McCarthy in any way shape or form. You could also now add in Joshua Hoffmans newfound utter contempt for the 'Septic Siblings' Hoffman had again made it crystal clear that the ten commandments had to be followed by the Dutch Courage tour party or else. So, as he wasn't happy then obviously 'Frog Splash' weren't happy. Back home Carlton Gooch was livid at the reports he was getting back, and no-one seemed to be having much fun.

"They're looking at dropping you from the East Coast leg and replacing you with the psychedelic rock troupe 'Avocado Toast' or the ace British rock and roll band 'Ruby and the Mystery Cats,' who are also on tour out here hup two, three. The only thing going for you is that it might be too short notice for them to get there from Florida, two, three." Ropes then cursed under his breath as he remembered that he hadn't collected Mac's suitcase from reception back in Los Angeles.

The Dutch Courage entourage drove on in silence. John was convinced he was being stalked Stateside by the girl he met in London after his TV appearance and the ghost of their previous merchandise seller and now really wanted a drink or maybe some spiritual guidance from Frog Splash. Mac was sat facing six months hard labour and was still waiting on news from his appointed lawyer Art Sales that he would get the green light to travel out of state to be able to finish the tour, but he too was also itching for some grog. Nocka Izzet was enjoying the scenery of the greens and blues flying by out of the skyline bus window as they travelled, and Brandon Slam was wondering where his next job would be coming from as he couldn't see the band lasting the way it was going beyond the next week.

I took the bull by the horns and broke the silence and the tension "Ok, Ok. We're going to calm it down. There will be less drinking. We will be grown up and responsible. Let's give a good account of ourselves from now on, starting tonight." The looks I got from everyone bar McCarthy said it all. It was written on everyone's faces, that look of 'I'll believe it when I see it.' "What's this we" remarked Slam. "There's two of us in the band that don't have any problem enjoying a laugh and a drink. But there's a difference between enjoyment and utter obliteration which you don't appear to have learnt in all forty odd years of your life."

In terms of US touring and days on the road, Los Angeles to San Diego was one of the easier drives. The route was a simple straight road, and the 'Dutch Courage' minibus took just over two hours to hit Old Town, San Diego.

Everyone was hungry like the wolf with the exception of the very hungover John Leonard who was at the almost ready to retch / puke / frothy spit stage.

As the bus drove down Mateo Street towards 'Bettina's American Fries and Pies' for food, John saw something out of the bus window that caught his attention. It was something he thought was the outline of a cardboard cowboy advertising something outside of a fancy looking building, but he wasn't sure what it was. On first glance it looked like maybe a huge clothing shop, but the bus had passed it at too quick a speed to get a proper look.

San Diego old town was very Latino in make-up. There were Mexican flags everywhere and across the nearby beach you could just about see the coast of Mexico. It reminded most of the band of cowboy movies, with small bars and white taverna's dotted around the sandy streets.

The bus parked to let the band and manager out. Home for the next twenty-four hours was another flea pit motel called 'Big Dicks Halfway Inn' which was only a five-minute stroll from Mateo Street.

As the bus drove off the first thing noticeable was that the humidity in San Diego was not as fierce as LA. The temperature was cooler and there was a nice breeze blowing in from off the sea.

The five entered the outdoor bar and grill for lunch to the strain of "Hup two, three, hup two, three."

"I don't feel too hungry lads." I offered as I caught a waft of grease and meat which nearly made me gag on the spot. "I've seen this cowboy place up the road. I'm just going to take a stroll up there if it's ok with you Guy and I'll leave you lads to your meals." "Keep your head down Mr Leonard sir." Said Guy Ropes as he held the thumb of his closed fingered right hand aloft to me and tried to attract the attention of a waitress with a peace sign gesture that he made with his left.

John Leonard wiped the perspiration from his brow and turned and walked away and started the ascent up Mateo Street, to visit the recently spied cowboy shop.

As he walked he could feel the alcohol sweats kicking in, as his blood vessels began to dilate. He reached into his pocket and put his sunglasses back on after wiping his greasy nose on his t-shirt.

'Why did this place have to be up a bloody hill' I thought to myself as I sidestepped some old woman ladled down with bags of shopping who wasn't looking where she was going.

I was just about to give up on the expedition, when suddenly the cardboard cowboy sign came into view, and I increased my walking pace to a still terribly slow one mile per hour.

Leonard ambled up the hill, saw the 'cowboy' sign outside the building but didn't bother to read what it was advertising. Had he bothered to do so, he may not have gone inside.

John arrived outside the door to number 2570 Mateo Street and what he had thought was a shop he could now see was a museum of some sort, and it wasn't doing much business.

The building was made of an impressive mix of terracotta-coloured ceramic tiles interspersed with traditional brick and from the street entrance a stagecoach was visible as it was parked just inside the way in. The clincher though for Leonard was the free entry sign that hung on the door.

'What better way to shift a hangover' I thought to myself, as I took two steps back to take in the name of the place. '…Than by seeing some cool cowboy shit,' I then had to step even further back to get the full name of the establishment into view.

The sign appeared fully in my line of vision 'Celebrated Saints Battalion Center.'

'Maybe its civil war stuff, which will be even better' I reasoned with myself as my eyes set on the word 'Battalion' which made me think of war.

I pushed open the door and entered to find I was the only person inside, there wasn't even anyone to greet you. I looked around and saw movement on the upper level, so I was the only soul on the ground floor at least.

As well as the stagecoach there was a silver cannon which was situated in front of a white wall to my right which had eight portrait pictures hanging from it. This looked like a good place to start my viewing.

I ambled over to the cannon. It had been well kept and was exceptionally clean and impressive. I pulled my sunglasses up onto the top of my head as I strained my eyes to look at the small, printed names of each of the portraits. Aaron Cowdery, Hannah Molokai, Spencer Porter, Dinah Roderick, Braxton Wallace, Anders Pateman, Antonio Boot, and the big cheese it said was the group leader Joseph Smith. None of them carried the tag of General, and there was women, were they even in the civil war? I guess they could have been nurses I contemplated.

As I turned, he was stood there. Unannounced, just stationary, staring directly at me, like I was the first person he had seen in twenty-five years. "Welcome to the All-Saints Battalion Center. My name is Hamish Blunt. Bless your heart. If I can help in anyway today then brother, please feel free to reach out."

Hamish was a short guy. Maybe around five foot five. He had chestnut coloured wavy hair and was wearing cream-coloured slacks, with a white shirt and brown tie. The clothing ensemble was topped off by some kind of crimson coloured smock.

I nodded my appreciation to him, and I moved onto the next artefact which was a number of black and white photographs framed on the wall and a reconstruction of something called 'Battalion Resettlement July 1846 to July 1847' which was made out of matchsticks.

My eyes began to read the narrative to the hanging picture frames. I read from left to right. 'Battalion marched two thousand miles, American West, Never Engaged In Battle…What the fuck? (That wasn't printed beneath a picture, which had me wondering if I was in the 'White Feather Museum') Twenty deaths during the journey west.' So, this wasn't about the civil war….All of a sudden I felt hot breath on the back of my neck.

"It's a moving story don't you think brother? Bless your heart." Hamish was literally a step behind me.

He carried on speaking. "Yes my brother. The soldiers of the Mormon Battalion made several contributions to the settlement of the American West. They improved living conditions and trails wherever they went. They helped build Fort Moorcroft in Los Angeles. Bless their hearts. They helped build Suttons Dam and witnessed the discovery of gold in them there hills brother. This prompted thousands of good people to migrate to the West Coast. Most army members reunited with family and settled with them in Salt Lake City, Iowa, or Nebraska. Are you from any of those parts brother?"

By now my hangover was raging. I was struggling to concentrate, but one word from his spiel had stuck in my brain and I don't think I could remember a single thing he said after the word 'Mormon' The cowboy outside the building wasn't a cowboy. It was a fucking Mormon. No wonder this place was empty.

I came to the sudden realisation that I had in fact set foot into a religious conversion centre. There wasn't anything to do with the American civil war here. My eyes locked onto another sign hanging above the wooden stairs that declared 'Family No Greater Joy – Welcome to the Church of All Saints'

'I decided to play this cat at his own game. "I'm from England brother. My name is John" Shit! Why did I give my real name. Hamish held out his hand

"Bless your heart" he said as we shook paws. "A lie in the house of God, is of course a win for Satan." Hamish bleated as we continued the longest handshake ever known to man.

"Welcome John. A friend and brother from the United Kingdom. Let me show you around if I may?" I don't know why I didn't run at that point, but I decided to let this kooky guy show me around the joint.

As the two men started to climb the stairs to the first floor John accidentally let out a short gust of intestinal gas through his anus. "Bless your fart" smiled Hamish. The smell of rotting meat, and fish heads plus old and crispy sick followed them up the stairs to the first artefact. It wasn't blessed anymore.

There was some cool pictures and interesting bits and bobs to see. We moved up onto 'Level One' And Hamish left me in some interaction chamber, where I could get dressed up from a box of ancient Mormon style clobber from the nineteenth century and go for an interactive 'Plains Ride' which was just like I was sat on a horse riding through some trail in America. At the end of the game, I had my photograph taken and had to leave an Email address to receive it. I left carlton.gooch@worldnet.net

I removed the clothing and laughed to myself. As I exited the Interaction Chamber, Hamish was stood waiting but this time a young woman had joined him. Her skin was immaculate and bone structure perfect. She also had an hourglass figure. If I had to guess I would have put a twenty-one years of age tag on her. That's what I hoped for anyway.

Hamish then introduced me to his daughter Belinda. "So, my brother, how interested are you in our faith and the good book of John Smith?" If I wasn't interested before, I was now. " John Smith, the bitter guy. Yes Ham. I am very fascinated by the whole thing. Engrossed, riveted even." Hamish laughed. "So, where abouts in the United Kingdom are you from brother?" He didn't wait for an answer. "See we Latter Day Saints have missionaries in London and Manchester. We would very much like to add Birmingham to that list. It has always been my mission. God spoke to me. In fact, I have been so fixated on being able to arrange this that the folks around here call me Birminghamish" It was a weak joke, but I let out a hearty laugh.

But I had heard the word 'Missionary,' and my clearly dirty mind went into overdrive. I began to gaze longingly at Belinda. She looked like she had two speed bumps stuck down her red dress. My hangover was clearing. It was indeed a miracle. "I can help with that. I live just down the road from Birmingham." (I lied) "So why are you here in San Diego my brother. Are you on vacation, sorry, bless my heart for that, I meant to say holiday as you Brits like to call it or for you a holyday?" I laughed again.

John told Hamish about himself and that he was the lead singer and guitarist in a rock band. He left out all the parts about drugs and excess drinking. He had also slipped his gold wedding band off and placed it in his pocket. He reminded himself to ask the question about it being ok to have more than one wife if you're a Mormon later.

Hamish looked overjoyed. "Oh, do bless your heart brother. It is Gods fate that we have met you here today. If you are serious about the missionary then we can move that along today. However, you would have to take my daughter with you. I would be insistent on that."

'Amen. There is a God and as long as she's legal, I will take her anyway I can' I silently thought as I stared even more intently at her, she started to smile back and began to twiddle with the ends of her long brown hair and if I wasn't mistaken she was blushing. "I've always wanted to make it to the United Kingdom." Said Belinda. "We'll make it all right." I answered as the smile on my boat went east to west.

"You Sir are a man sent from God. You want to be with my Belinda. The eyes don't lie. But to do so you must become a member of the Church of Jesus Christ Latter Day Saints to assist our quest brother. This my brother is non-negotiable. Our faith is very, shall we say, picky who they allow our sons and daughters to co-habitat with. You will need to be one of us. In taking on the missionary in Britain and to be able to take my daughter. That said, we could make this happen today. If I may say John. Your soul looks like it needs saving, reviving even. I see sorrow brother when I should see hope. I see sadness when I should see joy. I see Satan when I should see Jesus. Have a good look at Belinda. She is extremely excited. I can tell. I've never seen her this excited at a prospect my brother. You need to open your heart to accept the living gospel that is Jesus Christ. Bless that heart. How are you fixed to do that in the next twenty minutes, and then you can take my daughter and begin your new life with our blessing in Birmingham? And no charge!"

What the actual fuck. If I got this right, that if I were ordained immediately as a Mormon I could leave with this guy's daughter hand in hand. This was madness. This wasn't right, but the girl was hot to trot, she ticked all the right boxes and was fit as a butchers dog. I was in one hundred percent.

Hamish left to get prepared whilst I continued to look around the upper level with Belinda. We made small talk, and she held my hand whilst we looked at some old historical artifacts and watched exciting demonstrations on gold panning and a video about brickmaking.

When she first held my hand something happened. It was electric between us. I felt funny, my mind went fuzzy, and my heart skipped a beat. I heard a calling. Jesus was shouting that 'I owed him a tenner.'

I was nervous. I had begun to talk about how good it was that they had free parking there even though the entire sites car park was empty. I hadn't felt like this for years. Was this the effect of touring with 'Frog Splash' rubbing off on me? I hadn't even sworn for near on five minutes.

Belinda was talking "We believe that heaven is here on earth John. It isn't for after your life. It is for the now and it is how you live your life. You make and create your own heaven." At this point I had to turn away from her to hide my hard on.

As we came to the last item to view which was a life size cut out of the man who started the whole Mormon faith 'Joseph Smith' I got my phone out and took a selfie of myself with him. Belinda laughed and pulled at the hem of her short red gingham style cotton dress and then spoke. "You shouldn't take a picture whilst smiling with John Smith, else that is a win for Satan." I pulled her close and took a selfie of us both. She smelt of fresh strawberry shower gel and coconut shampoo.

Over in a room off to the left of the stairs I could see Hamish, who had changed into his Ministerial robes, where he was ready to ordain me. He beckoned me to head towards him.

"Yes my brother. To be welcomed into our faith you must first be baptised.

Bless your heart. If not, then Satan will do all he can to foil our plans. I do apologise, we were not expecting this to happen today, and we usually do all baptisms and that kind of thing in the church, but as you are on a tight time scale, I have bought this bucket of holy water to do the job. It has been blessed by my hand. Bless my hand and heart. This will have to do brother. Do you mind getting wet" There was no need for me to add a punchline to that question.

I didn't like to get down on his knees in front of men but this time I was playing the long game. I was now wearing a purple sash that Hamish had given me to put on for the ceremony. I was also holding a copy of the John Smith version of the bible that I had been presented with in my right hand. I bent down in front of Hamish and stuck my head down into the cold water in the orange bucket.

I heard Hamish say something about the 'Father, son, spirit and possibly holy ghost or mountain' before he pulled my shoulders back from out of the bucket which in turn enabled me to remove my head from the bucket. Baptism over.

Next it was time for me to place the bible I had been given on a silver lectern. It was a bit wet, but I placed it in the correct position as told. Hamish then launched into a speech about personal honesty (Nearly, check, I thought to myself), integrity (Check), obedience to law (Just about, check), Chastity outside of marriage (Not sure what that meant), and fidelity within marriage. (If that is sex. Yep, no complaints so far. Check) Pornography is a sin (Errr…ah) and he went on to say that drinking alcohol, tea, coffee and the use of tobacco and drugs were also forbidden. (I had been meaning to give up some of those. (two out of five should see me alright though.)

I just kept nodding. Then Hamish pointed both hands to the sky and shouted the words "By the power invested in me, I welcome you John Leonard, to the Church of Latter-Day Saints."

That was it. He came out from behind the lectern and hugged me. Belinda bounded over and kissed me on the cheek. I went in for the full-on smacker but was left looking like a gaping guppy fish. "Can we count on you for LSD on Friday brother?" Hamish asked of me. Now he was talking my language I thought until I found out later on in the conversation that Friday was the main day of worship, and he was actually referring to LSD as short terminology for 'Latter Saints Day.' He wanted me to attend the service at the local church.

I looked at my watch. I had only been here for ninety minutes and had been ordained as a Mormon and paired off with my potential future wife. The other lads will never fucking well believe this I thought, and I had a little chuckle to myself. "Sorry to break up the party brother, Belinda, err… sister? But I probably need to get back to my travelling companions. As good brothers they will be wondering what has become of me. I am sure they will have by now devoured their meat luncheon, those philistines, and sacrilege upon sacrilege, some hot beverages. But, despite their sins I am sure they will be worried."

I pulled my mobile phone back out from my pocket and saw that I had received messages that ranged from 'Are you all right?' to 'Report Leonard, report, two, three.' And 'Where the fuck are you knobhead?' Along with two missed calls.

Hamish moved quickly towards me and held my left hand. Belinda soon joined us both and she held onto my right hand. Hamish began to talk "Thou shalt not kill. Bless your heart. Thou shalt utterly destroy. Brother John. This is the principle on which the government of heaven is conducted, by revelation adapted to circumstances in which the children of our beloved kingdom are placed. Whatever God requires of you is right. No matter what that is. Although you, or I, may not see the reason brother until long, long after those events transpire. Now you have a blessed day, and may the good Lord bless your heart."

Hamish finally let go of my hand and finally left me just in the company of his daughter. It was true, I had entered the museum, church, conversion centre a physical wreck. But now I did feel different. I felt enlightened, my hangover had lifted. It was if I had a different outlook on life. Weight had truly been lifted from my shoulders. I grabbed Belinda by the hands and got lost in her sea blue eyes and uttered my best and smoothest chat up line. "I can't wait to shag the utter arse off you later. Praise the Lord."

Belinda and I arranged to meet later at a television repair shop close to the venue in which Dutch Courage were playing later that night. It had been difficult to agree to anywhere as coffee shops, bars, and vaping emporiums were out. I really had hoped she wouldn't be bringing her Dad as chaperone. If there really was a God she wouldn't and she would swallow.

John Leonard had walked up the hill to the 'Celebrated Saints Battalion Center' a quivering, sweating, hungover wreck. He returned to his colleagues spiritually enlightened though he still needed a few tweaks.

Mac, Nocka, Slam and Guy were all still in the taverna as John Leonard bounded back still wearing the purple sash over his shirt and carrying the John Smith bible beaming.

"You'll never guess what just happened to me? I only just got ordained as a Mormon" I yelled with a smile as I slapped the bible down so hard on the table that it made the dirty uncollected crockery shake.

I proceeded to tell all seated what had just occurred in the last one hundred minutes I had been absent from them. Guy Ropes just put his head in his hands as I then got the attention of a waitress, and ordered a beer, a coffee, a hot dog and began to roll up a spliff.

It seemed spiritual enlightenment still had some way to go with the Dutch Courage guitarist.

I got out my mobile phone and opened the picture gallery and brought up the picture of Belinda. I filled the rest of the lads in on what had happened at the museum. "She is tasty." Reckoned Brandon Slam in between sips of coffee. "How old is she John. You're not gonna get mixed up in Operation Dewdrop with this are you like?" chirped Mac handing back my phone.

I was about to speak when Guy Ropes handed me his own phone and gestured that I should listen to it. The voice of Carlton Gooch almost blew my earlobe. "What the French is going on now. I've just been woken up at four of the A M to be told we need to get a de-programmer out to you. You've been with a cult if I heard right. What are you playing at son beam. Religious people equals total avoidance Buddhist. Savvy? They are non-drinkers and head shrinkers. You are not to engage, get engaged if there's a bloody woman in tow or I get enraged. DO YOU UNDERSTAND."

I tried to speak but was cut off. The Gooch was still going ten to the dozen. "Jimi Jones, WACOMOLE, Manson the US of A is full of them 'I am God' nutters, and guess what, none of them have ever actually been God. Now deal with the resurrection and second coming of Dutch Courage and finish this tour without any more drama bwana. Can you be top banana daddy cool? Or do I have to come out there myself and if I do, the cost comes out of your pocket." And with that the phone went dead.

The gig that night in San Diego at the Rock Box went without a hitch. An away win for the British at last. There was no drama to report other than security asking to see John Leonard's girlfriend Belinda's passport to check her age everywhere the pair went.

There were no drugs, or alcohol, and everything went like clockwork. The Gods were once smiling down on Dutch Courage.

The following days flights were booked from San Diego International to Boston Sammy Malone Airport.

Dutch Courage found that they were flying direct. The flight across country would take five hours and cover 2,588 miles. The band were booked into cattle class with 'Siberian Airlines' whilst 'Frog Splash' were flying to New York, business class, as there was a T.W.A.T wrestling event that Walt and Budge had agreed to appear at for no doubt a considerable fat fee.

"Remember, don't let Satan into your life. Sin is a win for the devil brother, bless your heart." Said Hamish as he put his arm around John whilst Belinda held his hand. Both Mormons had come to see John off much to the amusement and ridicule of the others.

"Is he for real?" Mac asked the others whilst shaking his head. "She barely looks eighteen for fucks sake." "You're, you, you" said Nocka, "You're just j, j,..." "Jealous" Slam finished Nocka's sentence for him as they had a flight to catch.

John left Belinda and Hamish with the promise that Belinda would hook up with him in New York the following day for the final two dates on the US Tour before flying back to Britain with him.

Within two hours the band were through security, despite Nocka setting off the alarm again even though he was carrying absolutely zero metal objects. Guy Ropes had received instruction from Mac's attorney that he had been granted permission to leave the state to continue with the tour. Soon they were on the plane and in the air bound for Boston, Massachusetts. Macs luggage included.

John and Mac were again seated next to each other on the flight. Mac was eating some of the complimentary peanuts that had been handed out. John used the Siberian Airlines tagline and decided to 'Break the Ice' Leonard sipped his complimentary cup of Lemon Peel flavoured water then broke the ice.

"You going to tell me what happened to you and how you ended up being handcuffed to a park railing back in Los Angeles?" I asked Mac as he squirmed in his seat at the thought of it. "I can't fucking remember much. Hit the ale and Narcos a bit strong. There was this bird. I remember that much. All tits and teeth, well tasty and right up for a bit of Mac or so I thought. Well, we were having a great time, thing is I'm sure I've seen her before somewhere. I'm also certain that she kept asking about you, but I could be wrong on that score. It's all a bit hazy to be honest. She could have spiked me. I never really thought about that. That's what must have happened. She started to get a bit pissed off after we left some bar down North Hollywood way when I believe I told her you weren't coming out. But how could you have come; I didn't even message you. Then I'm not right sure what happened until I woke up the next morning busting for a slash." I just shook my head then tried to push my seat back, but it wouldn't move. I looked out of the window and did a double take as there sat on the wing looking back and waving at me was Mr Orange.

BOSTON

THANKFULLY FOR GUY ROPES, BOSTON, Massachusetts, was every bit as boring as its same named counterpart in the United Kingdom. For once, absolutely nothing out of the ordinary happened with the exception of Mac finally being reunited with his luggage. That was a shock in itself.

For the first time in several days Guy Ropes felt he could relax. His charges had behaved themselves, as there were no law enforcement to get involved with and no fines incurred. No damages to report either. The 'Septic Siblings' seemed to have calmed down, but was it the lull before the thunder? Only time would tell on that score. The next day could all be different in the big apple.

NEW YORK

Belinda's flight from San Diego was due in at eleven thirty in the morning. I just managed to get to the airport half an hour before it arrived. There was so much traffic everywhere. Christ, even the airport was like a zoo. There was so many people buzzing around. Where were they all going? There was so many destinations that this place flew to, and of course if they flew there, they flew back.

I found arrivals and saw that the flight I was interested in coming in from California was due in on time. I half expected Belinda not to be on it to be honest. I made my way to the bar and surprised myself by ordering an orange juice, which in turn surprised me itself when I heard the word "Seven dollars" being attached to it. In truth I probably could have had a beer for five, though of course this being America, it would have been a half of tasteless weak yellow coloured, foamy two percent beer.

Eleven AM came and went, and I moved along to the closed-door corridor in the airport that all new arrivals come out of. It was the clam before the storm. One second there was nothing and then the arrivals door opened and…pandemonium, as people exited with bags, luggage, suitcases, crying children, quiet children, briefcases or with a combination of everything stated. It made me slightly melancholy, and I started to think of my kid back home. I quickly snapped out of my funk as I realised people were streaming past me.

My eyes darted from person to person. Nope, not that one, too tall, no, too fat, then too male, and so on, and so on. Minutes ticked by and the volume of bodies were still coming through. Then, like a vision from heaven, I saw her, but she didn't look right, I rubbed my eyes and when I looked again, I realised it was Mr Orange pissing about dressed in drag with a brown wig on laughing at me. "That's not funny you twat" I shouted rather loudly, and some other people stood waiting for their loved ones turned to look at me with disdain as they then slowly started to inch away from where I was positioned.

The volume of people coming through the door dwindled from a tidal wave to a slow dribble, and I was just about to give up when I saw her. There she was, looking all vacant and lost and clearly out of her comfort zone. I waited several more seconds just to ensure that her Father hadn't come along for the ride. If he had he was being damn cruel holding himself so far back behind her.

Belinda stopped walking and started to scan the crowd for a familiar face, mine. I was holding a huge card with her name on and approached her and we hugged. The hug had a profound effect on me. (No, not that kind. Get your heads out of the gutter) I felt spiritually enlightened. Yes, I suddenly believed in God, and knew he was watching over us. However, in a dark corner of my mind I deep down hoped he wouldn't be watching me for the next couple of hours that I had spare back at the hotel room before I was due at the venue for the soundcheck for that evenings gig, as I was feeling rather frisky.

The band arrived early at the 'BCBE' venue in New York City. The club was still a prestigious venue to play despite the fact that it only held at best two hundred and five people. It was rundown, it stunk of sewage and the dressing rooms didn't have any more room for graffiti on the walls. Other than that, it was a privilege to pay twelve bucks for a bottle of crap beer in such a world-famous venue.

There stood alone in the queue, or line, (Do some Americans call it a queue of Charlie when they do drugs in a trans-Atlantic role reversal?) was a huge guy of around six feet seven inches high. I recognised the gait of the bloke immediately as I exited our transport, and walked up behind him, placed a stretched hand onto his shoulder and spoke. "Well, well, well, Chester Rataski, you lanky streak of piss. How the devil are you old chap?" Chester swivelled around and nearly took me out with his huge paunch. It was like the reversal of one of those annoying people who insist on wearing back packs at gigs, have two alcoholic drinks, forget they are wearing it and take everyone out like a collapsing rugby scrum whenever they move or worse bend down to pull up their socks.

Wow! Our ex-drummer Chester had piled on more pounds than gamblers on 'Grand National Day' I couldn't believe what I was seeing. There was no denying it. He was fucking massive. "I know you won two hundred and fifty grand on the lottery, what did you do, eat it?" I joked. 'Big Chest' as he had affectionately once been called by us just smiled at me. "Yeah man, but I could still do a job for you boys on the pots man. Who you got drumming for you now? I mean, I was pissed man that you didn't even have the courtesy to ask me. Of course, I would have said no, but it's the principal man. It made me pissed."

'Hmmm' I thought to myself. I'm sure Gooch said he had been contacted. Just as I was about to answer him, Nocka appeared at my shoulder. "The very man" I said changing track and ensuring I was talking to his good hearing side. Nocka put out his hand. "I'm, I'm, erm, I'm Nocka. Nocka Izzet. I'm half b, b, blind, and can't see out of my l, le, left eye, some, some, some people say I'm h, h, half blind that's, be, be, because there's only one eye in Nocka Izzet" As the two drummers shook mitts, Chester looked at me and asked about the possibility of a guest list for the show later as it was sold out and he didn't have a ticket. He may be richer I thought but he still didn't like spending money. Haleys Comet was seen more often than Chester was getting a round in.

We finally were allowed in the venue and Chester entered with us making himself useful by carrying some drumsticks and a cymbal. I got the feeling the guest list wouldn't be needed. We made small talk as we settled in the cramped, graffiti covered, damp smelling, dressing room. We tried to talk about the good times but found the silence break between the old war tales went on a bit too long.

At some point I had to leave to go and do the soundcheck and that's when Chester went and hid in a filthy stinking backstage toilet. I understand Chester remained there until show time in a desperate bid to avoid paying the ten bucks charge to charity that all people on the 'BCBE' guest list had to donate to.

I promised Belinda that I would return to the hotel straight after the gig. She didn't fancy a night of metal and indie rock. Couldn't say I blamed her as I hadn't really been up for it either. I left the gig before 'Frog Splash' even took to the stage much to Chester and Mac's chagrin.

Mac, Brandon Slam, and Chester decided to make a night of it after the show and managed an hour in a nearby Irish Pub imaginatively called 'The Shamrock' before they were all asked by the landlord Pat Downs to leave as it closed at midnight. "Where now?" Mac asked the local tour guide Chester as the three of them were stood on the sidewalk. Chester scratched his genitals, thought about it for thirty seconds and then answered. "Man, I honestly can't think of anywhere else that will be open at this time." Slam summed up what the two Brits were thinking "So much for the city that never sleeps. New York, New York. Everywhere is closed by midnight."

NEW YORK CITY, NIGHT 2, ARGYLL PLAZA SHOW

ERIKA PUCK HAD BEEN UNABLE to blag, steal or even give a blow job to anyone to get into the intimate 'BCBE' concert the night before, but she was sure as shit going to make sure she got in with or preferably without paying for a ticket for the last show of the tour. The venue for the final gig was the way bigger 1,700 capacity, Argyll Plaza which was situated in between a shopping mall and a massage parlour in downtown Manhattan.

The Argyll was an old theatre and the rumour that did the rounds that it was unofficially owned by the mafia.

Erika had made the iconic 'Tooting Hotel' on James and Bowen her home away from home during her stay in New York City. A bargain at only thirty-five dollars a night.

The 'Toot' (As it was affectionately known) was an establishment steeped in music history and many rock luminaries had OD'd or died fantastic rock and roll deaths on the premises.

Erika was staying in room number 911 right on the top floor of the building. She had managed to get the room next door to where mega famous 'The Nibble' lead singer Rex Everything had accidentally died in a tragic accident in 1978. This accident had involved an eight ball of dope, a satsuma, an ironing board and hoover with 0 to 10 strength suction attachment. The cause of death was blood loss and the carpet in the room still had the blood stains on it.

It was a good job she hadn't bought a ticket from a scalper the previous night as she had a lot of work to do. Erika had given up trying to get in at the small venue and went and scored some seriously good dope in the area Hunts Point instead before returning to the hotel. In the privacy of her room, she would, according to the runes, the cartomancy session, a further tarot card reading and even the tea leaves in her last cup of tea, be told that tomorrow would be the day that she would finally be together with the obsession of her life, Englishman John Leonard.

Erika picked up her makeshift voodoo doll of John Leonard. This one hadn't been as well thought out as the one she decided to leave back in London and was hastily constructed out of a checked sock that she had found abandoned in an alley way close to the 'Toot.' The features had been attached using some discarded chewing gum, using bits of grit out of the rooms carpet for eyes and said gum was also used to secure the hair which she had scooped out of the drain stopper of the rooms bathtub.

She placed the sock over her hand and began to talk to it whilst sat on the dirty stained sheets on the bed. "Tonight, we will be together forever John Leonard my love. God, I want you now, do you want me, like I want you?" Erika moved her hand and fingers to make the sock talk and put on a quite passable English accent if you were deaf. "Yes I want you beautiful pretty lady. I want you as my wife. I want you so bad. Kiss me Erika" Erika moved her head down to her hand and French kissed the sock. When she came up for air she then checked the time, saw that she had plenty of it before she needed to get to the venue for the gig. "Why don't you take me now then John?" she said to the sock sat staring back at her on her right hand as she rubbed off some of her lipstick with her left hand from the socks makeshift lips. Erika and the sock stared into each other eyes and then without any warning she pushed the sock down her underwear and proceeded to play with herself vigorously.

Thirty minutes later and Erika lay back content as she lit two cigarettes that she had in her mouth. John the sock had made her come good, twice. She took a drag on the cigarette and blew a plume of blue smoke into the atmosphere and then put the second smoke into the socks mouth. The sock let out a cough, so she removed the cigarette. "Sorry John, I forgot you don't smoke anymore." Erika smoked both of the cigarettes herself and then asked the sock if he fancied taking a bath.

An hour later, Erika had cleaned herself up and put on what she thought was her sauciest killer outfit of a low-cut black top, black miniskirt, black thigh boots with matching black stockings. It was still early in the afternoon, but she was clearly excited, so decided on a trip down to the venue to see if anything was happening. She thought she might be able to catch one of the bands prior to sound checking and sort her entry out for later. Someone was bound to let her in as she looked and felt like a million and one dollars, twenty-nine cents.

The two-minute walk to Seventh Avenue / East Twenty Street Subway attracted a number of wolf whistles and stares from men of all ages. Behind her dark shades, Erika knew she had worn the correct outfit.

That evenings venue, 'The Argyll' Plaza was only five stops on the subway. In reality it could be walked in twenty minutes from the hotel but not in these heels thought Erika.

She exited the subway and walked the two blocks to Law and Border, the street where the venue for the gig was situated. As she got closer she could see a white coloured transit van (Some say it was cream) that was parked with its engine running waiting to access the currently closed parking structure at the back of the venue.

It looked like 'Dutch Courage' were in the van as she recognised the muppet that she had chained to the fence a week or so back in California sat in the front seat drinking a beer.

Erika increased her walking pace as much as she could in those heels to try and reach the van before it entered the parking lot. But it was difficult to gather pace in those heels. Just as her stride lengthened the gate opened and the van pulled in, then the gate had closed again by the time she had got there.

The parking lot was a hive of activity. The 'Dutch Courage' van had parked next to another smaller van and venue staff were stood around waiting to move equipment from various parked trucks into the old hall.

That's when she saw him. John Leonard. He looked so scrummy. Granted he was slightly balding, but he looked hot dressed in blue jeans and an open neck plain white shirt. He was helping a young girl out of the van. They then kissed. It was a deep kiss with a bit of tongue. 'Maybe it was his daughter' Erika tried to kid herself. She continued to watch from a distance. Leonard was holding hands with this 'girl' whilst talking to some massive eight-foot-tall baboon who was holding some drumsticks. The baboon clapped his hands, then shook hands with John Leonard. This slip of a girl looked like butter wouldn't melt in her mouth, but we all know what has been in her mouth Erika thought to herself as rage made her body shake and her blood pressure rise like mercury in a thermometer on a bloody hot day.

Erika felt so stupid. How could the mother fucking runes be so fucking wrong? And the tarot card reading had turned over 'The Lovers' card albeit on the second or was it the third attempt after 'The Hierophant' (This was discarded as she didn't know what it meant or stood for and thought she had already removed them all from the deck) and 'The Fool.' 'Oh my God. That came out second. The card of 'The Fool' Erika Pucks body began to vibrate with anger and then released more adrenaline which caused her blood vessels to dilate and made her cheeks, chest, and upper neck to flush red in colour. She grabbed hold of the chain link fence of the parking lot and started to shake it for all she was worth causing it to shake rattle and roll, but no-one heard her. Even the tea leaves had been wrong, 'Those lying mother fucking tea leaf bastards' screamed an enraged Puck.

Erika glanced over to where the vans were all parked. Everyone who had been in them had gone inside and the first wave of equipment had also been moved with them. Erika was about to leave when she saw, the huge guy who was carrying the drumsticks appear back in the parking lot. She began to shout his way. "Hey, Lakenstein, High Tower, yeah you, you on stilts, big, tall guy, come here a minute." Erika beckoned Chester over with a wave. Chester in turn saw some gothic looking chick waving at him like she was trying to land a plane and bounded over towards her position at the locked gate.

"Are you with that Limey 'Dutch Courage' band?" asked Erika as soon as Chester was in earshot. "With them, man, I use to be in them" replied Chester whilst pretending to bang on some pretend drums with both hands using the sticks he was holding. "Yeah right. Then tell me big guy....Who was that scrawny boring straight looking cunt that the guitarist was all over in the car park earlier?"

Chester Rataski was slightly taken aback with the language. "Hey, tone it down Lady. She is his new girlfriend. They only just met. Love at first sight if you believe in such mushy trashy bullshit. Hey I'm available though. How about we…..."

Erika started to kick and punch the chain link fence whilst screaming the word "Motherfucker!" over and over. Chester took this as his cue to leave and was about to call security for assistance when he remembered he still hadn't yet sorted his guest list credentials out for later so sloped away as only a guy his height could.

Puck stormed away from the venue just as a guy up a ladder at the front of house was adding the letters S, O, L, D, O, U, T, to the billboard advertising that evenings gig. Erika stopped, checked what the guy was doing and swore again loudly. She hadn't bothered to buy a ticket for that nights gig either. But it was written in the stars she would be joining John Leonard today. She should be there as his guest and now even that was in tatters. Why had everything gone wrong. Why were the mystical powers lying to her?

Erika formulated a plan. Barney on reception at the 'Tooting Hotel' had told her that he could get anything / anytime for her for a price. She needed to see him urgently and put that to the test, but first she needed to procure a bottle of vodka to ease the pain welling up inside of her that she was feeling.

Just by the return journey subway station was 'Liquor Nice' a twenty-four-hour off-licence. Puck stormed in and left with a half-bottle of 'Hangover One' vodka wedged into her underwear. The bottle felt cold against her skin. Fuck the brown bag to drink it from, there wasn't the room to add that as well in her knickers. She did however get some nuts in there.

This was indeed a dark day for Erika Puck. She felt that she had lost someone close to her. Her current feelings were like someone important in her life had died. She needed to numb the pain and started to drink the neat spirit from the open bottle. The burning sensation on the back of her throat made her feel alive. For now, it was back to the hotel for Erika to regroup and re-plan the night, everything was so good just one hour ago and now it had all gone to shit.

Erika from America sat on the train making the return journey back to the station by the 'Tooting Hotel' Her brain was doing somersaults. The alcohol hadn't made its way into her blood stream yet to hopefully calm her down. She was still apoplectic with rage and began banging her fists on the window of the carriage in which she was situated scaring most of the other passengers. But, In true New York City style, no-one wanted to get involved and most breathed a huge sigh of relief when she got off at her stop.

At least she still had her 'John Leonard' sock in room 911 to take her frustration out on.

Ensconced back in her room at the 'Tooting Hotel' Erika was still downing neat Vodka, the vile taste being offset by a mouthful of salted peanuts every couple of swigs. This was one of the few things she had learnt to do during her stay in London, which was to drink like a local. Them Brits knew how to absorb alcohol if they were good for nothing else. Soon she stopped wincing in between slugs as the harsh spirit numbed her throat like an anaesthetic.

Erika was lying on the bed. She checked her cell phone for the fiftieth time since she got back to the hotel two hours ago as tears streamed down her face and ruined her previously perfect make up. A picture of John Leonard (Albeit taken from some distance) stared back at her when suddenly there was a knock at the door.

She knew exactly who it would be. Erika jumped up off the bed and made her way to the door of her room stepping over a check patterned sock that had been torn to pieces with a small penknife. Erika was still holding the phone with the photograph of John Leonard still illuminated looking back at her. Erika began to get angrier cursing loudly before she finally opened the door.

The doors and walls at the 'Tooting Hotel' were as thin as a size zero model. Stood there in the dark hallway holding a tote bag which looked like it contained some kind of heavy object was Barney from the hotel reception. He entered the room without invite and pushed the door shut.. "I have those two packages you wanted." His accent was deep guttural New Jersey. No-one would mistake this guy for a French man. He threw the tote bag onto the bed, and it bounced once before coming to a stop on top of a mascara-stained pillow. He then carried on speaking "I think you'll find it's you, not this John guy who is the cock sucker" and he commenced unzipping his trousers as Erika dropped to her knees in front of him to repay some of what she owed in the deal made with Barney.

Back at the 'Argyll Plaza' The doors were being readied to be opened for the gig and some fans had formed a line / queue (Delete as applicable) in anticipation of the final show of 'Frog Splash's' "Die a Thousand Deaths Tour" All seventeen hundred tickets had been sold and security were getting into position and were testing the airport style metal detectors that were permanently ensconced at the entrance doors were working prior to opening up to the general public.

"Can I talk to you, urgently. I've got something to get off my chest." Mac said to me. "Oh" came my lame reply. He continued. "I saw the band contracts back at your flat. You put me, your old best mate on a wage to do this shit for fucks sake. We started this band together and I wrote half of all the songs, yet you appear on tele once and then go behind my back to rip me off in cahoots with that slime Gooch. Did he put you up to it? Anything to save a quid that bloke. It's like having Chester back in the band having him peering over our shoulder all the time. I'm not happy and I won't be continuing with this after we get back unless my terms are improved, and I'm made an equal partner."

I stood back and started to nod my head before I replied in kind. "Dear Mac, I've got prayers with Belinda. We will talk about this later. No-one is going anywhere, so let's chat after the show, though I will say you've been lucky to be paid anything following your behaviour and disappearances in California. It's a good job for you it hasn't been pay as you play."

John Leonard walked away briskly leaving his one-time friend feeling like a broken football….. deflated.

Back stage was also a hive of activity. Mac was wondering around looking for his bass guitar or catering, which ever appeared first was cool. He was, however, getting annoyed that he was still being asked by people on the tour to see his credentials as there were various staff of the crew who didn't realise who he was. This was on account of him virtually missing the first half of the tour on the West Coast.

He had cleared out of the dressing room whilst Leonard was holding court and talking about God with Chester, Belinda, Slam and Nocka. Guy Ropes had also got bored very quickly and had gone outside to smoke his pipe. Mac didn't get his old mate Leonard. He thought this sudden instant conversion to religion was some sad pretence just to get in a girls knickers and a way to now talk his way out of ripping off his best mate.

'Frog Splash' had a minder called 'Bucky' who was stood in front of their dressing room door even though they hadn't all arrived yet. As Mac stood staring, the door opened and out walked a man in a white satin suit, who was clutching a mobile phone in one hand and putting his hand through his hair with the other. It was none other than Dutch Courage manager Carlton Gooch, one of the last people Mac had wanted to see. Their eyes met in the backstage corridor.

"Are you looking forward to Porridge in California dickhead?" was The Gooch's opening gambit. "And I'm pleased to see you too Gooch" said Mac as he put his fist out for a bump. "A fist bump Buddhist, a fudging fist bump, I ought to bang my fist in your spiffing face. You've cost me thousands on this tour in bonds, fines, police call outs, breakages, and Buddhist knows what else. You can't behave yourselves for five pigging minutes you doughnut. Be a groover, not a loser. This is no way to run a business dosser. Do you hear me? It's no way to run a business." Mac looked hard into the band managers eyes and tried to stay composed. "You could take it out of my ten percent wages you fucking rip off merchant." Carlton Gooch didn't like confrontation and hadn't brought his minder Bullock along for the trip. He started to put his hands vigorously through his hair before responding. "Well life isn't fair is it Martin McCarthy? Look at hedgehogs. They live for two years or so and hibernate for half of that, then die. Things in life aren't fair in the slightest, some people are born Tottenham supporters Buddhist. Is that fair? You fudging well signed the contract Chappy, have got to see the other side of the world for freeman's and talking of a free man…. You wouldn't be one bwana if it weren't for the fantastic plastic flexible friend held by your old pal Carlton Gooch. Capeesh! I can call off my lawyer if you wish to find one to defend you back in Cali. So, think on dear boy." Mac walked off in a huff as The Gooch stood hyperventilating whilst simultaneously running his hands through his ever-thinning thatch faster and faster as he really wasn't one for conflict without his seven-foot minder.

Two hours later and the majority of fans had filed into the venue. You always get the ones who come late having had a cheap drink elsewhere in town but this being New York City if you did that you risked missing a lot of the show. Not getting there early was a no, no, as security was thorough in checking each and every person who attended the show.

Dutch Courage were just about to start an interview in their dressing room with a college radio presenter by the name Kate Blanche. Kate was punky in appearance and was wearing very tight-fitting black jeans matched with branded 'Perverse' make baseball boots. On her top half she sported a band t-shirt of up-and-coming American indie band "Toxic Syrup" who those in the know reckoned would be the next 'Blessedness' Mac didn't even know there'd been a first 'Blessedness.' She also had many ear and facial piercings, a couple of tattoos on her left arm and impressive breasts.

"I bet you must have been stopped getting into the gig. You must have set the metal detector off with a face like that" laughed Mac.

"Any road, who's the band on the shirt?" Mac aggressively asked in between swigs from a red bottle of branded beer. Kate took it all in her stride, as she naively pushed out her chest to show the drunken Mac a better view of the article of clothing he had referred to. "Tox. You must know them right? Burt Novocaine is the singer. The next big thing if you ask me guys." "Yes I believe I'm indeed looking at the next big thing." Leached Mac still ogling the interviewers chest. "But hey I'm here to ask you stuff." Kate said as she hurried into her first question. "If I were to ask you for three words that you hate most in the English language, what would they be?" Mac responded instantly. "Please. Drink. Responsibly." Kate didn't seem to get the joke and her next question was just as mundane. "Who would you not like to get stuck in the lift with?" Mac again was straight in with an answer "The lift repair guy." Kate looked Mac straight in the eyes "And how do you know your lift repairer is a man?" Nocka tried to insert himself into the interview "P, P, P, Per." "Person! Lift repair person." interjected Slam.

Whilst the interview continued backstage, 'Chelsea Bird' had taken to the Plaza stage to play twenty minutes of cover versions before doing an overlong version of the one song that he was world famous for. He had more filler in his set than a chain of DIY shops but had gone down well on the West Coast, so he was invited to play on the East side. He was happy. His appearance money made sure he was well on the way to becoming female.

Forty-five minutes later, Bird had finished his set and he and his equipment had long been cleared from the stage. Roadies though, were still moving gear about. The stage lights were flashing on and off producing wonderful colour schemes and amazingly there was a hum of anticipation amongst the audience for the next band, Dutch Courage.

Outside of the main hall punters were milling around the venues foyer, paying through the nose for popcorn, hot dogs, and watered-down two percent beer. Some were looking at the over-priced merchandise booth. 'Frog Splash' had the merch covered. You name it, they had it. Tee shirts, long sleeve and short, hats, boxers, thongs, playing cards, socks, and even condoms which bore the legend "Stay Safe – Make Sure You Splash With the Splash" But absolutely no-one was going to buy that 'Frog Splash' green coloured ironing board they had.

The hallway at the 'Argyll Plaza' smelt like a fair ground and that was what the owners wanted, a carnival like atmosphere once you had entered the venue, having turned out your pockets, gone through the metal detector and undertaken two security frisks. It was less hassle to get on a plane.

The majority of gig goers were in the main hall chatting, listening to the DJ spin some tunes, and waiting patiently for the next act as the roadies continued to do their thing on the stage.

A spotlight was now flying around the auditorium and dry ice was pumping out across the stage.

Away from the lights, the tours stage manager Lou Boggs was walking to the dressing room of the next act due on stage in precisely four minutes time, Dutch Courage.

As the Plaza was a decent sized concert hall Lou had the walk down to one hundred and twenty seconds each way. He had practiced it three times when he arrived with 'Frog Splash' earlier in the day. He checked his watch and found he had arrived at 'Dressing Room 2' precisely three seconds early. He counted off the seconds in his head and then knocked the door twice. "Dutch Courage to the stage, Dutch Courage to the stage." He shouted at the closed single hinged interior door.

Lou had dealt with it all over the years. Bands ignoring him, band members going missing, various managers of all descriptions being rude to him, gofers running around bringing all manner of items to the band and getting in his way. He had heard on the touring bands grapevine that these Brits liked a bevvy and he had seen first-hand how unruly they had been at some places on the tour. Therefore, he was on his toes as he didn't know what to expect from them. Would they be good or badly behaved tonight?

In this instance by the time his balled fist had retracted back after the second of the two knocks, the door was opened by an army looking Major type almost immediately and the band trotted out with the older man shouting "Hup two, three, hup two, three."

Stage manager Lou turned on his heals and the British band followed him as he switched his torch back on to navigate the five men following him back to the stage. The corridors were pitch black as the house lights had all been dipped a little early in anticipation of their impending appearance.

The five men passed roadies some of whom were stood talking to each other backstage having done their bit for the time being then passed another who was re-stringing a bright frog green coloured flying Z guitar which must have been for the headline act.

Belinda had decided she wanted to watch the show from the crowd and had departed for her position shortly after the band had completed the interview for local college radio.

John Leonard swept his hand through his hair and felt the nerves kick in. He pulled his t-shirt from under his arms as both sides had stuck to his pits due to sweat. He usually had a few alcoholic drinks in him before he performed but not tonight, he was stone cold sober. Mac looked a dishevelled mess and even in the dark you could sense him sweating out some toxic mix of perspiration and booze. Nocka was taking it all in his stride, though he did trip over a small metal box which had been left on the floor out of his view on his blind side. Brandon Slam was jumping up and down as he walked and doing some other strange limbering up exercises.

Boggs walked onto the stage as the band held back hiding out of the public gaze. More and more dry ice was pumping out. He pointed his torch to the sound guy at the mixing desk and turned it on and off three times to indicate that the band was in position and ready to take to the stage.

The stage lights dipped and then the house lights went off completely which created a low hum of anticipation and buzz from the gathered throng of indie kids and rock fans. The intro music then started. It meant nothing to Lou, but he had the words 'Steptoe and Son – Old Ned' Intro written on his show itinerary.

'What the hell is this?' thought Boggs to himself, unaware of the British 1970's comedy show of the same name as the slow-paced music started. It featured the sound of a ukulele and piano being accompanied by a clippety-clop of some coconut shells being hit together to imitate the sound of a horse walking. Every fourth bar there was some trombone joining in for a few notes. 'These Brits huh. It sounds nuts' he thought as a huge seven-foot-high bloke pushed past him to occupy a standing space by one of the speakers at the side of the stage. 'Must be the bands guitar tech' Boggs further thought to himself.

Nocka was the first to leave the group huddle and made his way on stage to get behind the drumkit, Mac broke away next and bounded on stage drunkenly waving to each and every pair of eyes that were set on him. Brandon Slam and John Leonard walked on with arms around each other. Slam pulled away and walked towards the microphone to address all those assembled as Leonard waited for his actual guitar tech to pick up the instrument and place it around his neck. Those things are heavy, you didn't want him to put his back out before he'd strummed a note did you?

I walked up to my amp and to my waiting guitar. A roadie ran on to help me with it as if I were some kind of paraplegic or some incapable old person. He quickly left the stage as he had appeared having placed the guitar and strap over my neck. I was shocked. He had been the only American who had done a job for me and not waited for a tip.

I glanced down and switched on the guitar and plucked a power chord. It sounded good, so I plucked another. I looked down at my monitors and the levels were reading perfectly. The sound had been as clear as a bell at the sound check and nothing had affected this despite the mass of humanity who now had farted, coughed, generated heat and done whatever else the public do that makes wood-based instruments go out of tune so easily in large open spaces. This was going to be a good show I could sense it. I strummed some more chords, Nocka hit the snare and toms a couple of times as Mac plucked a couple of bass strings in between hits from his latest bottle of grog. We seemed to be match fit.

"Hello citizens! You are New York and we are Dutch Courage from Britain. We are happy to be here. You should be happy too so try telling it to your faces and pin back your ears. This is our first number. One, two, three, four…" cried Slam as we launched into the first song "You've All Done Very Well."

On completion of the opening song, which seemed to have gone down well so we went seamlessly into "Teenage Pricks" This went well too and garnered some decent cheers from the watching crowd. I watched on waiting for my cue for song three as Slam wiped his face with a towel, a towel which looked cream in colour and not milk white as our rider requested. Heads would have to roll for that. Slam began to regain his breath and then spoke some more to the crowd.

I quickly looked to my left as I took some water on board from a bottle of water that was on my speaker stack and amazingly saw Carlton Gooch talking to Chester. I doubted that neither was offering to buy the other a drink from the bar. Gooch saw me looking over and flashed me the thumbs up. I smiled and strummed a chord on my guitar, still waiting for the cue to the next song from the vocalist. Someone / something shouted out from the crowd. It sounded like a wailing banshee, but I couldn't quite make what was being said so ignored it. The shouting persisted as Slam commenced the introduction to the next song which was a seventy second banger called "Kite" that we had put together during soundchecks on the tour. I still couldn't hear what was being hurled our way verbally. Who-ever was shouting was now stood fairly close to the stage as their voice was more prominent.

Nocka tried counting the song in, but I took over from him after 'two' and Slam kicked in with the vocal. "Fags and pills, Pints and spills, ciggy burns, never learn, god sake, head ACHE….. High, high, high tonight, high as a kite"

The New Yorkers were soon out of their seats, enthusiastically jumping up and down and clapping along in time. We had them in the palms of our hands and everything seemed to be going fine when suddenly I felt like I had all the wind knocked out of me. Not only was I winded but I staggered backwards as a burning sensation seared its way through my rib cage.

I looked all around me, and everything suddenly appeared to be happening in slow motion and life's lens had gone from colour to black and white. There was peace and then pandemonium, but worse still I had missed a chord change in the song we were playing. The vocal to the song had stopped though. What was going on? We should have been on verse two which lyrically went "Rollin' up a big fat spliff, trying to counterbalance the sniff" Then I noticed there was no drums playing either and now my breathing started to get heavy. I could feel my heart punching like a jack hammer against my chest, sweat began to bead upon my forehead and drip down my cheek. Something wasn't right, but I couldn't fathom out what? Everything was playing out in front of me without any sound.

Now there was chaos at the front of the stage, it looked like fighting had broken out amongst the punters as a large empty space had opened up where only moments ago bodies were happily crushed together dancing to our beat of indie rock.

By now all I could sense was feedback from my guitar. I turned to look for our drummer, but the stool was vacant. Nocka had for some reason hidden himself inside the bass drum. I glanced to my left and then another sharp burning sensation ripped through my body. At this point my legs went weak, I tried to shout for help, but I couldn't form any words. I instinctively put my hands down my body to the area of pain. I felt something warm and sticky. What was it? I couldn't remember anyone throwing a pint of piss at me, so I brought my hands back up towards my line of vision. My hands were completely covered in something dark. It looked like blood. What the fuck was going on? For a moment I was hit with confusion, and then I commenced the second seeing of Gods light in just a couple of days. My strength then deserted me, my legs buckled and then everything went to black.

The majority of the crowd in the Argyll Plaza had loved what they had seen and were cheering wildly. This was an act right? British slapstick humour at its best?. Two crowd members sat in the upper balcony even remarked at how good the special effects had been. They were stood up clapping as the Dutch Courage guitarist fell to the floor and other members of the band swiftly hid behind nearby speakers or jumped off the stage. "Ow man this is awesome; they must have spent too long in Hollywood bro." One guy wearing a 'NYC' blue baseball cap said to his pal wearing a red 'NYC' baseball cap who in turn high fived his buddy shouting "Super impressive awesomeness!." Blue cap spoke again "We've had unplugged recordings before, but this show must be being recorded for a plugged album, as someone has plugged the guitarist" The pair high fived each other again and then low fived for good measure.

Lou Boggs was horrified at what he had seen or what he thought he had seen. Was New York suffering another terrorist attack like one he had lived through in the nineties? He shook his head briskly, but it wasn't a dream. The carnage was still there and stood positioned at the front of the crowd right by the stage was a hooded figure dressed all in black. A figure who appeared to be waving a gun around having previously pointed it stage wards and fired three or four times.

Lou instinctively ran onto the stage when he saw the British guitarist fall to the floor and it became the last thing he ever did as another gunshot echoed around the Argyll Plaza.

The music had abruptly stopped as the screaming started, and more shots were fired as the crowd parted like the red sea. Security personnel that was used to dealing with crowd surfers disappeared as they decided they weren't keen on taking on any gunmen at twelve dollars fifty an hour.

Keeler Boyd was a twenty-four-year-old music fan. He was six feet tall, blonde haired and was wearing his favourite blue flannel check shirt and jeans. He wore a pendant around his neck which was inscribed with the words 'Dodged a Bullet' Keeler had been stood beside the assailant when they had opened fire at the stage and brave as a lion or stupid as a fool had tried to tackle the perpetrator. He was rewarded with 'a bullet' he couldn't dodge as it ripped through his neck at close range and lodged into the flailing arm of another fleeing customer.

Many fans were now cowering under their seats when they realised it wasn't part of the performance, and many more had streamed out of the venue in terror. More shots were heard as fans jammed the 9-1-1. police hotline and firearms officers were immediately dispatched to the Argyll.

The hooded assassin now needed a way out. They were sure the target was down. They still had ammunition for the Beretta handgun they possessed which had been surprisingly easy to fire with extraordinarily little recoil and had been pleasingly accurate.

The first shot fired had gone wayward as some fan had accidentally bumped into them as they took aim but the next three would have won the fluffy toy first prize the next time the carnival was in town as they hit their target with deadly accuracy.

If the stupid have a go hero in the blue check shirt had waited just another thirty seconds, for the assailant would have to have reloaded then he would have still been alive. He couldn't have known the handgun was down to its last bullet prior, but the black hood was surprisingly quick on the draw. It was an unnecessary kill as the perp had no beef with anyone else as meat was murder. The beef was only with Dutch fucking Courage. And where was the courage when it turned hairy? The drummer had squeezed himself into the bass drum, the bass player was cowering behind a speaker praying to a God no doubt that he probably had little to no belief in just ten minutes ago. As for the singer, he jumped into the security pit and fled shielding himself behind two Hi-Viz wearing security guards.

The hood had now reloaded and fired again at an area that was producing a tall man like shadow on the stage. They then grabbed a nearby diminutive emo girl who had been stood rooted to the spot like a white rabbit in the headlights crying in fear.

The hood placed their gloved hand over the mouth of the emo girl. "Shut the fuck up Emo kid or I swear to fuck I will put you out of your misery. Is that what you want? You all want to die anyway right" The Emo girl tried to shake her head, but the grip of the Hooded menace was tight.

By now the New York Police Department had started to arrive outside the venue. Paramedics were also quick to the scene. Officers on the street were having difficulty trying to clear the punters streaming out of the venue away to safety.

The radio crackle that came through to first responder Officer Vinnie Acierno reported that intel from inside the concert was that they were possibly dealing with a lone wolf attacker. None of the law enforcement gathered at the Argyll Plaza could understand how the perp had managed to get inside the venue and beyond the metal detectors with a firearm. Still, they had, and whoever they were, they needed to be dealt with, fast.

Acierno had spotted a backstage side door that had been kicked open and jogged towards it cradling a Remington Model 619 shotgun, a version that was kept in all NYPD squad cars. Once inside he could see steam still rising from the stage. There was also a prone man with a broken guitar strapped around him being given mouth to mouth resuscitation from behind the speaker stack by what looked like a noticeably young woman.

Another shot rang out in the hall followed by more screams. Acierno looked around and could see a pair of large feet which were attached to some long legs, neither of which were moving. The now stationary red stage lights were fixed on them, but the rest of the body was hidden in darkness.

Acierno bent down into a crouching position and ensured that his radio was on silent. He then removed the safety from the shot gun and manoeuvred himself around the onstage obstacles towards where he thought he had heard the last shot ring out.

The police officer reached the drum kit and was rather surprised to see someone squeezed into the bass drum. "NYPD Sir. Are you ok, are you hit?" Nocka Izzet locked his good eye on Vinnie Acierno. "I'm, I'm, I'm, I, I, I," Acierno moved on before hearing the answer to his enquiry. Time was of the essence.

Acierno reached the side of the stage and peered out into the stalls. Apart from two bodies that appeared to be one male and one female lying motionless on the dancefloor, there was also, he noticed, a pile of black clothing that had been discarded amongst the usual debris of the show, such as empty plastic cups and food wrappers.

The police officer surveyed the area and scanned the upstairs balcony but couldn't see any sign of life. "Carnage" he whispered to himself before reaching for his radio to report in "This is Officer 892016. The downstairs of the venue is clear. I repeat the downstairs of the venue is clear. Please send in back up to clear upper level. At least four people down in lower level, maybe more. Send in the paramedics. No sign of the perp. They could have left with the escaping crowd. Repeat must have departed with the escaping crowd." Up in the balcony seats Mr Orange was sat with his head in his hands. He was joined by three new associates, one male and one female and former stage manager Lou Boggs all of whom were covered in blood.

WHO SHOT JL ?

FOLLOWING THE SHOOTING THE NYPD launched a manhunt, but the question remained. Who shot John Leonard? Hey, Who shot ya?

THE RUNNERS AND RIDERS

ERIKA PUCK – ODDS ON FAVOURITE at 4-7. Unhinged lunatic who had a stalker like fascination with the Dutch Courage frontman. But could she find a gun in New York City at short notice and manage to get it inside a seemingly fortified venue? That and you are expecting a complicated didn't see that coming ending twist right?

Budge – 3-1. The Frog Splash singer was none too happy at Leonard barging into his dressing room and being disrespectful about American sport, Christianity, and Jesus. We know he had served time in San Quentin Prison. You may recall that this revelation was accidentally provided by his one-time drug dealing friend 'Medical Bill' earlier in the tour. However, being a devout Christian, 'Thy shall not kill.' Unless of course it was his day off being a Christian.

Medical Bill – 3-1. He could get his hands on crap drugs that don't work but could he get his hands on good guns that did? Why was he in San Quentin Prison? What had been his crime? Did one of Frog Splash hire him to take out the obnoxious John Leonard? This is America. Anything is possible!

Guy Ropes – 6-1. The Dutch Courage road manager was at his wits end and being ex-army was very capable and familiar with military hardware. Had he been pushed to the brink by the bands antics on the tour? Being trained with the British Army he should be able to handle a couple of drunks with his little finger. Who-ever committed the act would surely need army training to escape the scene and evade police capture. Was Ropes this man? Just what did he smoke in that pipe?

Unknown Sub – 10-1. The Argyll Plaza was rumoured to be owned by the Mafia. Had someone unknown put out a hit on Dutch Courage? If so it was the only hit the band would ever have. The chances of anyone wasting money on this extreme course of action is remote. They hardly left daughters pregnant on tour or stole your wife.

Chester Rataski – 33-1. Big outsider. Literally. Was he that frustrated at not being asked to re-join the band when they appeared to be on the up? Would that make you annoyed enough to kill? Granted he had the capital to outsource the job having won a quarter of a million dollars on the lottery, but being tight as a ducks chuff you can hardly see him paying someone to do the job when he could get close to the target for free to do it himself.

Carlton Gooch – 100-1. Why had he turned up in NYC out of the blue? What business did he have in New York? The Dutch Courage tour had been costing him a fortune. Was this enough to push him over the edge? Was the Buddhist thing all an act? Did his Chinese links stretch to more than a half share in the 'Lucky Wok Restaurant' in Croydon?

PLACE YOUR BETS NOW PLEASE……..

LETS REWIND THE NIGHT

8.13PM THIRTEEN MINUTES INTO THE EVENINGS second support bands set shots were fired in the Argyll Plaza towards the stage and then indiscriminately at members of the crowd.

Two hours earlier. Mac had tried to have his conversation about band money with loved up, newly ordained Mormon and fresh god botherer John Leonard. Leonard brushed McCarthy off as if he had been a crumb on an old sweater.

6.37PM Mac had about his person what could only have been described as an illegal cigarette. He went outside of the venue to the parking lot and climbed aboard the bands transport where he knew he could chill out and have a quiet smoke in peace. He had some serious thinking to do.

As he smoked the dope stick to the nub he then left the van and noticed a vaguely familiar figure loitering around the closed entrance to the car park. He walked a little closer towards the figure quickly as it looked like it was a she and that she was quite possibly flashing her breasts at him though he hadn't got his glasses on to be sure. 'You just don't get this kind of behaviour from the women at gigs in the United Kingdom' thought Mac whilst chuckling to himself.

When he got to the gate his demeanour dropped "You!" He shouted as he recognised the attractive girl with rosy, red lips standing the other side of the gate. "Hey handsome. You gonna help a lady." Erika asked quizzically.

"You're hardly what I call a lady. It was you that chained me to that fucking fence." Mac shouted wagging his finger at the woman. "Oh, that was just me playing. You know high jinks bro. It wasn't my fault you passed out on me. How do you think that makes a girl feel? Look bruh I haven't got a ticket to the show and can't get in." She held her bag up, letting Mac see the bottle of spirit that was easily visible in it.

"They won't let me in with this either. Have we got time for a wee party before you have to go on stage?" Erika shook the bag. It seemed heavy. Mac thought hard and responded "I'm not really into that to be honest. You know pissing on each other. It's not my thing." Now it was Erika's turn to be confused.

Mac looked around to see who was about and then when he noticed the area was free of security he opened the Emergency exit gate which just had two thick set rusty old bolts to negotiate. He finally managed to open it and Erika Puck shoved past him. A shout then went up from two security guards who were making their way over towards them. Mac decided to front them up and show his AAA pass.

By the time Mac returned from dealing with security Erika had disappeared into the theatres labyrinth of backstage tunnels until she found the appropriate toilet to change her attire in. It was here she put on a black hooded outfit that came down to her knees. It had a tight waistband, which is where she lodged the second-hand Beretta handgun that she had procured from the concierge at the Tooting Hotel for three hundred smackers and a slurpy blow job. She then left the restroom and continued exploring until she could find her way out of the backstage area into the crowd. She didn't want to hang out backstage with the risk of being caught and thrown out of the venue without completing her mission.

THE RESURRECTION AFTER MATH

FOLLOWING A TIP BY AN unnamed source, Erika Puck was tracked down to her room at the Tooting Hotel where she had barricaded herself. The siege that followed lasted just two hours before she decided that death by cop was a better finish to her story than several life sentences for killing what was in truth a visitor to the country.

After a silent prayer Erika charged at Police who were positioned all around the landing of the nineth floor of the Tooting Hotel and was instantly shot dead by New York Police Department markswoman Gaye Barr, thirty-one, with a single shot to the forehead. Barr was later cleared of any wrongdoing and awarded a 'Distinguished Law Enforcement Valour Award' Only in America could you get a medal for shooting someone stone dead.

The headlines in the US media ran riot and read as 'SHE DON'T GIVE A PUCK.' 'MAD WOMAN KILLS SIX IN NYC GUN SPREE' Amongst the victims of Erika Pucks sixty-minute gun rampage at the Argyll Plaza were stage manager and Frog Splash employee Lou Boggs, fifty-one years of age. Music fans twenty-eight-year-old Moe Lester Saville, a chef from Park Slope in Brooklyn, Regina Fluoride, twenty-one, a design student from Gramercy, Manhattan, Wenger Bowderstein, forty-six, an accountant from Hell's Kitchen, Manhattan and show guest Chester Rataski, forty-six, unemployed from Astoria, Queens. Five other people were also treated for gunshot wounds and one other was seriously injured after being trampled underfoot of fleeing concert goers.

Martin Mac McCarthy returned to face trail in California but on arrival was informed that all charges were dropped. He was rather annoyed that they couldn't have phoned to tell him this decision earlier which then would have saved him the cost and time of a flight across the country. He erroneously voiced his displeasure and this opinion in court. On doing so he was charged with contempt, thrown in jail for twenty-four hours, fined one thousand dollars and deported from the country.

Mac returned to Britain and tried to sign back on the dole whist waiting for musical inspiration to strike him. His claim was disqualified, and just three months later his driving licence was as well after an arrest for drink driving. Who said drinking and driving was so much fun?

He never challenged the deal he signed to be a member of Dutch Courage and currently drinks anything alcoholic whilst sat waiting for the phone to ring with the television off in a darkened room.

Guy Ropes later quit the music business and drafted a book about his time in the British Army which he called 'Learning the Ropes.' To this day it remains unpublished.

Belinda Blunt returned to her father and the church in San Diego and continued to have treatment for post-traumatic stress disorder after giving John Leonard mouth to mouth before and then after the shooting. She never returned to New York as it was also the scene of her favourite dress being ruined as the blood never washed out of it. She was currently halfway through an intense First Aid course before Covid struck. She refuses to be vaccinated.

Belinda's father Hamish ended up using church money to invest in a toilet manufacturer. The novelty church bell cistern sold well and made him flush. He is currently under investigation by local law enforcement agencies for fraud.

Nocka Izzet found that being scared shitless during the shooting at the New York gig helped cure his stutter and can now talk freely. This proved to be handy as he ended up with a job in an insurance call centre, where he still works today. In the evenings he delivers fast food locally for the delivery company 'Goober Eats' He also had a small novelty hit with a cover of Paul Hardcastle's techno classic which he renamed "Covid N, N, Nineteen" where recording the chorus vocal, the stutter would have actually been beneficial.

Brandon Slam decided music wasn't for him and eventually returned to performing his first love magic. If you call 07965 696969 you can book him for, as his business card states 'Weddings, Parties, Anything' His favourite trick these days involves walking down a street and turning into a pub. He also put a considerable sum of his savings into a Ukrainian Holiday Company that specialised in trips to Kiev and several other towns and cities in the southern and eastern regions of the country. As at year ending December 2021, the business was doing a bomb.

As for John Leonard…. Poor John was shot three times at the infamous 'Argyll Plaza' show. Twice in the chest and a headshot where a fourteen-hour operation was undertaken to remove a bullet lodged in his grey matter. Today, he currently remains to all and sundry brain dead and on a life support machine at Kings Lynn Hospital Center. The address is 246 Second Avenue in Rochester, NYC, 30153 if you would like to send flowers or a get well soon card. The doctors believe there is little to zero chance of recovery. But what do they know? The British consulate in Washington DC continues to foot the bill despite Carlton Gooch running Fund-it campaigns on the internet for Leonards Doctors fees.

Carlton Gooch visited John after he was moved to 'Kings Lynn' and was discovered by a nurse recording a few pings and bleeps from the life support machine that was assisting Leonard to live and breathe. Gooch promptly had these sounds added onto the release of a rushed Dutch Courage single called "Elixir" which was remixed by the happening chart sensation act 'The Substance Sisters' and became a minor chart hit in the United Kingdom and Luxembourg.

Not long into the next year came some disease called Covid which went on a world tour and forced nearly all of the entire world's population to stay at home apart from bizarrely the residents from the place where the disease originated.

Carlton Gooch remarkably cleaned up financially during this period where people couldn't do anything except stay at home and wait by releasing a 'Stay at Home and Have Your Own Music Festival' kit. Punters just couldn't get enough of it.

Here's a breakdown of the instructions to the £44.99 game which was released by the Gooch's own Asteroid label.

HOW TO HAVE YOUR OWN FESTIVAL FUN KIT

THANK YOU FOR BUYING YOUR own festival from Asteroid Idea & Design Store (AIDS)

Festival contents include: 20 crushed used cans of beer. 20 plastic pint pots. (We recommend the pots to be stamped on by foot after drinking the contents from and be discarded in the room where you stand. IE Anywhere but in a dustbin to help with making your own in-house festival vibe.)

General Rubbish / Trash which you should liberally throw around your living room or wherever you choose to hold your own indoor festival to assist in making the scene look authentic.

Blank cards (Included) to print the names of your stages IE Elysium, Promised Land, Wanker Stage etcetera. (Pens not included)

How to Play: First. Set up stereos (Not included) in all of your rooms of your abode you are using for the festival. These will enable you to have different stages available to go and listen to different music throughout the festival.

Set up your best stereo system in your living room, or biggest room in the property, take card and write Stage one and preferred stage name.

Then select eight well known compact discs (CD) to play of established artists from your own personal collection (These are not included)

The smallest bedroom at your festival site should be designated for Stage Two. Select a further pick of eight CDs of lesser/ slightly unknown bands for this. However, if you wish for a big special guest for stage two then it is ok to mix in a CD from your stage one selection.

You must then select a running order and start to play a disc on each rooms stereo. These must be continued to be played at the elected times over a ten-hour period.

A third stage could be utilised using the smallest and least used room at your property (We advise on using a shed, greenhouse, or outhouse for this) It is advisable to play any folk acts or unsigned bands on CD-r on this stage (Not included) as experience indicates that hardly anyone at the festival will bother to visit this area. This may require a battery-operated stereo if using a shed without electricity mains. (Not included)

When changing over the compact discs please wear the enclosed 'Stage Crew' T-shirt. (Black. One size fits all)

If using battery operated stereo and the batteries run out, then please wear your 'Stage Crew' shirt to replace them. You may find that they ran out ages ago whilst you were dancing around in stage one or two. If this has happened you may be required to make an announcement to the crowd to advise that certain acts or all acts in this arena (If you have no further batteries) will not be performing. Please use inflatable microphone (Green. Not suitable for children under four years of age) to make the announcement.

Once your acts have been sorted and disc one has commenced playing, you are required to personally start getting into the festival vibe as a punter. To do so we recommend drinking copious amounts of alcohol and we suggest that you should visit each room at your festival at various points of the day to listen to the tunes playing between noon and 10PM. These actions should be repeated over a three-day period. (Standard festival duration)

At the completion of each day, the trash / rubbish should be picked up and placed in the orange refuse sack provided. Whilst carrying out this job please wear the enclosed black baseball cap marked 'Cleaner' (In white) (One size fits all) You are then free to go to bed.

On waking up for day two of your in-house festival, you will need to select another eight compact discs to play and re-distribute the trash collected from the orange bag around your property to create the atmosphere and realistic festival setting once again. This will be the same requirement for day three.

Further instructions: No festival really ever happens outside your front door. For authenticity you can select 2 options. 1) Bed & Breakfast / Hotel Option: Inflate an air mattress (Not included) and place it in the smallest space in your home. EG A pantry would be perfect. This becomes your home away from home for the duration of the festival. Please then smoke forty cigarettes in this environment very quickly to provide that perfect nicotine / stale cigarette smoke smell for your pretend hotel room that most cheap B and B's in the UK possess. (The more Potpourri you encounter on arriving at a real hotel in the lobby the worse the smell will be in your room)

Or select option two. Camping Festival. Erect your own tent in the garden if indeed you have one. (Tent or garden) You should then walk around the garden for a minimum of one hundred laps prior to feeling the need to use the toilet (If female) or use the included plastic milk bottle provided (Men) This is all about creating the correct festival ambience for each gender.

*Disclaimer footnote. To create the perfect festival atmosphere with your kit you also need one hundred and twenty cans of your favourite alcoholic beverages, which aren't included and need to be bought separately.

Once drunk at your festival, ensure the cat, goldfish and any photographs of family members and friends are easily available. These will be required for you to have rambling drunken conversations with as you move from stage to stage to listen to your favourite artists throughout your time at the festival.

Also enclosed: Two coat hangers. These can be used to create a merchandise area. Attach T-Shirts (Not included) and display.

And whilst the metaphorical cash registers were ringing for Carlton Gooch and his Asteroid Ideas and Design Store, ka-Ching, cha-ching, the man who wrote the songs that were selling for him was trapped lifeless in another country three thousand, four hundred and fifty-nine miles away still attached to a machine that was breathing for him which was going ping, beep, ping, beep, ping, beep, ping.

Fast forwarding to the year 2023 and there's now a Dutch Courage tribute act by the name of 'Liquid Confidence' doing the rounds on the UK pub and toilet circuit and immensely popular they are too.

Strange old world isn't it.

THE END ?

THE DIFFICULT SECOND BOOK: LAZZA'S THANKS LIST

You for buying of course! And most definitely; Mrs Ogden Author, M + D, Rhiannan, Sarah at Mirador, Tim Trab (Master Artist) Dudes Punk Rock Radio Show (Nuneaton Crew Rock Radio – Check it out) , Kingy for his Thingy Kingy videos and art, Dave & Owen of ECL – Estate Cleaners Leicester – The Green Clean Machine, for setting me on my way with festival experiences, The Wheelers of the Albion of Burton for invaluable support, Dom Warwick of Vive le Rock (Despite his taste in terrible football teams), The Ogden LA Supporters Branch in San Pedro, USA, the lads at the Drunken Duck, all the great Mod, Punk & Oi bands for inspiration, Valerie Kobe Chung, Garry Bushell for being bothered and all sporting teams of Leicester that carry the Fox crest. Anyone who has been interested. Peace be with you.

WE WANT THE AIRWAYS
Email: lazzaogdenauthor@btinternet.com
Facebook: Lazza Ogden Author (Search to befriend) or…like at www.facebook.com/lazzaogdenwritessomewords
Twitter: Lazza Ogden Author @AuthorLazza
Insta: Lazza Ogden Author Instagram.com/lazzaogdenauthor

Amen

Printed in Great Britain
by Amazon